Redh<

Ian Enters is a novelist, poet and dramatist. Weidenfeld and Nicolson published his first two novels, 'Shadow' and 'Up to Scratch'. Outposts and Envoi published three of his poetry collections.

He was the dramatist and director of his own plays 'Minos' and 'The Loathly Lady' and has directed many community productions.

He directed, adapted and wrote the librettos for 'Lulu', 'Twist', 'The Highwayman', 'Stocksbridge Dragon', the Musical.

He wrote and produced 'Forty Nights and Days' and the opera 'Avalon'.

He organises and delivers projects and events for the Friends of Coleridge and gives talks about a wide range of poets and their biographies.

He has recently published 'Word Hoard', his translations with commentary and notes of Old English poetry.

Ian Enters

Redhead

Start a fire and you will be burned

Macadie Books

Chapter 1

The dwarf stopped, hot and beery, by my bench today, here by the river in Bristol at the renovated dockside with the pleasure boats moving slowly at their anchorages and the quay bubbling in the sun. The dwarf showed me a fist of dull brown coins and asked for silver. He smelled of fish and urine. His upper lip was beaded with sweat and encrusted with a sore.

"No home, no place to go," he muttered, looking away from me along the quay. I gave him a little money. "So bloody hot," he said, still avoiding eye contact, and shambled off. Last time it had been so bloody cold – no in between on his pendulum.

"Swing low, sweet chariot," I sang after him, but I would not carry him home.

At least I had a place to go and I had briefly considered inviting this man of restricted growth back with me to the digs the first time I'd met him on the begging prowl, but I had been too short a time in what passes for the normal world and the landlady, Jane, would rightly have objected. She would have talked about the Tower House Hostel, the hospital, the trust between the doctors and the community care scheme, that rules were necessary and that I was lucky enough to be given a sheltered place. I had dismissed offering the invitation then and now I just watched the big-headed, short-legged man waddle away. The singing died in my throat.

I prefer the word 'dwarf' to a 'person of restricted growth'. The latter sounds like a bonsai tree, a deliberate pruning of mind and body. It shrieks of victim. Who has restricted your growth, old dwarf, hot and beery, cold and hungry? Who has determined that you should be old as a dog is old before taller humans have realised their middle age? By giving another label, I take away your last shred of humanity. I am called sponger, scrounger, inadequate and misfit, but I expect such terms. My mental disturbance is much the same as your physical difference from the supposed norm. Just one chromosome short of a shilling, otherwise all is in place, hunky dory and ready to meet the chasing wind, the sharp rain and the sudden sun with confidence.

A woman laden with shopping is eyeing the end of my bench and now she has come over to ease her varicose veins even though I have spread myself wide. She can't find the flaw in me by looking. I am almost six foot tall; dark hair curls over my collar; fat is generally confined to my paunch; hands are long and thin. 'Like a pianist's mitts,' Mother used to say with exaggerated tight red lips, laughing despite the cold in her head. She was always snuffling and sneezing, my Mother. Now, when I consider her condition it is all too clear that Father kept her in viruses each month. I read in the paper only yesterday that bacteria are coming to kill us all and not before time I reckon. They are able to adopt a host, adapt to a new lifestyle, work cuckoo-like on other offspring and eventually feed off the life blood. They do all this in insidious degrees with good manners and the wit they were born with. These are the core skills for survival. I, on the other hand, handle change badly, expect others to follow my lead and end up weighing whether a tramp-dwarf is higher or lower in the human scales than I am.

I would not start from here if I were you, down near the bottom of the ladder. I can hear the counsel from the past, but shall ignore it. Belief in equality shrivels rapidly out on the streets. Starting is blind and carries past, present and future darkness with it. This start is as sterile as others, but I have a story to tell and the dwarf is part of it, as is the way the chestnut tree by the trinkets' bazaar shows its candles in cauliflower white bravery. The Guardian on my lap is of the same colour with creeping black worms slithering across it, pretending to hold today in their passing. I have considered giving up the newspapers, having already rejected advertising hoardings and the television, but it is a habit of my old teaching days to steal the wet-wet look at the weird world.

I sighed and looked up at the tree, stretching my legs and crossing them at the ankle. I heard my wife from pre-Dartmoor time automatically warn me of thrombosis from cutting off the blood supply and I settled more firmly, pushing back on the rest and flicking open the paper. It was good that the sun was shining, the water lapping and that my tobacco was scented sweetly, even if it had been cultivated by the destitute of another land. These things could sometimes stop me crying; sometimes they made me cry; at yet other times all I could see were individual black flecks that make up newsprint in an ash-filled sky.

I turned towards the shopper. She must have been seventy five, old enough to be my dead Mother. Her hair is silver and her face puffy and pink. I felt drawn towards her and shifted along even closer. She eyed me suspiciously, but I smiled encouragingly. She looked back at the concrete beneath her feet. I coughed and spoke,

"Three years ago I was teaching art in Leeds. I told the children to bring in images they saw like this," and I jabbed my finger at the photograph on the front page of the paper. "They blocked them in light and shade; they developed lines to represent and to distort perspective. I showed them colour mixing and compared pictures from the past with contemporary images. At the end of each month my bank account caught up with my overdraft and I pretended that the passing on of technique was important."

"It is important, teaching," the woman said, gathering her shopping to her and lifting herself up. "I've a bus to catch," she said.

"I used to believe that too," I rushed on before she could move away. "Education – the bastion of civilised behaviour. I'd never accepted the lecturer's thesis at college about de-schooling, revolution and putting the power in the hands of the next generation. She said schools were institutions of social engineering to keep the masses quiet."

"I must go," she said and pulled away, smiling and nodding at me reassuringly. It is the way I speak that keeps them hanging on. I decided to finish what I had to say, anyway. There were other passers-by to pick up a flavour.

"Children deserve a cultural heritage, but their eyes are dead and their behaviour belies and beggars my beliefs. Their minds are literalist, representational propagandist, demanding of linear movement and clear consequences. I live to betray such certainties and schools encourage conformity. We should not conform." I stood at this point, raising my finger. "We must examine the images we are given, capture their inner meaning and intentions. We must bring the habit of analysis to bear on the horrors we are shown to keep us quiet." Nobody stopped. There was more avoidance. I quite understood. My messages are painful to hear and anaesthetised brains reject laser truth. I picked up the paper and started to show it. Quod erat demonstrandum.

"Here is a young man lying naked in death," I announced. "His handcuffed wrists and ribbon-cut throat belie the small smile on his lips. Can you see another's fettered arm caught by the cameraman in the side of the frame? There is another body, unchosen by the photographer or editor, lying alongside, packed against his fellow civilian. And there is the lie, the evidence that the camera always lies. The unchosen one is the reality. The picture is the game."

Still the procession of shoppers did not waver and I slumped back to my bench and my eyes flicked from face to anxious face. I could see in them the rows of smiling corpses stretching from Dubrovnik to Sarajevo, across the beautiful country of green forests and cool glades, from Kuwait to Somalia across bleached sand and bone-white mountains, from Afghanistan to Kosovo, Iraq to Syria, through Serbian strongholds of berbers to barbarians. And as my eyes photographed each person I placed a coloured band upon each hand, showing the judgements I had made on the outward show of their inner cultures. Now all people were festooned with butchers' rosettes. Perhaps they would be hooked on walls and their differences anatomised so that the few living creatures might view their deaths with equanimity. For the dead are no longer human. They are no longer counted, no longer important.

Last week I had written to the paper, but the editor would not have printed my letter and so I had not sent it, assuming the irony would not have been observed. Now I recognised that the irony had been too clumsily driven, but there it was. I carried it in the pocket of my patched blazer.

'Dear Person,

Your coverage of the terrible carnage in Forevereverland was sexist in the extreme today. That a young woman should commit atrocities is neither here nor there. Almost all people can terrorise, destroy and murder if sufficiently numbed by their conditioning and conditions – men, women, girls and boys, Renamo, Somali, and, of course, our own ministers with much rubbing of hands and blindfolds. The list is endless of person's dehupersonality to persons and the process of contempt for people gathers pace across the globe. Dehupersonation leads to dead minds. Oh for some values of respect and worth for our fellow sufferers, but my hands are tied with rent arrears, my debt to society, my need for medication. What are yours tied with?'

I even signed it as a politically correct ambassador for minority rights and concluded with a heartfelt postscript:

'When I pray I ask for my mind to be filled with unselfish and supportive ideas so that when next I meet others I do not taint their hearts with my hatred, my wounds and despair. I do not foist my powerlessness on others. Do you recognise another's need for self-respect on shis journey into the dark through the dark? Just tell the Redhead to keep away from me. I try to be impartial and unprejudiced, but he has done me injury beyond your knowing.'

I had signed it but had not sent it and now, having reminded myself of it, I hesitated to look up lest the Redhead was on patrol. I quickly convinced myself that I was needed back at Tower House. Elizabeth in the hostel would be crying over the baby she supposedly lost in the blitz. I could not help her much, nor wished to do so, the truth being known, but being there was better than out in the impersonal places. I would offer her cigarettes, but Jane told me in no uncertain terms that whatever I did I should not sub Elizabeth for a gin or fags. Fat Elsie was told too, but the old crone was a devious one – wouldn't put it past her breaking into my room and nicking my money. But when the red veins pulsed at her temple and her eyes filled I had to think of my Mum and feel sorry. A lot of old women I've met use this similarity with old Mothers to win sympathy. I've noticed it in shopping queues. They're hard as the cheese-parings on my feet. They scuttle past me saying, 'Just a loaf of bread,' and then jaw for twenty minutes about the weather and how their Rita should never have gone out with him in the first place.

I had been sitting on this bench for too long. It is dangerous to be in one place for me. I need to inhabit many nooks and crannies, hideaways. I stood up, shoved the paper into the wasp-haunted waste-bin and started walking towards Exchange Square. Once away from the pedestrian precinct it is difficult walking in Bristol. Cars and buses monopolise the roads and pavements dwindle to narrow ribbons at important corners. Two abreast is a luxury and I approached the blind turns carefully, pushing my shoulders against the stonework of the Castle Inn and inching round. I did not wish to be confronted by the Redhead and I always checked for escape routes, but once clear of the exhibition gardens I accelerated past the high-rise car-park and on towards home.

How the word 'home' reverberates. It is the great 'om' of inner security and sanctity where Elizabeth drops her aitches like an archetypal cockney-sparrow woman and Elsie heaves her bulk from room to room, turning sideways in doorways. 'I'm not staying with men,' I'd said to the social worker at the clinic. 'I had enough of that in prison.' I'd had more than enough straight after prison, but I couldn't say about the Redhead then, couldn't say it now, just kept my eyeballs swivelling for him. I'd put up with fifty contagious women with leprosy, other than my wife, before having to share with a Redhead, but I worried about the dwarf out in the world. I worried about Elizabeth and Elsie in my world.

A door opens inside my head when I walk the streets and inconsequential pictures and prattle follow me. Weigh my words as feather-down. The scales my wife used were too exact, although heavy, substantial, producing solid judgements in the long run. I reached Gloucester Road with a basic depression gathering low over the Atlantic. I used the front-door key and did not feel my spirits lift with customary householder pride. I knew that one day all things would come together or the centre would not hold. If the former, then the dwarf would be given his place in the sun, his mind washed clean of all resentment, and the Redhead would disappear in the sunset offering his own scalp to the darkness. If the latter, Elizabeth would end up strung on a meat hook inside the kitchen with her thin hair wrenched from its undyed roots and her hunched birdback stretched over a cheese wire, while Elsie hogged a mound of glace-cherry eyeballs from a sticky knicker-bocker-glory glass until a stroke froze her body as her brain seems to have been frozen.

Meanwhile Jane's husband, Peter, was hacking out old plaster on the landing by my room when I hauled myself up the long stairs to the attic. He paused to sup tea from a Mickey Mouse mug and grinned at me.

"We'll have this neat and clean in no time," he said. He'd finished my room in a week, scraping off the thick green wallpaper, making good the holes and then suddenly the white and pink were there, bright like a new-born baby's room. For a while I felt an intruder with my stinking old habits of pipe and shabbiness, but then Doctor Rhodes suggested I was embarking on a fresh course, needed freshness about me. I felt at home for a short while, naively believing in the power of appearances.

Thank you Renamo for destroying this idea. I saw you smiling in my paper years ago and how could you be a murderer with such a smile? Your babies foetal in rows of matted blood and bones were pretence surely, for you were full of words of reconciliation and love, were you not Renamo? It would have been possible to gather all the dead children into one mound, cover them with a magic skin to produce Elsie. She carries her twenty four stone like Bunyan's pilgrim and the dead children within her writhe their angry spirits through her fat red lips. She calls me pig and would like to squeeze the life from me with her great bulk. When I had asked Jane how Elsie had come to the hostel, she had rightly refused me information, but by a nod and a wink I guessed that her anger was not burning off her fat, but feeding her growth. The more the dead children in her loathed their murderer, the more layers of fat accrued around her, pushing down the fires within, asphyxiating the love that might have appeared possible once, before her Redhead had flung the featherless tiny fledgling of herself from her own nest, leaving her bare skin and bone with lashless bulging eyes.

Elsie, you may hide your vulnerability in fat and shout at me and call me pig, but you and I share more than you would believe. I said this to Jane, but she quickly interposed, a definite woman, challenging my rapid conclusions.

"How do you account for her little girl hair and dress then, John? If she's so angry with men, why does she wear frilly things?"

I tried to explain about safety in infantilism, but she refused to listen. "We all have our crosses to bear and we either manage them or we don't. Some of us give them to others to lug along and that's your way. You try to implant your own unhappiness in others and say the whole world is evil because evil has been done to you. Get a grip on your own life!"

When I first moved into the hostel she would not have spoken so to me. She had shown respect for my teacher's standing, for the pictures and poems I had brought with me.

"It's all Elsie and Elisabeth for you, isn't it?" I said and she laughed, poked a strong red fingernail towards my chest.

"You can wriggle all you want, John, but face yourself

you must or it's downhill back to the hospital for you."

"You've been talking too much with Doctor Rhodes," I muttered sulkily.

"Don't need a doctor to tell me you're too caught up in your own head to see the world straight. But I won't have you worrying Elsie. She's enough on her plate."

It is important for roles to be defined in my mind. It is worrying when people move beyond the expected responses. Jane had moved from the impersonal to a probing concern that heralded a desire to manipulate and control.

"Keep up the outward show and leave the inward to its own devices," I said. "I am happier with the daily niceties of polite enquiry about weather, food and did I sleep well last night."

"Did you?" Jane asked, smiling at me despite the coolness of my tone.

"What?"

"Sleep well?" She invested the words with such warmth that I blushed. I am a forty five year old man feeling like fifteen and I hastily rummaged for my pipe to cover the confusion.

"You shouldn't do that," I said. "It's changing the rules."

"Oh run along with you. Where's your sense of humour?"

I left her to trudge back to my room. Rules are rules, I thought. There are cold words and hot words. It is best to shelter behind the cold. My Mother and my wife, Monica, had both taught me to hide. Even in mid-summer with the heat bubbling the tar beneath my old boots, it was important for distance to be kept and the frozen lake to remain untested. It is commonly believed that frigidity is ice without passion. I tell you differently. Beware the coldness. Beneath, brooding and stoking up immense fires, lies murder. It is revealed through the burning head of flame that spurts from volcanoes locked in deep snow and ice. It is far more destructive lodged in freezing chains than when channelled over customary sun-soothed ground. There was that about the Redhead which confirmed my belief absolutely. His skin was white as morning snow, but flecks of fire pocked his surface and from his crown sprouted the flames. If the sun don't shine, then hide from the Redhead, who thinks he is the sun.

I walked up the last flight and remembered a bus ride I made with my toddler daughter, Joanne. We'd been wrapped up warm against the February chill, sent off out to go to town for a new radio because Monica had a head cold and could not go. There was a light covering of slushy snow on the pavements, but I held my daughter's hand and did not let her skip into the gutter. We waited for the 87 in a patient queue and clambered on the crowded bus. Joanne had launched herself towards the stairs as I paid for the journey, but I caught her arm and took her downstairs to empty spaces either side of the aisle. She had not wanted to come and pulled back.

"Upstairs," she demanded. "Daddy upstairs." I reached the seats and popped her down, turned to sit myself and she was off. She stumbled as the bus lurched forward, bounced against a passenger's thigh and knocked her face. She screamed and I caught her. It was nothing serious, but would she stop her howling, her demanding to go upstairs? But I said no and heaved her on my lap where she gasped and sobbed.

"Wouldn't have hurt to go upstairs." I heard a woman whisper behind me and I turned bright red then, wanted to yell at her that it would have hurt. Children had to recognise authority, do as they were told. I did not want to breed a fascist thug, scrabbling for power because limits had never been defined. But now, when I remembered the tiny incident, I realised it was my wife's words speaking through me. I had dearly wanted to gather my daughter up and take her to the highest point in the land, to show her every possibility and every freedom, but such madness had to be quelled, driven underground into acquiescence to the outward show, the rules because the ice was upon me, choking back the free flow of blood into a trapped furnace.

I opened the attic window and Joanne's tearful face dissolved. The traffic roar intruded and a breeze lifted the council tax form on the table by my bed. I would give it to the social worker on Thursday. She said I should not pay, being a patient in community care.

"Leave it to me. I'll sort it out. Don't worry."

I try not to worry, but forms have always made me freeze. People who pass judgement are terrifying to me and forms, their instruments, are insidious, creeping through letter boxes or on screens like spies. Why then had I found myself so cabined, cribbed and confined, so dependent on others and not my own person at all if authority frightens me? I picked up the form, twisted it in my hands and placed it on my illegal ashtray. "No smoking" says the notice on the wall, but I lit the blue touch paper and watched the officialese flame. My stomach clenched with the terror of it and I could hear Monica scold me, my Mother scold me and the firm tread of my Father pulling off his belt. But they can't reach me here on top of the bus, on top of the world, a free spirit at last. I could see other trapped creatures writhing in the flames spurting from the pink form. They were black little dragons with tiny needles in their wings and, if I put my finger just there where they fought to quell the paper into ashes, they would lance me, pricking me to pain again and again. My fingers danced in and out of the flame and I flicked my thumbs against forefingers, scoffing at the searing. This was such a small Redhead, a tiny spurt, no power to hurt or heal. I looked round my room for things to burn, but it was not time yet and I did not wish harm to befall anyone other than the Redhead.

"Fight fire with fire," I muttered, crouching over the ashtray, pretending to be an alchemist searching for gold, but I knew I was pretending and that was important or so Doctor Rhodes always said.

"If you know you are pretending, then the pretence will stay unreal." A mantra for inside my head, but the Redhead is real even though others might call him pretence. I defy anyone to define reality. It is tested in the fire of martyrdom and, by definition, martyrs are dead and can not share their knowledge of the real God with their spirits flitting over the planet like chimaeras.

And this fire came from thinking about my Joanne and fat Elsie, I thought, sitting on the side of my bed, the smell of ashes harsh in my throat. I opened the attic window and brushed the black smudges outside. Elsie's eyes are like shallow blue saucers; her face as pale as Wensleydale; her hair bubbles blonde over a bulging forehead. She wears rose-printed cotton dresses and light blue cardigans with the elbows gone. She calls me pig and smashes her great forearms against the table so that the eating-room shudders, but whatever hurt she carries inside can not equal mine, I think, for she does not have my sensitivity, nor my powers of extended thought. I closed my eyes and heard the Redhead's voice. 'You are a fucking snob,' he said and I flinched from him. I would have to make amends because respect was what he was after and there was no respect in my head for Elsie, but I could pretend.

"I am fire under ice," I said clearly out into Bristol over the rooftops. "She is a blancmange, but I like the taste of blancmange. It is sweetness and light." Insincerity is all, I thought, but did not say aloud, because the Redhead was a liar himself but might accept my lie as truth.

There was half an hour until the evening meal. The day had passed and I recalled Doctor Rhodes' advice to spend a little time each day facing the past through music, pictures or an object. I normally tried to paint, but now thought of my old jumper, stained with oils and smelling of white spirit, baggy and torn. Monica borrowed it one morning. She took it from the chair by the back door and wore it for the quick run with the spaniel out on the field by the allotments. Mist covered the top of the hill, even shrouded the pylons so that only the hiss of water static told their presence. I watched her shape until it disappeared through the garden gate and sat with my toast imagining her thin bones wrapped in my thick jumper as if I were her protection. When she returned through the back door, the wool was beaded with white and a dank dark smell wafted in with her. I smiled as she flung off my painting jumper, her nose wrinkling in disgust.

"Kept you dry, didn't it?"

"I didn't wear it for sentimental reasons," she said. "It stinks to high heaven and is through at the elbows."

It ended in the bin. If I had it now, I think, I would get leather patches for Elsie and for me. Were they still sold in cobblers?

"You can sit too long reading meaning into trivia," said Doctor Rhodes on another occasion. "Have something lined up to do."

I had the evening meal in fifteen minutes and, until then, the last few overs of the test match. The opening batsman was playing a journeyman's innings with an apprentice at the other end playing out the day. The commentary lacked focus. Boil Boycott talked about the difference between swing and seam, while an off-spinner tried to finish enough overs to avoid a fine. In the distance, like the roar of traffic, the crowd hurled Mexican waves around the ground, hot and beery. I slapped off the radio.

"How dare you take my jumper for less than sentimental reasons and without permission?" I shouted, the hot words boiling out. Then a few deep breaths and it was supper time.

Chapter 2

The doctor was wrong. Once started with the observation of an object I could not turn my brain off like a convenient domestic robot. It had to travel on even after the sausages and chips, the plums and custard, the cup of coffee and Elsie's violent disapproval of my table manners. I was presented with the washing up sponge. The roster was on the wall. It was my day. I shivered over the pulpy grey dishcloth, the green scourer. I buried my arms in the soapy water up to the elbows and leaned, looking through the steamy window at the uneven patio Jane's husband had not finished. I would prefer to lug stones, dig out holes for setts, chop off obtruding roots rather than follow the roster. The significance of the sponge was out of all proportion in my head. It brought to mind a beckoning finger towards pain. It lurked behind an alarm clock. There was a nail inside my gut that twisted into my intestines, dragging me towards a horror I could not name.

"These things have to be done, John," Jane said, keeping me at the task. "Routine helps the world go round."

I think of William Blake's engraving of God

encompassing man in a triangle of fire. My spirit is trammelled in fairy liquid. The spirits of our age are dragooned into numb marching through wastelands.

"How bloody stupid I am," I whinged. "It is just a silly little job." I grabbed the pots and started to sluice them clean. There is no relationship between one scouring pad and another. The reality of this mushy sponge at 'this moment of now' could be held away from previous times that no longer existed, perhaps never did exist. The answer may be to deny any context for daily behaviour. Dogs and cats are like that – here and now and never think backwards and forwards. Stay locked on the immediate sensation – squelch, scrape and sluice. Thou shalt not be afeared of the big bad wolverine of work.

I sloshed through the pots with a rictus for a smile and no words. My companions in the hostel winced away from me. Even under my stern injunction to stay where I was locked to the brown-spotted sink in the brownly decorated communal kitchen, I travelled back to living with Monica and the children. Through the window I could just see the old man in his blue donkey jacket reaching his pigeon loft. Soon the port holes would open and the grey flitting creatures would flap through the misty sky like ghosts or moths. The cabbages were shining like seaweed and the hawk would rest up, even his vision clouded. The peregrine would leave the hundred pound racers alone. I became at one with the birds, flapping and wheeling on an invisible thread, the pretence of freedom in my brain.

"You need a bit of company," said Jane, wiping down

the units. "But I'm off out. It's aerobics. What about the tele with the others?"

I knew that she meant well and that my medication was due the next day, but I rejected her suggestion. "Is it art therapy night?" She knew it was not. "A quick pint round the corner?"

"Benefit day tomorrow," I said. Upstairs I had just enough tobacco for a pipe before bed. To smoke it was all I wanted to do. She gave up on me to settle Elisabeth in an armchair and to find Elsie's ball of wool. I shuffled past the shrieking silly picture set and returned to my eyrie.

If the top of the skull is carefully removed, each stitch unthreaded with a sharp needle so that the skull is lifted clean along the forehead's laughter line, what is seen but the whirled walnut whip I bought for Monica in regret for my anger with its bloom of grey upon it? She sank her sharp pointed teeth into the laughter lines of chocolate and revealed the white cream. With a delicate pink tongue, she dipped and licked, dipped and licked as a ruminative snake does. Flicker, flicker little fork, how I wonder at your sweet-corked taste-budded tongue and the sour poison under the hollow tooth. There would be another form soon, another Child Support Agency enquiry and more coils wrapped around my unresisting body.

A chocolate lover and chocoholic are much the same. I can dream of a solitary glorying in cloying sweetness. Chocolate eating and having sex stimulate the same hormones. I read this in a woman's magazine in the hospital waiting room last week. Monica loved her Terry's dark and I could not compete with a sophisticated coffee cream. Don't dip the tip of your tongue in my grey cerebellum, oh sweetness seeker, oh doctor of the mind. I will turn your teeth sour, your breath foul, as I turned Monica into a fetid cowlike snake, drooping over her mounded belly, working her prey through the pulping of her long gut from a distance, a monstrously long long distance from her long long body.

Skeins of smoke wreathed from my pipe and I closed my eyes thinking that tomorrow would come more quickly with my pupils covered. If I could only find the open door on the landing of my brain and close that too, I would be able to cope in the small place, in the dark, where visions could not come. I would slide into bed and huddle under the duvet like a silly child. It was the closest to action that I could reach.

Slowly I undid my belt and began to slide down my trousers. It was the medication that gave me the pot of fat above my belt. I wished it were not there. There was a knock at the door. I could tell who it was by the rap of the ring on the board, the hesitant scrape of the knuckle. If I called for entry I would be discovered with my trousers at half mast and my shirt rucked up – the central part of me clear to view with its folds of fat and the way hairs sprouted from the small of my back like fungus.

"Wait on, old crone," I called and wondered what had brought Elisabeth from the fug of the television room and up the stairs. I shambled into my clothes, packaging myself. At least when she peered round the door, I was decent.

"A little tea," she whispered as if I had been engaged in holy work and so I had, I thought. I had been observing my human decay in a world of ideas and distorted memories, pondering the chances of immortality. I wondered what role I should assume with my trousers on. Should I appear seer or sap, sage, savant or savage? There were too many fanatics with dreams for my future happiness and their sects were standing up like organ grinder's monkeys claiming the only truth lay in the melancholy moans of the mindless. Yet if I replied to Elisabeth as if I were an old man without aspiration and with only this week's benefit payment to expect, she would not offer me tea and sympathy. She needed me to be strong, above her in the hierarchy of the house, so that her small deceptions could never appear threatening or part of the battle for power. I suspected her motives. She believes in pain. It is the factor to remind her that a memory of living hurts again and again. How long would she wait for numbness or the small plywood coffin flicked to the undertaker's shoulders like a greengrocery box?

"A cup of tea would be as nectar from the gods," I said. "Two spoons of sugar would complete the treat." She gaped her mouth and shook her head so her watery eyes blinked.

"I saw them coming," she said. "In the shelter, huddled in blankets, eyes tight shut against the muck, I still saw them coming – great throbbing beasts with wings blacker than the sky and stars like searchlights seeking, seeking my baby to smash her to bits."

"Nothing like a cup of tea to steady the nerves."

She leaned towards me full of confidences and plucked my sleeve.

"Have you noticed it, the way those planes look like sharks in deep water? They put the fear of God in me – wouldn't catch me up in the air." "Wouldn't catch you out of this house, would we, Elizabeth?"

"I saw them see," she went on. "You tell me I couldn't not through all that earth above me and the concrete tunnel walls, but I could tell. Terrible scenes down there. They'll tell you different, but underground was a death trap, hardly safe. It's what's hidden inside that counts, isn't it? Inside them planes was bombs. Inside my pram was my baby. Inside the shelter was me, but no place for baby – oh no, not for one needing fresh air one storey up the escalator with the other babies. They told me to leave her there, couldn't take her down any further, quite safe, they say, but I saw them coming and went for her – too late – much too late. Swan prams are best. They're strong, but not strong enough for a rolling bomb."

I had to quieten her, put my hand across her mouth, not roughly mind and say firmly. "You've told me this before and yes I did know your baby had blue eyes. I did know they were coming for her because you left her, but you had to, no reason to feel guilty now." Her skin is like old paper and her tiny shoulders are working up and down under my arm. "Steady now, Elizabeth. Put it out of your mind." I inched my hand from off her purple mouth and she gasped,

"I was to blame, brought her into the world through the split of my legs and left her to die on another landing."

23

I'd lay odds the old girl would die a virgin old queen, but who wanted to check the hymen was intact? She used to haunt the old Kings Road in London, lugging a newspaper pram load from nowhere to the corner of Oswestry Street in the dark. If questioned, she'd say that the lights had gone out all the way to Marble Arch, but she'd see them coming one way or another. How did I know? Elizabeth told a different story to Jane.

"There's no need to try to impress me," I smiled as warmly as I could. "A cup of tea would do twice as well as this old tale." She twitched then like when the body has a reflex spasm and I knew we'd finished the panics for a while.

"Oh I am pleased. You seemed so down earlier. A nice cup of tea, that's what he needs, I said to Elsie." She closed the door carefully and I heard her on the stairs, humming. My depression had given her purpose, but I could not stay bitter when the chipped mug arrived with its scoured and rusted spoon. It was hot to sip and took thought from me. In between sucking up the brown sweetness, I looked up at her hopping from slipper to slipper on the new carpet.

"It is nice up here. It's better than my room."

"He'll be doing up your room soon. He's working his way down. Have you thought of a colour scheme?"

"I've always wanted an attic room," she said, scurrying to the window gap and back to the bed.

"Not this one you don't. There's no view and the traffic row comes in."

"I wouldn't mind. I'm used to noise. There's been noise all my life. I'd have you know I was born near a dockside in London, near where Canary Wharf is now

– Isle of Dogs way. Funny how I've ended up in Bristol, near another place for ships. Not much call for ships nowadays. There used to be tankers, can't tell me nothing about tankers, and the row from them steel hawsers – set your teeth on edge two mile away."

I swallowed hard on the tea, wanting it to be gone, her to be gone. She was beginning to crab in on me and soon she'd have her baby and the nightmare would start all over again. Ever since Dartmoor I had become jealous of my patch, whether the single narrow bunk, the chair in the hospital lounge or this hostel room. I needed my space. If somebody came within six feet of me, I could feel the threat, the breath overpowering and their need for recognition swelling into a boil's yellow bald head.

"Mind you," Elisabeth went on. "When the war got going after the false peace and I was wanting out, there was no way and I wouldn't let my baby go. Other Mums might say it's for the best, but she was my first baby, my job to care for her and where's the harm in that?"

In silence death comes, like a thief in the midst of mayhem and murderous flame. He would dance from the fire with a smile on his lips and his face would be white as ashes. With gimlet eyes he would bore through my soul and freeze my heart into ice. Redhead is fire and Redheads are ice. Redheads kill in a frozen trice. Here is her baby. Now it is gone. So quickly she vanishes like a brand new song. I think it propitious to listen to this old frail woman. I share her fears. Every shadow has her baby's name upon it. So we have tried to avoid the sabre toothed tiger and the warmonger and both have failed. She plants her screaming pain in her own death as her own baby. I bury my fear in concrete. My feet are encased in stone. My legs are covered in thick knotted cords. My torso is swathed in dark blue terylene cotton mix and my sparse head is shrouded in a net and scarf. Only my face is naked and, looking now at Elizabeth's pinched cheeks, I think I too will wear a smidgeon of powder and a smear of lipstick on my puckered lips. Hiding in another's personality is my favourite haunt. It avoids meeting people.

"If," Doctor Rhodes had explained, "it is necessary to avoid human contact and I recognise that all of us need time for ourselves, then displacement activity might be the answer. Let the other's words wash over you, keep a polite face and another vision behind the eyes. With practice it can be done." I put the mug on the table by my bed and looked at it carefully with its inner staining. I remembered seeing a docker's dinner table from the nineteenth century at the local museum. It carried more utensils, more hope of a satisfied appetite than the dwarf's paper bag. His clay pipe, flint and pouch spoke of time to sit. Elizabeth mentioned carriage pram and I interposed.

"A plastic bag would have been so much better." She looked blank.

"Better than my pram? You've to keep plastic bags away from babies."

"It is impervious to rain," I explained. "He bought three jam doughnuts and kept the old bag to carry his next meal. It was a poor decision."

"Even with the blackout on I could walk my baby in her pram to settle her down. There's too many rocking and patting backs all hours God gave them, when a gentle push along a pavement settles baby quickly enough."

"There's grease in hot doughnuts and they weaken the paper. His tin of beans fell through and rolled into the river. You should have seen his face."

"I don't know what you're going on about," said Elisabeth. I took pity on the old woman and tried to fill in the background, but she was not interested in what happened to the old dwarf's dinner. "You're a funny one and no mistake. Mind you I can tell a story or two. Make your hair stand and true too." I did not want her back on the old course, having steered her clear.

"I'm sure you could," I said. "But not tonight Josephine. Besides your story is always the same story just told from a different angle." She poked her cockney nose in the air, mortally offended.

"As if you can talk," she said. "Doesn't matter how often it's said, if it's important."

"I'm not saying it isn't important, Elisabeth, but another time eh?"

She was so small, so tight, so clutching of her unhappiness, so bustling in her sharp twig-snapping twitches. I know I should have helped her tell the full story of her impossible little girl in London and how she'd died, but I hadn't let her finish and that was the end of it. It would come again, in time, in many variants, but I refused to sub her story in payment for the tea.

She picked up the empty mug and left the room, making sure that the latch dropped and that was good because normally it needed a strong pull and lift at the end of its swing to jerk the metal tongue into place. I knew if I mentioned the sticky flange to Pete, he'd be

27

there in a jiffy, cleaning out the thick paint, loosening the screw, smearing just a smidgen of thin oil and then open and bang, open and bang, flick and close for ten minutes.

"It'll be as good as new and half as expensive now, old mate," he'd say. Open and bang, open and bang you bugger, I thought. How you would flex and flip the door into your shape, just as I could imagine you flexing between Jane's legs and flipping her, an easy self-satisfied rhythm.

"Ship-shape and Bristow fashion," I, acidic with jealousy, would say to the Bristol man.

"Aye aye, sir," he'd grin, because there was no side to him, no realisation that I was close to mocking him with his practical can't see deeper than two coats of paint, call a spade a shovel mind. But why should I even think to sneer at Elisabeth with her sparrow's feet and wings scrape, flit-flapping through the house? Why should I prevent Peter from carrying out his landlord's tasks? The petty studpidity of the powerless old male mate, I thought. There he was, the man of the house when I did not want a man near me. He had his drill, his paint roller and his woman. Here I was, a middle-aged patient in the house, no longer a man, just plagued with old sores and old stories. I turned on my side away from the door and blotted out the traffic roar. It was time for a picture in my head.

High tide on the river tonight and the tall lights are deep in the black water near where the little man sleeps. He hides himself each night in a corner of the building site below the derelict church, between crumbling brick walls beyond the flood defences. The bulldozers are slowly working their way towards his corner, but he is safe for a few months more. If I were the painter I pretended to be, I would paint the thin slice of silver light cutting into the bulbous head of the dwarf, crouched in his low shack, while a bulldozer, like a frozen dinosaur, poised to rip the earth. I would show each fissure between the broken bricks as chasms into other broken worlds. Oh I could see where the bombs had fallen, even though bomb-sites belonged to my childhood many years ago.

"Well it's not a bloody photograph is it?" I said to the wall. "It's understandable if I bring a little of my own history into the matter." Too selfish to listen to Elisabeth's fantasy history, weren't you? I thought and hunched back over in my bed to see the thin line of light beneath the door where the landing light always gleamed because Jane said people might want to find their way to the loo in the night. It really was kept on all the time because Elisabeth woke up crying so often and the night-light soothed her. Well let's be honest about it, shall we? I stretched out on my back and watched the ceiling revolve, little flecks of white in a grey sky. Slowly my eyelids closed.

Tomorrow I will get cash at the post office, visit the doctor for medication and see things more clearly in that order.

Chapter 3

"Why do I have to come to see you once a fortnight for medication? I can give myself a bag of pills, even use the syringe with some dexterity. It is my body and mind, my right to decide whether I stay scrabbling after snippets, trying to build little clues of understanding. If I wish to be attacked with panic, betrayed by strange visions, then I am a free man to suffer or reject suffering."

I waited at the clinic, rehearsing my speech of independence. There is another voice, however, treating my place in the roll-call as a form of willing worship. Others might attend a church for the benefit of their souls, I came to the hospital as an acolyte to the science of medicine. In a short while I would partake of communion at Doctor Rhodes' rail and all things would be laid bare to me.

"John Edwards," the nurse intoned, reading from a clipboard, and I bowed my head over my magazine, pretending to read the letters about cancer and the sun, waiting to hear my name again. "Is John Edwards here?" She said, looking round, and I stood up quickly, not wanting the third time of asking. "Doctor Rhodes will see you now," she said, nodding quickly towards the doctor's room.

On my best days I managed to stay in conversation with the man for forty five minutes. I looked forward to speaking to a shadow by my side. But there were times when the doctor was obviously busy, could only administer the jab and wish me well. I have told him how precarious this made me feel, how ineffective the medicine was without the personal counselling. Last time I came he afforded me just ten minutes and even suggested the nurse could give the prescription if necessary. I should not have complained. What seems complicated and frightening to me must be mundane and obvious to him. I asked him once whether he had ever been surprised by a patient's words. He'd said he often was, but I contended that surely he could recognise the patterns of warped thinking in advance. He is a humble sort and said each mind was different and alone. He told me about Charlie then and how he'd discharged himself and died, propped against the bar of the Trafalgar Arms. He'd known how we'd worked in the hospital garden together. I pretended not to have heard. He should not have passed on such information even though it was kindness that motivated him or was it? There are always layers of reasons why anybody shares such news and Doctor Fletcher might have wanted me to confront a reality so that I might decide to avoid drinking myself to oblivion.

"Why does the jab have to be rear end?" I asked. It troubled me, dropping my trousers, turning and slightly stooping. "I had a frightful pain in my buttock the other week – must have hit a nerve."

"Over in a second and lots of padding there," was all his answer. "And how are we today?"

It is a strange feeling to have your brain rinsed out fortnightly. There is no sudden feeling in me, just a gradual lightness in the forehead and, when I look around at the posters on the wall or the doctor's veined hand, there is a renewed definition as if the external world was convincing me of its reality again. I suppose that towards the end of the fortnight I lose that sense of proportion and crystal clear vision that a normal brain should have and when I do the exercises linking lines, finding odd words in lists and picking out false from true, it does not come so easily. The medication moves through the cells removing all traces of dust and dirt, the dog-ends in sticky litter bins. It is as if only the facts remain and they have no power to hurt or be reinterpreted.

"My major concern," I said today, "is whether the treatment will cause long term damage to my brain. Should we not be cutting back the dosage?"

"That depends on how you are at the end of a fortnight," the doctor said. I looked at his lined forehead, the way his glasses slid down his nose as he scanned my notes, the tapping of his finger on key points. "You have managed well this time?" He asked and I had to shake my head. The last two days had not been good and I remembered how I'd shouted at passers by in the street from a bench. It was time for the confessional, but the doctor explained he had no time, suggested I write down my worries. He told me to be in touch if I wanted to talk about Charlie. It seemed a good idea to my renovated mind.

I committed a crime. I have done time. My wife left me and has custody of the children. I have suffered a breakdown. I am now on the mend. I paint pictures and write picture poems. I smoke my pipe and pay no tax. What more is there to write? I do not want to know more than this bare outline as I stroll out of the hospital, across the double carriageway with the grey barrier in the middle, over the dog-dirtied verge and down Chesterton Road to the art therapy. Today, I have decided, I will paint a pure white beach with palm trees. There shall be a sky so blue that my eyes ache even to think of it and wherever I look an expanse of emptiness will stretch into the unthreatening void.

"It's my new start," I said to Gladys, the therapist. "And nobody's there."

"Perhaps you could add detail later," she said. "Get the general feel. Landscapes need to be broad."

"You sound like me," I told her, delighted by the recognition. She was black from Lancashire, in her late twenties, wore loose-fitting bright clothes, loved parties and worshipped a cat, but her voice was saying teacher words and I felt kinship.

I told her about Charlie and we agreed that life goes on, that even as we battle with the past, the present manages to set up new challenges. She told me about her grandmother in Liverpool and how her mind had gone into a mush, but she did not realise, how could she? She'd taken her into a home for a trial period, but as far as Mum was concerned, every day, every minute was a new trial because she only had now in her sights and even now was dimly held.

"You know," said Gladys, "She keeps asking

me who I am and why she's there and what's for tea when she had it two minutes since." "That sounds like me or Elsie or Elizabeth or any other person in extremis."

We shared perspectives like equals. Immediately after the medication I find it easy to identify with others, can laugh and cry readily, but in proportion to the situation. When ill, I can be reduced to quivering sobs by dropping a saucer on the floor.

I first noticed this tendency to overdramatise trivial matters when teaching.

"I want every pencil back in the block, lead sharp and unchewed, thank you very much." I watched them return with hawk eyes and saw pupils deliberately push leads against bench tops to snap them. "I'll snap your head off young man if I see you doing such a thing again." They began to wind me up: a paint tray left unwashed on my desk; orange peel shoved into the easel mounts; chewing gum, always chewing gum, stuck on the whiteboard where I held it at the top. It seems so silly now, makes me feel pathetic in its telling, but pettiness and perfection are near aligned. I sometimes cried at the end of the day, standing in the store-room, seeing how my stock was being destroyed. Towards the end I was ready to use a ruler on the fists of children, bellowed at every little falsehood. I left the artroom red-faced and trembling, locked it meticulously behind me even though the school had an open access policy. They would not spill a drop of paint while my back was turned. And when the inspectors came, I tore up the letter telling me my grades as did all the other teachers out of solidarity, but my action was from fear. The quality of teaching is not strained and I was so strained that the fibres in me were like violin strings wound to snapping tension. I burned the letter in the storeroom and flicked powder paint into the heart of the blaze, marvelling at how the colours changed … almost like firework flares.

I worked all morning in the studio at building blocks of neutral light colour across a wide expanse. Over and over again I tracked my brush, trying to leave no trace of its passing except the subtle tinge of blue or pale primrose. It was as if a mist had gathered from the sea and all swimmers had departed because of a shark warning. There was a quiet reflection in the haze where the sun had been and I was outside the picture, able to view it dispassionately. Then Gladys showed me illustrations from the Greek myths, suggested the Cyclops story and I could see the final picture. Nobody, Oudeis, clutching to the belly of Polyphemus' sheep, bleating his way from the black cave to the sheer shingle, peering through bonfire clouded eyes, matted wool and morning mist towards his far ship. But how to convey that he could still see the burning timber sprout into the giant's forehead, grind its flowering glans into the single eye until the pupil oozed like sperm and then shrivelled into tar and steam? My clean mind recognised that image as an earlier picture, one to inform through past experience, but not to deflect Oudeis from survival. This picture would show survivors skulling over the sun-blue sea and disappearing in a heat haze.

"I can stay focussed on the important moment after medication," I explained to Gladys. "Later I become confused, try to incorporate everything into one canvas. Can you stop me doing that? Tell me when the picture's done."

"Well I don't know John," she said. "You have to decide the intention in the painting, not me. I take away nobody's right to mess. Who knows where it's going better than you?"

As I cleared away, I recognised the justice in her words, but worried about the power it gave me. I was happy when not picking at the scabs, but how could I stop doing so when the anaesthetic wore away?

By the weekend the old carapace was already growing round me, my protective covering and disguise. My plastic mac was on my shoulders, the sieved soles of my boots were leaking as the Bristol rain blanketed in from Avonmouth, but I needed the drip down my neck, the soggy socks to remind me that I was a creature caught in the whim of the weather. I'd come from the hospital again, taking up the doctor's invitation to a talk and I needed time to think about the situation. Charlie, my old mucker in the hospital gardens, used to say,

"Can't do nuffin about the wevver and thank Gawd for small mercies. We've fucked up all else." When nobody sits on the old school bench, it must be holiday time and raining. The dampness in the seat of my trousers was uncomfortable.

"To be pissed on," I used to say to old Charlie. "That's what we're here for, old fucker."

"Oh no we're not," he'd crow. "We're here to piss on ourselves!" Then, laugh? A drain, hackle crackle down the tubes. We pissed ourselves to prove him right.

I was smutted by the rain and the clouds were becoming visible above the mist like grey pillowcases bulging on washing lines. The grass was spider-webbed and I was not doin' nuffin' wiv the wevver old Charlie boy and still it hissed out of a steel sky while I smiled and cried at the same time because Charlie was a funny man who'd died.

"I know you and Charlie had a good relationship. "The doctor had said. "It was why I agreed for you to work in the gardens for that time. You helped each other, but Charlie was never going to make it out of here for long. He needed too much support."

Still steady on the medication I smiled and told the doctor not to worry. Old Charlie had gone to a far far better place than we could ever dream of, being stuck inside this cave of human greed. I could see Charlie putting his wiry back into his oars, rowing away like a good'un over the shiny sea.

"Come back to me this time next week," the doctor said. "You may want to talk later if you get depressed before our next appointment."

Talk? I thought. What bloody use is talk when the words are so slippery that nobody understands what they're driving at. Just press a button and let the standardised forms trickle through the standardised mouths in bland self-assurance. We are sorry to have to announce the death of the well known raconteur and wit, Charlie ... but I did not know his surname ... I could not use the words. I was bound to silence. Let another write his obituary because those who control our language, control our lives. I had cast the television into outer darkness. I read newspapers through a lens of suspicion and advertisements were like enemy mortars in my head. It was enough that Old Charlie was dead and there would be no public sorrow at the loss of the finest backchat from London, washed up in a mental hospital in Bristol.

I tried to keep my brain clear, but it felt confused already, just a few days on, but I could still pretend to a sort of reason and was not yet filled with fear. In fact, I decided, at this stage I was a valuable commodity if others were only to know it – a dispassionate sensibility, ill disciplined, but free to produce ideas and ideas are needed, oh dead and unhappy creatures that we are. If normality depends on a restricted code with a selective access to an organised file manager, then abnormality lies in opening up files in the normally hidden parts of the network. There is immense potential lying behind the normal show, but a sudden invasion from the subconscious areas can blow the system. If the gradual use of drugs could enable the opening of unused doors in the brain without destroying it, then there was a chance of finding new perspectives. Was I fooling myself to believe that my revealed cranium could produce inspirations skimming like shoals of fish leaping free from giant trawler nets? There was no certainty that I would be able to walk through a door, even when it appeared open to me.

"It is a question of passive or active living," I told the swooping seagulls, as they bombarded the litter with shrieking cries. As quickly as it had come, the rain rushed away on a flapping wind. The awnings over the bric-a-brac shop belched and heaved. Liquid gold spilled over the cobbles. Refracted light shone through my pupils like a rainbow and the sailors walking on their pleasure boats were distant wraiths. I would sit and let others act out their aggressions and their greed. Others moored at different places as their whims took them, docking without condoms, believing theirs were the safe houses.

For every person striving to possess and change the world, acting out a strange conviction that influence on events is gained by doing, there are millions receiving a meagre subsistence from nature without the imprimatur of paid work. The dwarf was quickly out along the quay after the rain, working his passage along the motor boats. He gathered meagre pickings from the boating Berties, but worked hard. His large neck was red beneath grime; his sweater was the dark green of jungle fatigues. I once owned a shiny shirt in such a green given to me by my stroke-numbed grandmother. She talked like this small man, sideways, as if guilty, from a mouth corner with a little dribble on a fat lip.

"How did you get your fat lip?" I asked. Did giving a little silver allow a significant question? The active world is all buying and selling. I gave him silver and asked the question.

"Fuck off," he said and stumbled away, rubbing his face with an open palm, nowhere proper to go. I should not have paid before receiving the goods. There was no come-back. I lifted myself from the wet slats and followed, sorry for what I'd done. I, more than most, should know to avoid personal questions.

"There are rooms on those boats," I pointed out just as the harbour master put-putted tut-tutted past to check an idle hawser on an idle boat. I pulled back my waving arm.

"I'm seasick on boats," the dwarf flubbered through his lip. "And I can't stand the smell. Have you noticed the stench along here? It's sewage, that's what."

The children of leisure were playing in the evening sun, winking and smiling, confiding and joking on the stage of their boats in the bright golden sunset, while deep in the water the sewage was rising, killing the fecund with death and decay.

"Is that right?" I asked doubtfully, peering into the scum touched and churning water. There were no dim torpedo shapes writhing through the blackness and I could smell nothing but the tar and the dwarf's staleness and beer.

"It's all crumbling – Victorian pipes are corroded and in twenty years we'll all be shitting straight into clay and then watch out for rats and cholera."

"You're a cheerful old bugger," I said. "It's not Calcutta." This was the ancient port of Bristol, the true capitol of England. Forget about the excrescence of London, the outdated fort of York. Here in Bristol had been the open road to the new world, the network to commerce. The city would adapt, would find new ways of ferrying sewage safely, I thought.

The dwarf stopped walking and thrust his head

towards me, his hand pumping up and down in emphasis. He was a big man, thick-torsoed, solid-legged, bunched forearms like a pocket Hulk.

"If they stopped worrying about what things looked like and put a bit of time into what things are, I might have somewhere to live." I took two steps back and he followed me. "Fastest growing economies are in the East. West has had it – no foresight, all money-grubbing by the rich. Won't be rich soon. More computers in Calcutta than in whole of Wales. Don't know what you're talking about and nor do they." I had shown an ounce of sympathy and he saw it as weakness. Acid was churning through his stomach lining and farting up through his mouth. His spittle landed and ate into flesh.

"Who are they?" I asked because it all boils down to them, to us and me, the divisions and connections.

The fat bottomed man swung away from me and shook his ponderous head. It was all 'them' to him and I was part of 'them' even to ask. Now when he shuffled on, I followed him, a metre or two behind him. He knew I was there and his shoulders hunched against me. For a moment I felt like smacking him across the head and booting him in the rear. He was only a shrimp after all with a fart on his warts and a fuck to his flux. He expected it and I could do it. There was reason enough to do it because he was weak, could have no redress, would have his view of existence confirmed again. He was used to such treatment.

At the end of the walkway I watched him lurch round to the building site and through a gap in the fence of

41

hoardings. He did not see me peering round the corner when he disappeared into a black crack between broken walls. I knew that was where he lived and went on back to Tower House, feeling I'd done a good turn in forgiving him his misshapen ugliness.

I often do not like myself. I blame the medication.

Chapter 4

Very little happens for a very long time. There is the gradual building of fantasies. They feed on tiny actions. I painfully exclude what might have been, but the visions intrude and conversations bubble from the strangest places in the strangest contexts, because nothing is happening except fear of something terrible happening all the time.

"I have hidden, I must tell you, little man, oh dwarfman, behind Cleopatra's needle and seen her lifted like the Duchess of Malfi on the spike of her warlike pride, easing her lusciousness on the sword of her lust, splashing the ground with her heart's blood in cenotaph wreaths." I made a mug of tea and still nothing happened and there was no dwarf to hear my words and so I returned to self-communion with the radio intoning over after over of Test match cricket. It is a dangerous trade, but what alternative when words are caught by all and sundry, twisted and reworked by the Redhead and then spread on their way like stubble fires sparking through fields, flames urged on by harassing winds? The commentators console, tell stories of past deeds and present woes, but within their trite descriptions there is room for a deep malaise to grow like mould on a damp wall. Time passes almost imperceptibly until I have reached last November with its ritual remembrance of time before and time before that time.

The grand parade of crick-cracking marching boots have crisped in clean trim along Pall Mall. I have followed from lamp-post to lamp-post, skulking behind the thinnest of metal railings to watch the smooth placid faces of the robot men and women glorying the past in their strutting and every individual carries a memory and every memory is a distortion and the distortions are bred from fear. I scratch a mole on my left wrist where my watch used to be. It always irritated me. A previous generation had met flame with flame, fire with fire, until the whole known world burned and now they march with a dark red flame on their chests as if there is pride in the deaths they wrought. My father was one such marcher, each year his uniform tighter around him, each year the medals burnished to catch the sun, each year the rain.

I was born in London, worked in Leeds and now am in Bristol, but my head still stays in London when it can. It is, after all, the Lords test match and there have been testing times even after the wars were ostensibly over to the cheers and street parties of my parents' generation. In London the students were shot by the police when they launched a home-made rocket at the Big Ben clock. Here were the Irish laddoes led off in arm-locks, headlocks, cufflocks, with the cabbies whistling and sticking fingers from their windows. Were they not, with their brogues, threatening the prime minister himself? And when out of Arsenal belched the bloated cloud of a bomb, I saw the horse's legs shredded, the toppled Britten's soldiers crack like lead on the leaden road, but nothing ever happened. It was always over there.

"You Bastards! You Bastards!" screamed old Granny Duffy as she stood by the eel and pie stall. Her granddaughter, Sarah, had been caught in the cross-fire and her pram was no tank to survive. A Basque separatist tried to translate for the evening news. He was introduced as a government spokesman for Home Affairs, but his language was gobbledegook. At this time in history, it has always been thus. Babies are two a penny. Now Elizabeth could tell a story about her baby – your baby, my baby. From where has the child sprung, fully armed, hair of snakes, ready to spit and cry?

"My baby was only two months old," said Elizabeth once, before I could move away and let the ball spin harmlessly down leg side. "Two months old when the Germans came." A full two months and nothing happened – just build-up, just fearful expectation, just scratching away at the imaginary psoriasis.

I listened to the cricket for the full day. It was like sitting through the full three hours of the Good Friday service when, as a boy, I became part of the church choir and earned enough for two knickerbocker glories in one morning. The opener scored eighty five painstaking runs until forward short leg took a one handed catch, which should have been disallowed because he was encroaching his shadow on the batsman's ground. It was a particularly black shadow. Brave man, I thought, standing in the way of the square cut or drive. With his dismissal, there was a mini-collapse and the end of play total was two hundred and twelve for six, with the old ball yet to swing. Six dead in one day is a lot happening. It is exciting listening to cricket while on and on the traffic roars and the earth turns spitting God on his cross suffering for sinners and me spooning ice-cream into a greedy mouth. Out of suffering comes considerable advantage for the spectator. He is so much happier for it not being him on the cross. When the ball whistles past the helmet, missing by a whisker, it is good to be nodding sagely and calling for limitations to bouncers. How many nails are allowed in the palm of the hand for a secure crucifixion? Two bouncers in an over are more than enough to put the wind up the average defender of virtue.

It is summer time and the key question is why did a normally attacking batsman get bogged down by the spinners on a pitch of even bounce? Given the weather forecast of rain for the weekend again, don't you feel the only chance for England was setting a big total in the first innings, which would have involved more adventurous stroke play to entertain the large crowd, and bowling out the opposition twice in the rain-reduced time? How many does England need to be safe?

With these thoughts ringing in my ears with the prospect of sound-bite satisfaction tomorrow, I closed down the radio for the day, wishing to miss the news. When I reached the eating room, however, the television was already on, with the bulletin sniping. I sat with my back to the screen and chewed noisily.

It happened when I returned to my room and found Jane there before me. She had used her pass key. She said she never would and now she had. She was angry and her hands were bunched under her armpits to stop them flailing out at me. Doctor Rhodes had said I could not have a better landlady or a better place. I was about to be battered and wanted to disagree.

"This is no bloody way to live," she shouted when I walked in. "Pete here has made your room really nice and now it's a fuggin' mess again." She had hidden her husband behind the monster of her anger, but Pete was there leaning against the wall by my pictures.

"Nothing that a clear-up won't mend," I muttered, kicking at the clothing on the floor.

"Don't talk daft," she said, pointing at my pictures. "What do you call these? Moonshine? They're bloody obscene."

"Murals," I mumbled. "I'll cover them up, if you like."

"Elizabeth said I ought to come up here. She said you'd been painting on the walls – disgusting stuff."

"It's art," I tried to defend myself. "You may not like them, but they are strong and clear. They say the simple truth."

"I try to be open-minded," Jane said, flushing up. "But I'll not have naked men buggered on my wall."

"He's not enjoying it," I said, as if that made it better.

"It'll be covered up or you'll be out. I'll tell Doctor Rhodes you need another place. Pete," she turned and shot an order. "You paint it over first thing tomorrow. And," turning back to me, "while we're about it, what

47

about these?" She pushed her hand out of the velux window and brought in a pair of my socks between finger and thumb. "Just look at what this bastard has done." She said, her forehead wrinkling in distaste.

"I put them out to air," I covered up, letting the ball go by outside the off stump, not ready for the nip back.

"Air?" she scoffed. "They're stiff as boards and stink to high heaven. They need soap and water. We do have a washing machine downstairs. No wonder the whole room reeks of feet. I doubt if you've showered for a fortnight."

"I'm sorry Jane," I said, hoping she would not notice the corner where I'd stubbed out my fags on the lino. At least the foot smell had masked the taint of smoke and ash. I slumped on the edge of the bed, wishing they would leave me alone, but not showing it because I was suddenly scared I'd be out on the streets again, finding refuge in the dwarf's hutch. I peered up at Jane. Her beautiful brown eyes rolled. She pushed long fingers through her deep red hair. Then I did not want her to go, but wanted to be held by her, soothed and cooed over. It would be wonderful to be forgiven. To feel my face snuggled against her soft mohair jumper. To be a child, found out in naughtiness, but learning a Mother's love is stable.

"Look," she said, shifting to a more reasonable attitude, her arms on her hips so that her breasts sang to me. "You're a nice man underneath it all. You're a talented man. These pictures are well painted; I don't deny you that. You need to get them out your system, but that's why there's art therapy. If you want to paint a mural, why not pick on something nice? You could paint, oh I don't know … a jungle scene with lovely plants and tiger's head and things. If you want to, just ask. I like pictures."

"It's not so bad," said Pete, appearing at her side and grinning his chipped mug grin. "I've seen worse at sea."

"You've always seen worse," said Jane, mock anger now, and I saw how Pete's arm had snaked round her waist. His broad fingers held the top of her black leather belt and was tugging at it speculatively, one finger sliding down, reaching for the silk. She did not wriggle away.

"They come here cos they're ill, Jane," he said as if I were not there. "We've to expect a bit of muck. I'll be back tomorrow." He pulled her away from my bed and led her out of the door without a backward glance and I hated him with all my heart, my guts, my liver and my soul. I knew in my heart that the Redhead of my hatred might be counterbalanced by another power and Jane was such a possibility, although I had my suspicions that her hair was henna augmented from week to week.

With them gone, I spent time picturing Jane with no clothes on. I had often painted nudes, was always ready to be amazed by the difference between the clad and unclad body, how even the oldest face could crown the sweetest frame. But I knew Jane to be honest. There was consistency of beauty in her body and her pubic hair was a dark invitation. Others might see her as plump, but not in my eyes, oh no! I had seen her, you see, although she did not know it, nor would I tell it abroad. The bathroom was two floors down and only a step away from my landlady's bedroom. She had thought herself alone. Elizabeth and Elsie were, of course, downstairs and

49

she thought me at the pub, but I had returned because somebody like the Redhead, but not the Redhead, had talked to me. Jane had walked to the bathroom, eyes front, breasts firm, buttocks tight, skin shining like silk just as I reached the top of the stairs. I could hear the hot water running and the hot blood was beating through my body. I am a painter, of course, and do not despise the careful observer. Even the peeping Tom may be justified if he wishes to portray nakedness without shame or the inevitable change in the cast of the body when another's gaze is upon it. I had felt myself honoured.

I turned reluctantly to the mural. I traced the lines of the paintings with my finger, the way the hot penis resembled a stinkhorn fungus, the way the orange red hair of the attacker stood on end, the way the man beneath twisted his arched back and how his round eyes bled. It was a jungle scene. Then I pinned my eiderdown across the wall. I could see Jane's point. Pain should be locked away and only parcelled out in small pretty boxes to a special clientele. I went to bed, remembering how I'd hastily covered up my shrivelled body when the old crone came and how I'd forgotten to mask the wall.

Before I went to sleep, a little chilled under a blanket, I wondered when Elizabeth had noticed the paintings. Although I had completed a great deal under the hypnosis of Test Match Special, there had been evidence enough the evening before. She'd given no sign. Tough as old boots, I thought, giving her a little credit for hiding from me. I also considered that Jane should not have told me the source of her information. Not that I was the sort of creature to take violent revenge, but how was Jane to know that? We live in a precarious world, although nothing happens to most of us most of the time.

Chapter 5

Elizabeth spoke with me this morning as if nothing had changed. I could almost believe that Jane had received her information from quite another source, but a lifetime of deceit brings covered and covert faces. Her faded blue eyes did not focus when she presented the inevitable mug of tea. Every day she brewed and presented, brewed and presented tea. It was her security ritual and I found it catching. Hadn't my mother many years ago brought me a cup of sweet milky tea each early morning?

"Cup of tea dear. Mind your eyes." Crack of the light switch, struggle from the blanket and the scalding sweetness cutting through the previous day's nicotine.

"So what is death?" I asked her and spooned in two more heaps of the refined white.

"That's a stupid question. Just sup your tea." It was water off the duck's back to threaten obliquely. I assumed the guise of a prophet and smudged the yellow from the corners of my eyes.

"I will tell you because you are old and will soon be meeting this death that haunts our streets. I would have expected you to know and recognise him better than I because you are always ready to lament the loss of your baby daughter to that foul thief of time." I noted the way her bottom lip turns in towards the upper and how her gum shows purple above false teeth and continued. "But nonetheless, old woman, I shall tell you what little I know so that you may observe his arrival and not be taken unawares." I became avuncular and thought of Bunyan. I too had been ignored and ridiculed. She would receive the pompous puritan words as if from the pilgrim's scrip.

"What are you talking about?" She asked. "Why don't you talk proper? I'm not going out on those streets." I will not be diverted, I thought, warming to my task.

"First of all," I said, "you will know this Death by his hair of flames and his face of leprosy. He carries a large and potent stick with which he infects his victims, breeding inside them his parasites, his succubi and incubi, his creatures made in his own vile image." I could tell she was seeing the picture on the wall in my words. I smelt her fear, the snuff of dried urine, the staleness of mouse droppings. "Remember your little baby, Elizabeth," I said with sudden clarity of purpose and her cheek whitened, her eyes widened. Soon she would shrivel, begging for redemption. It was only the floury pastry of her sagging jowl that caught my tongue and bade me stop.

"Don't you talk about my baby," she said, pushing her beetroot mottled hands over her face, palms forward, ready to ward off the death in my words.

"You see," I crowed triumphantly. "You do recognise him. You know Mr. Death as well as I. In fact you saw him only yesterday and escaped from his clutches by the skin of your teeth, the lift of a latch and a flap downstairs.

Will you be so lucky today?"

"It's better to think of being alive," she muttered, her hands slowly fluttering down like petals to land on the bedside table.

"I agree. Better to forget betrayal, better to forget the passing of false witness, better to forget the red man and his victim on the wall."

"I don't know what you're on about," she said, wincing towards the clean paint under the attic window. "You've been right funny these last few days. I don't know what's got into you."

"Let bygones be bygones," I said and stretched out my little finger to take her little finger in an embrace. I shook it up and down. "I am the witch in Hansel and Gretel and your finger is far too thin," I chanted in time to the shaking.

"Oh don't be so stupid," she said. "Drink your tea."

We had a few moments of comparative silence. I like to draw hot tea into mouth by sucking equal amounts of air and liquid from the edge of the mug. The result is slightly cooled tea and an anticipatory whistle. Mind you, I could still hear Elsie stomping in her room. There is little to obliterate the thunder of an elephant indoors.

"One day she'll come through down into the kitchen," I said, "and then what'll Jane do?" The old woman said nothing. Perhaps she did not accept the truth of my preliminary statement and, therefore, the consequent question would not apply. More likely, she was bemused. I continued. "She will ask Peter to build another roof, will Jane. Peter and Jane are so self-sufficient, so able to cope, just like creatures from the reading scheme. They will hire a joist to lift Elsie from the floor. Fortunately she will not land on either of us, but will form a mountain of white plaster on the carpet. They will spray her with water from the garden hose until the plaster sets in a cast. They will set her on a pedestal on the payshio until her bones knit in the jelly of her flesh and then …" Invention petered out. I did not want to resurrect the angry fat woman who spat hatred at me, but neither did I want her brooding presence statuesque in the garden for ever and ever. I became matter of fact. We all had to live together after all. "I had intended walking to the shop for my tobacco today," I said. "And when I reach the zebra, I shall ride him all the way to the door. Shall I buy your Lambert and Butlers?"

"You and your jokes," she muttered. "They'll be the death of me. I shall come with you," she said, picking at the buttons on her coat with its mock-fur collar even though it was burning hot outside with the paint blistering on house railings like Mother's skin when she caught her arm on the flaming gas ring. God she could scream and she did, rushing for lard, no margarine, to cook it nicely for tea.

"Bloody cold water, you stupid bitch!" yelled the man, hurtling to her side, dragging her to the sink with the wooden draining board. "You old wife, you old tail, you old burnt-out fool." But he shoved her arm under flowing water until her flesh began to cool and the puckered lines of bubbling fat set in a puce and red ball.

"I always have my coat on," she said when I ventured to suggest that a light cardy might be more appropriate. "If I'd a summer coat, I'd wear it. Clothes keep you cool." Her little drystick bones walked in the shadow of her clothes all day, cooling her with sunless ease. "Natives wear lots of clothes," she said.

"Natives of where?" I wanted to know. "Most of us are natives of some sleazeasy somewhere. Even travellers are lead-besotted natives of the road."

"Oh you know what I mean," she snorted. "Look at them Hanifs, them Indians with their baggy old clothes. They worship cows and don't even kill flies." I thought she might have adduced the widow, Mrs.Caddiacino who sold the local rag from the kiosk at the corner of Maynard Street, but when would Elizabeth have spotted her so far from the Tower House, all of quarter of a mile? She wore Mediterranean black olive and her moustache matched. But the Hanifs were altogether another matter. Silk and shimmering, gold and darkness, delight of mystery on spice-laden shelves, the mother and three daughters drifted lightly from the shop and hovered above the squalid pavement while their father, in waistcoat and white linen bags walked proudly between them, his bandy legs giving a nautical roll. "He went to Mecca," she said with a ring to her voice. "That's why his beard is red."

But he is no flaming head. I touch my chin where my beard is beginning to grizzle and wonder which colour I would turn. "It's henna that does it," she said. "Every week I see them, but they don't see me watching them walk past the house with him out in front and the others following on behind, all dressed up in their finery and I wonder where they're off to. Is there a temple or a mosque down the road?"

56

"Are you coming or staying?" I asked, suddenly petulant. Her mind was too nimble for mine, so nimble it stayed on the high tightrope with her teetering steps finding a strange way from Hinduism to Islam without faltering. My words they stumbled and tumbled with every new old thought that dived into my brain. I could scarcely make a full stop now without a grenade exploding and me finding myself in quite another country where the japonica trees bloomed despite rows of victims huddled on the steps leading to what was once a library and city hall and now served as hospital and mortuary.

"I'll find my purse," she said and carefully counted out enough for her L and Bs. "Unless it's your treat," she said.

"It's nobody's treat," I muttered, "but I'll buy your fags. Just keep the kettle bubbling." She carefully undid her buttons and smoothed her dress as the sides fell away. She was relieved. I could tell. She hated even looking out of the door as if she might be one of the people on the pavement. Being above the fray, peering from a window from behind lace curtains was more her cup of tea, if the truth were known. When she was on the level with other people, she could still see her baby with her arm across her face and the hole where her belly should have been.

"She would've been all of sixty," she said, her eyes rheumy.

"That's a short time in the age of myths and your maths are beyond my comprehension wife of Methuselah," I said. "But perhaps there is time for wounds to heal or fester!" She huddled more closely into her coat and sniffed loudly. It was time to crawl out into the big world before my shoulder received the water once again.

57

A think in my head, a slow realisation and I've reached Dingwall Road. The fish and chip shop was closed because it was Monday and the fish had a day's release. All over the world's fishing grounds, fleets wind in their long rods and wish the small fry a day's respite every Monday. The keep nets are rolled into the holds and sailors play three card brag to give chippy shops time to scour out the old fat and scrub the marble tops clean. A newspaper flapped along the gutter and a stained plastic fork rattled under my foot.

I looked carefully at the opening times on the grey board and saw it was not Monday at all. Having collected my giro, it was Thursday again and the closure was caused by an altogether personal affair between the Greek Cypriot and his ulcer. For a moment I was nonplussed, stood in negative equity with the calendar whirling past me. Then I felt reassured. It is only the workhorses who recognise themselves through knowing the date and time of their passing. My road directions and markers are necessarily more haphazard.

"Closed due to illness," I read aloud from the notice on the door, and, in another hand, saw scrawled across the window-pane: "Salmonella can be fun!" I shook my head, unamused. Some sixties' hippy throwback from Hair had planted his mark for the sheer callous hell of it.

I turned angrily, pointed at the cruel words and spoke to blue fug and hissing wheels. "This man's trade depends on folk buying his brown paper-bag fish and to spread doubts about hygiene might appear just a joke, but could have serious consequences for his future and his family. He does have children: two sons and a daughter with glorious black eyes and acne. I am appalled at the harsh judgements implicit in this scrawled message. There may be racist undertones, but I must tell you that I have been reading about the new Health and Safety regulations in the paper and, when all is said and done, the stringent requirement to keep people away from food, cooked from uncooked, plastic round everything, particularly ham, can only lead to fewer fatalities from food poisoning. This is no Glasgow butcher, you know, and fish in batter is one of the cleanest foods around. Boiling fat scalds all the germs out of a fish. At a time when a grenade can remove twenty children in two seconds, it is good to read of the government's insistence on expensive hygienic practices for small businesses. This Greek Cypriot has enough on his plate without sneers from potential customers. I want you all to join me in condemning the power behind the pen of the man – it would have been a man – who wrote these words."

The cars continued to slide along the road and there were no other passers by to enlist and so I took out my handkerchief and rubbed at the words, but they were hard to remove and smeared across the glass. Besides one or two other pavement walkers appeared out of the blue and looked at me strangely. I didn't want to draw attention to myself any longer, so I moved on but, by some freak of inattention, I did not reach the zebra crossing and the corner shop, rather I turned left into Mason Street and faltered down towards the city centre and the river.

I became aware of the sky. It was gunmetal grey blue and haze misted the roof tops. Bristol Cathedral, the Council House and the Wills memorial building danced in mugginess below and out of the fumes rose mighty coloured balloon ships billowing up from the Gardens, grazing the unicorns and mounting above the towers in a stream of variegated colours.

I cry you mercy great whispering giants. I fill your wings with magical powers. I wish to clutch the trailing ropes of your progress. May I be carried up, up and away on your beautiful yellow Sunlife balloon into the real blue of a real sugar frosty sky? I stumbled at a trot down the long hill, my eyes continually caught by their colours so that I turned and pointed, ran backwards, sideways and cricked my neck with catching sights behind the stark buildings. I hardly heard the curses, but gradually came to realise that other adults did not share my childlike enthusiasm. Sadly, they had seen it all before and had lost their capacity for wonder.

"You will never be philosophers," I told bag-laden women queuing stoically at the bus station. "Bet you wish you were in one of those balloons – better than a bus." I received no response. Even a riposte that the balloons were wind drawn and therefore unlikely to travel to the right destination would have cheered, but no. They all glowered at me with burning eyes, jealous of my freedom, no doubt. I picked out one young woman in a red dress for particular attention. "You could put your basket in that big basket under the red balloon and sail off to your dreams." She looked fixedly past me and the

175 bus pushed its boiling air to a halt beside me.

"Is he being a nuisance to you, Miss?" I did not wait for further comment. Money was burning a hole in my pocket, but I needed a companion. I would go to the dockside and buy the dwarf a drink, I decided, quite arbitrarily. It seemed important to celebrate the defeat of the air, the overcoming of the great Wills Whiffs. It was not every day that a sparkling cavalcade brightened the city centre.

"It is pints on me," I said to the little man, "as long as you tell me your name." He nodded his great head as if I spoke the most normal words in the world.

"That's right," he said. "Don't let the buggers get you down."

"You can talk," I said. "Face like a wet weekend most days."

"Today," he said, spreading his plump palms, "I shall smile."

He is like a child like me, I thought, with his sudden zest for spotting balloons between the tall buildings. He waddled over the road, avoiding traffic by miracles, to point at the monsters overhead and I saw how the pedestrians covered their mouths and grinned, pointed and warbled at his obesity, his gestures and shouted words. With me, they had kept their distance, made covert and destructive comments. They had not ridiculed me. A burst of hard rock spilled from a CD shop and, to take away the ridicule from the little man, I cavorted into the precinct and danced, twisting my buttocks and pointing my arms and toes like a Rowlandson cartoon. In another context I might have appeared normal, but here it was an embarrassment because my pelvis no longer swivelled as it did long years ago with the hipsters slicking and the soft shoes swishing.

Suddenly the dwarf was standing squat and solid level with my waist and I stopped moving.

"Don't fuck it up," he pleaded. "You won't be served."

And so we processed along to the Christmas Steps staid and sedately as a pair of nuns. We looked in the music shop and compared flute prices seriously. We inspected the clothes of Yesteryear for moth until the owner, scratching his backside, emerged. Before he could speak we were off, rabbiting down the stone steps like knock-down ginger kids.

"It's Petrograd," I screeched, swaying and waving as if to the fleet. "They'll bring food to break the blockade. Where's the pram? My God, I'll save the baby from the guns this time." I rattled forward at the crouch and then stiffened for I heard the military drums. There was no escape. "The trouble is." I turned to the dwarf. "They're in another league. Half a league, half a league, half a league onward … where are the Russian guns?"

"What crap you talk," said the dwarf. "I'm thirsty. Where's that pint? My name is … " And, for crying out louder than the seagulls over the deadheads, I can not for the life of me remember. It is not Rumpelstiltskin; it is not Rapunzel. It is ordinary and dull. It is – that's right – penny dropped – normally does when the chips are down. It is Martin, Martin Beverall. See it on a card, on a shop front, at the end of a letter your sincerely and there is sod all difference from other names.

62

We slid into the Sugar Loaf like a pair of criminals and he lurched to a table near the door where he could prop himself and be as high as any other human, while I addressed the bar. It was lunchtime crowded and the barlad was taking orders for ham and chips, chilli con carne and salad, burgers and a cheese and pickle sandwich as well as pumping beer into tall glasses.

"I'll take it separate," he said, pushing a raffle ticket at a man with a thin rash of spots on his neck. "It's fifteen pound eighty for the food, eight thirty three for drinks."

"I just need a couple of pints," I said.

"Be with you in a sec," he said, disappearing up some steps. I moved back to avoid the elbow as the served man wheeled with his drinks.

"Cop hold of this one," he said to a friend in a suit behind me and I felt darkness pressing in around as another muscled into the bar, moving between the passed glasses.

"Now who was next?" The barlad said with a fixed grin and the newcomer leaped in. It's testing time, I thought. Speak now or else for ever hold your peace.

"Hold on," I said. "I was next. I was. Two pints," I said. "That's all I want. It's not a shipping order."

"No call for language." The barboy looked me up and down and I didn't know what I had said.

"Oh give him his drinks," the intruder said. "I need to order food." He was doing me a favour and it stank, but I just stood there, Elisabeth's tenner at the ready. Money talks louder than any mouth of mine.

By the time I reached the dwarf again I was trembling. The froth slurped over the top, but there was nothing I

63

could do to stop the twitch. Even the dwarf noticed something was up.

"Where's the sunshine gone?" He said, burying his upper lip in beer.

"I've seen him again, Martin," I said. "I try to tell myself he's gone away, lives somewhere else now, but I know he's still around, Martin."

"Who?"

"The Redhead. He was through in the other bar, but I don't think he saw me, Martin."

"There are lots of red haired men." The dwarf was dismissive. He knew what it was to feel hounded, but he could not pity a fellow sufferer. His was a far worse case. But I had seen my torturer forking up the ketchup bottle with his freckled mottled hand. I'd seen him grinning back over his shoulder at an unseen friend.

"This is a bastard pub," I said, suddenly angry. "I don't want to stay." And I didn't want to say the dwarf's name again. It sounded like an insult at the ends of sentences, a joke tag. "Does anybody call you by your name?"

"Please yourself and no." The dwarf shrugged and huddled over his pint. He was not moving with a full glass and so I spent fifteen minutes alternately sipping and slipping round on my stool to inspect the clientele.

We left that pub and I had intended making my way back through the market to home, but now the black drudge of depression had seized me by the throat.

"Hang for a sheep as for a lamb," Martin said. "Drown your sorrows." I had the rest of Elisabeth's money and another ten pounds – my money for the week.

"You only live twice, Bondy baby, and where hell is is

64

where you are," I agreed.

There are four pubs from Christmas to Kings' Square and I was not used to swilling, but the dwarf was another story, becoming ever more confident, ever more loud until he was ejected by a barman in The Three Feathers with a tattoo of a parrot on his forearm.

"I only want a bleedin' drink," he shouted across the bar, his lolloping great head almost resting on the counter, his fleshy grey hand thumping down.

"You'll get a thick ear," said bonzo with the bird.

"Pick on somebody your own size," sneered the dwarf and that did for him and he bounced on the steps outside, singing raucously. "I love the way you move me!" His fixed grin was so wide I could see the black holes where his wisdoms once rotted.

"Are you with him?" asked the bouncer with a thumb like a banana. I nodded solemnly. I'm no Peter. "You're a pair of shits," he said, matter of fact, brushing his hands down sharp trousers. "Go stone your heads on meths – no stinks in here."

My God, he's judged it to a fine art, this barman. My pocket was empty and my bladder full, while dwarfy never had more than fifty pence to start with. Rook us and roll us out in the hot mid-afternoon. We staggered along the road, over the littered square gardens and, in a fit of nostalgia for lost friendship, I flung an arm over the little man's shoulders. He started laughing, cackle cackle cough crackle and my hackles rose. Where was I and why was I patrolling Bristol like a tramp? I'd a place of my own and no need to panic. The man with red hair had not followed me. I pulled up short and span the dwarf

65

towards me. He almost fell and I steadied him with my hand as best I could, but I was unsteady too.

"I get twitchy," I said straight at the little man. "When I'm twitchy I don't know what to do with myself and then others come and use me. You're a user and you've nicked Elizabeth's fags."

He kept laughing, thinking it was a game, and I slapped his face, not hard, just to bring him round to my way of thinking. But all he did was wobble like a wobbly man and come back for more, laughing still. And then I hit him hard on the nose to shut out his cackle and it did. His nose ballooned and blood gushed. He clutched at his face and hunched himself away from me, his shoulders heaving. And then I was terribly ashamed, fumbled for my handkerchief, shoved it at his face, apologised. He stumbled away from me and I cried after him.

"She shouldn't have snitched. She shouldn't have told Jane. I'll buy her fags later. It was my fault." But Martin Beverall did not look back and so I marched away, my head drumming like a steel band. The pavement beat at my soles and my back sweated so that my shirt stuck and froze. I pushed my finger round my collar and looked at the black goo. I had washed my neck that morning, I was sure, but just a walk in the street had turned me rancid. The pain in my side was back and the pain in my back was inside. Each step was painful, swivelling on my hip close to where the stitches had barely healed.

It took the sudden pain to make me realise fully the cause behind what had happened. It was neither

Elisabeth, nor Jane. It was not the dwarf nor the barman with the parrot. It was the Redhead. It was the death head. It was the sod who buggered me in Dartmoor and sliced my side. I would be lucky to escape his attentions on the journey home, but once back at the safe house, if I could only slip in past the great fat Cyclops' wife called Elsie, past the shrivelled shell room of Elisabeth and reach my attic, I should be able to shower, be able to pull out my old grey suit from my wall cupboard, wear a white shirt with tie, and pretend to be robot man, the dependable, not deplorable.

Elisabeth was waiting for me on the landing by her room, her arms crossed and her eyes haunted, greedy for her nicotine. She believed I had failed her because she had coughed on me.

"It's quite deliberate," she said, her voice unnaturally calm. "Two times out of three you're as good as gold, run an errand as well as Cedric next door, who is two pence short of a shilling, but never goes off course, and then, when I know I should have buttoned up my coat and come with you, you let me down; you let yourself down. I should have seen the signs, but I think of you as an educated person, a grown man. I should be able to trust you, but then I watch you wander off the wrong way and then I'm pinching myself for a fool."

She was so steady in her voice, so wise and careful in her words, so matronising that it was easy to ignore her thin fingers pushing up her sleeve, nails nipping into the blue-grey arm.

"I wish you wouldn't do that," I said, my head aching

and reeling with the guilt and the beer.

"At least you can feel ashamed," she said and her nails made white half moons on her slack skin. "The idle don't bother and the rich don't care."

A skewer had been inserted above my right eye. A steel rod had been stuck in my belly. I needed aspirin and sympathy, but neither was available; neither was deserved.

"It's not the Lambert and Butlers," she said, her eggshell voice beginning to crack, giving the lie to the negative. "Don't think it's that. It's being let down. It's like being jilted. I waited for you and you didn't come. There have been too many men drinking the cider and leaving me all alone."

She was eighty five years old and then some, with papery thin skin round pale lashless eyes. Her hair was a mist of grey over a red scalp and she talked like a tart. I suddenly realised that, for all her apparent goodness, her motherly concern for my morality, she was trying to hurt me, to assume power through my temporary weakness. For the price of twenty fags she could start to bully me and then where would it end? Where did it ever end when once you passed the baton, gave another the power to make life miserable?

"Remember the tea-cosy I gave you for your birthday. It's not been all one way traffic."

"One swallow doesn't make a summer, John." She shook her head at me, her eyes filling for the next ploy.

"You shopped my picture on my wall," I blurted out. "I've tried to give and forgive. What right had you to spoil my wall?"

"It was dirty, nasty and dirty." She winced back from me as if I were contaminated.

"So's smoking," I muttered and shuffled past her to mount the last flight to my room. Besides I could hear the door opening below and feared Vesuvius erupting from the black cavern of Elsie's room.

"But what about my fags? My money?" Elisabeth wailed behind me. I hadn't even a shred for a roll up, so how could she expect cigarettes from thin air?

"Get 'em yourself," I sneered. "Jane said we weren't to sub you."

"You dirty bastard! You effing tea leaf. It was my money; they're my fags." Her claws would have been in my face if she could have reached me and now there was the subterranean howl of Elsie joining in.

"Wha's the battard dunnayou, dearie?" She was stomping up a flight and the house shuddered with me. She was panting like a sea elephant, but she would never make it to the top flight, and by tomorrow she'd be back in her normal coma. Pray God she'd be back in her cocoon of fat.

I staggered on up. I'd been on my feet too long and my knees were water. Already the lights were going off inside my head and there was only a small cell left in which to huddle – such a small grey cell with a single bulb dangling on a frayed flex that another inhabitant might consider for a noose, but not me. My heart has grit in it. It rubs me sore all the time, but it keeps me alive, keeps me kicking others.

Valkyrie was on the stairs, winding and turning up

through the tower, muting acid and spitting fire, leather wings and beak of iron, but I would cheat her nicotine stained fingers. I would hold the golden rock of love out to the far sunset with light glittering in the mineral grist of its heart and shout out to the heavens for safety. With a grinding of a winch and a rattling of chains, the huge drawbridge would be lifted, leaving the batty cat clinging to the serrated edge, shrieking, before she tumbled into the black moat beneath, her witch-broom broken and her magic eaten away in the rot of her hatred.

I reached my door and could only hear the roaring of the sea. It covered up all the messy mouth of the old crone and the fat slab slob. The Cyclops could heave and shout, brandish fists in the air, pluck boulders from cliffs and throw them far out into the cream flecked waves, but my ship was sailing away far from the scrabbling beasts of fury. They had no dignity in defeat, none at all. Their legs were knotted with varicoses and their faces empty as moons. When they remembered things from the distant past, they switched into malevolent spiders with poisoned fangs. The cell inside my head had no room for hurtful words. I turned the lock upon them. I would listen to the roar of the sea, the high wind over the headland, rushing through the pine forest with its scent of resin.

"All right I'm sorry. I'm very sorry," I bawled through the locked door. Sweat beaded on my forehead with the noise pain. "I'll pay you back, but not now, not now." And the words echoed from the lookout across the wide water. Sound travels further than rocks over water. They heard; they must have heard even in the red eye of their storming. They must have heard.

"It's all very well saying you're sorry, but what does that mean when it's at home, eh?" If I could hear her, she could hear me and I could sense the creeping weakness in Elisabeth's voice. When all the stridency is said and done, sparrows depend on crumbs.

I stumbled to my bed and the dangling bulb flicked off so that I could only just see the barred window in the corner with my eyes closed. Jane ought to see about the dripping tap. I couldn't be expected to manage any bleeding thing.

It is an understandable protection from the community to give the vulnerable a "fresh start" after the pain of illness, but I must watch Elsie to discover the roots of her disease. In her history lies the seed of why she weighs twenty -four stone and calls me pig in public. I may be accused of prying, digging into the blancmange mound for my own self-protective purposes. This was true of my motives initially. Her threats needed effective counter armoury to negate the bawling cavern of her foetid mouth.

What was it then that awoke another interpretation of her hostility? Who gave me the clue to realise she was more hurt than hurting?

Her bedroom was larger than mine with flounced curtains at the early morning window. Her bed was huge, mounded with a frilled duvet under which she lay like a stranded sea lion. I could hear her breathing from outside the door. I whispered "Elsie" as I tiptoed in the room, my head pulsing with each painful step. If she were awake, my story was ready. Peter was due to test the fire alarm that day and he'd asked me to check that Elsie knew. It was a poor excuse for breaking and entering at six-thirty in the morning, but I could say the thought had slipped my mind in the pressures of the previous day. Besides, it made no difference as long as the poisonous mountain did not invade the heart of the woman into a bawling panic, wakening the police on the same floor.

The sun was filtering through the curtains, touching silver on the bedspread and the floor. Her dressing table was covered with two hairbrushes, a box of tissues and large tubs of Baby's powder with pots of zinc and castor oil cream alongside. The room smelt of my babies. I almost withdrew.

My attic was poky, low-roofed and grim compared to this palace. "Only the best for the best," Peter had said when telling Elsie that her room was next to be decorated. I approached the bed. It was a shock to see her face so clearly, framed by a pink pillow, light spilling on her cheeks like milk. I like to sleep buried deep under all covers, but Elsie was on her back, eyes closed, snorting through her small nostrils like a train panting at a station. It made sense to be on her back. How else could she regain the vertical from the horizontal except by shifting her legs over the side and pulling herself up on a heavy chair-head. I almost tripped over it in the gloom away from the window – a chair weighed down with what felt like piles of magazines.

It was her face, though, that caught my eye. It was smooth. Her features were regular and bright – a small perfection cradled in a sea of blubber. I had come for a sub to carry me over a bad time and there was her purse by the bedside lamp. I picked it up, clicked open its small claws. The sudden noise cut through the regular snort and wheeze, but up it started again. I was tempted to take more than £5.00, but restrained myself. I had prepared a small note, explaining what I was doing and how I would repay when my Giro was through. I stuck this scrap of paper by the other notes and looked back at Elsie as I turned to go. Her eyes were open, gazing full on me. They were puzzled, the large eyes of a child awakening from a pleasant dream. She could not fail to see my darkened shape and scream. Slowly I inched my finger to my lips, pleading for absolution and silence, and she stayed still except for a small smile upon her lips – gleaming lips. I began to back away, but suddenly her hand seized mine as it pulled the purse away from the table. I was dragged towards her bed like a doll or teddy bear.

"Take it easy, Elsie," I whispered urgently, but she pulled me until I landed full on her chest, staring into her face.

"What you doing then?" She asked. Honesty was best.

"Getting money for Elizabeth's fags. I'll repay later – soon as Giro is through. Didn't want Elizabeth messed around anymore."

"Look at me when talking," Elsie's breath washed in my ear. I had not realised I was trying to look away, but now I felt her grip on me increase so that I was forced round until my face was lodged an inch away from her face. "You're a thief pig," she whispered.

"No, Elsie," I said. "Just borrowing from a friend. You are my friend although you call me pig." I had thought her entirely ugly, not just obese, her body full of stench and every pore oozing dirt. It was not so. Her eyes were dark blue and her face held an inner glow, warming her cheeks now so that the silver turned to gold.

"Bathtime yesterday," she said, her face lighting to a glorious smile. I should have known. Just once a week, three handlers in white overalls arrived. Their backs were strong as tensile steel. They bathed Elsie as if she were an infant.

"She can not reach between her legs or round the back, you see." Jane had explained to Elizabeth when she thought I was not around. "In hospital she received a blanket bath every day, but that's more than we can give. She likes her bath, she does."

I would not like a public bathing. I would hate the intrusion, the use of my body like limbs separated from my brain and heart. But maybe, when your body is so extremely distorted from the truth of you, it is possible to cut off mind from flesh and revel in the tactile pleasure of soaking and soaping.

"She's like a baby in the bath," Jane had said. "It's warm, secure and a symbol of the loving she has never had."

Now her eyes shone in the dawn as if brimming with tears. I changed my story quickly.

"Just came to check you were all right," I whispered. "You were angry with me yesterday. I'll be on my way now."

"You're a naughty pig," came her voice, gentle, low

and musical, each word clear as a bell.

"They're taking her off medication," Jane had continued. "But it is steady as she goes – could blow up into a balloon, but we don't want her brain turning to mush. Her rehab depends on losing some fat, but we don't want a zombie."

Slowly, her eyelids fluttered and closed. Her grip loosened, stroked my hand and then relaxed. Her breathing became regular again. I eased myself away and left the room. In the shadows of her brain, this reality would be a dream conjured from the pills she had to take. It made me think about the sort of woman Elsie was, behind the mask and the angry vitriol that burned against me every day.

Chapter 6

Elisabeth did breakfast in the safe house, making a fuss of it.

"Easiest meal," I said, clutching my head. But she moaned about the toaster being bust and how the grill only burns on one side.

"Don't want it burnt any side," I said.

"You know what I mean," she said. It was trivia time.

"This marge is for cooking not for spreading," I said and she sniffed at me, so I shoved on lashings of marmalade.

"You're a pig," said Elsie suddenly and I wondered for a moment whether she remembered the previous afternoon and the bedroom intrusion, but not so: it was the normal insult. She turned her body fury on me. Hate her body, then hate me. Shove her hate deep inside the cavern of her mouth down the gullet of destruction into the gorge of guilt and the acid bile of digestion until I too, with all her other children of despair, would lurk like Jonah in the whale in the long intestine of her bulging flesh. Jane said it was good she spoke her anger against me. And I wasn't to take it personally. All the rest of her savagery seethed and bubbled within. If I helped her speak her anger, she might find a way forward.

"Carte blanche to annoy her is it?" I asked, but that was not what Jane had in mind at all. Just being in the house was enough to set off Elsie in all her blubbery wrath. I reminded Jane of William Blake telling his wrath to an enemy and to a friend. Which was I to be and Jane said, "Friend of course." I was not so sure of the diagnosis and suggested "acquaintance" might be as far as I could stretch, but the soft scent of the early morning bedroom and the immense gentleness of the sleeping woman were an invitation to absorb the slings and arrows for Elsie's sake. It was hard, though. I am a private person and like to build my own walls around me. Why should I try to scale another's fortifications?

I hate communal eating with a cannibal, but it was one of the terms for staying out: halfway between hospital and home. After all between breakfast and the evening meal I was free to, free to … Well what is a person free to? Driven to, haunted by, hurt by, but free! A joke word, but I supposed I had more freedom than most. Take the holy golden grail of regular employment and stuff it against the grindstone of despair until all the gloss has been raked into dust. Bring out those old kitchen scales, the ones with the lead weights and the black dish. Place all your weights on one side, even press your whole body down and you will not shift, will not budge for one tiny instant the Larkin toad squat upon the dish. There is no money to compensate for being dragooned through ritualistic behaviour leading to destruction and the workers, poorly educated and highly trained, robot through their lives without a bald thought about why or where or how.

An example: the man at the benefits is one tired and crumpled paper bag with soiled through shop use etched on his skin. He hands me the disclaimer and helps me through the forms, but still tax worries happen and here is the brown envelope on my plate again saying final demand to fill in the form explaining why I had not filled in the one before and the one before that.. He said last time that I did not have to pay, being under medication and in the care of the community plus on benefits and unwaged for so long, but still the revenue officers don't believe I can be broke and broken, but here is a note with the form claiming that because I was no longer in hospital I was liable and possibly owing money from previous earnings. The man had not known at the office at all and the social worker knew sod all because, if they were once confident, strong in what is right and wrong, they would recognise how the powerful keep changing the language to keep the weak guessing, inadequate, prepared to rely on the voice of authority, the bastards with the cream. But still the benefits' man pretends he has the world under control, follows rules and regulations for the good of all our precious souls. He takes the calls, ignores them and derives what little status he has from legalised hatred of the underclass, but at least my trap is of my own making even though I've lost the key. He does not even recognise the bars and does not see that his world is chaos dressed as order, sham in a policeman's clothes.

"Nothing to pay with, is there?" I said through a

mouthful of toast in a matter of fact way as if I did not care, but I did. Perhaps the last step to freedom, the key to my door, was to stop caring about the bloody silly rules that kept cropping up and crapping on my feet. My bowels still turned to water with these imprisoned officials spitting out their frustrations like cobras at the mealy-faced victims in their job-seeking queues. They can track me down and find I had worked freelance for two months doing art classes trying to keep Monica in clover, but they can't recognise my fall from grace, my collapse into inadequacy.

"Aaaah!" I screamed, flinging myself sideways, clutching my side. It hurt like bloody hell just to be touched, but Elsie's finger was stabbing me like a rapier. "What the hell are you doing?" I sobbed, trying to catch my breath and staring through watery eyes. Her face was a weeping moon covered with spread fingers. All I could see was her mouth working like a goldfish. All I could hear were strangled gasps.

"She wanted the marmalade, but you weren't listening. You never listen," said Elizabeth rushing round the table to pat the rocking mountain on the back, to proffer a tissue. "It's all right ducks," she said. "He's just got a bad side, didn't like it being poked."

"She needs putting away," I said, easing myself back on the chair, keeping a wary eye open for more brutality, wondering again whether Elsie knew more than she was letting on about the "thief pig" incident. "She didn't mean it." Elizabeth carefully wiped Elsie's cheeks and then leaned over the table for the marmalade and knife.

"Here you are ducks," she said cheerfully, loving to feel wanted, to be Mum for a moment or two. "You just put that inside you – better in no time."

I eased up the corner of my shirt, caught a glimpse of the dressing, still in place but slightly stained. It was a wound that would not heal. It suppurated at odd times under stress. The mark of the Redhead would not go away.

"Did I ever tell you what happened when I went to the GP with this lot?" I asked Elizabeth, knowing that I had, but she wasn't the only one with repeat stories. "It was hospital for the mind and GP for the body – a step into the world again, or so Doctor Rhodes said, but this GP did not want to know about me: too bad a risk on his neat fund-holding scheme. He did not piss about with pretending. You know what he said? "There are top people, middle people and low people," he said, "and you are one of the low." I was stunned and let his gloved hand poke at my scar while he continued. "You've inherited it from your parents like as not and so there's no fault implied – just the way you are."

A bloody doctor said that to me while he inspected and prescribed. I made a note of date, time and exact circumstances. I told Doctor Rhodes. I complained officially and he denied it all, there being no witnesses, I could take it no further. The press didn't want to know, didn't believe me. I could hardly believe it myself, but I remembered Jew-baiting, nigger-sneering and paki-bashing was not the sole preserve of the working classes. The doctors in Auschwitz had taken the Hippocratic oath."

"And you think Elsie should be put away just because she poked you in the ribs – an accident – you didn't hear her ask for the marmalade." Elizabeth's feathers were ruffling up for battle.

"She never asked," I said defensively. "Not so anyone could understand it."

"You're so selfish, you are." The intensity rose. Spoiling for a fight on her own terms, she was. I could see her point, but it didn't mean I had to give in to the accusation straight away.

"I get a finger stabbed in my side and it's my fault," I wailed.

"You make me sick," said Elizabeth. "Not an ounce of goodness in you – just spit, spit, spit. If anybody should be put away, it's yours truly, not Elsie."

"I shouldn't have said that," I admitted. "Elsie doesn't deserve to be put away. She does no harm. It was an accident. I'm sorry Elsie – can't say fairer than that."

"You're a pig," mouthed Elsie and her face mottled to purple fury. It was impossible to believe that three hours before I had gazed an inch away from the same face and thought it beautiful.

"I know," I said, wondering what Cyclops would do. She reached a great ham hand over the table and grabbed the tissue box, but then I looked more closely. I would have to stop making false descriptions of this woman. Her hands were small, neat and precise. These were clues to show that Elsie was transforming into recognisable woman.

"Pig! Pig! Pig!" I heard through the heaving sobs and I could tell the heart had gone out of the insults, but she had no other words to use. I returned to my story; it needed the coda although neither was listening.

"I changed my doctor, still on NHS, funds no consideration, just underfunding, but I preferred to be treated as a slab of meat in a row with other slabs, not liking the class system. When I mentioned it to Gladys Mitchell at the art therapy, she showed me her tape recorder. Do you know what she does? She carries it round to collect evidence ever since a policeman called her not just a cow but a cowpat – brown and shitty see. You did know Gladys is black and from Lancashire, didn't you?"

I'd messed the whole point of the postscript – should've put in the West Indian bit earlier – never was a good raconteur, not like Charlie, who told me the whole story – different names, different pack-drill – back in the hospital. How did it end? "They just don't know differences can be fun!" What a punch line! It socks a hole right through the twisted guts of the narrow-minded.

Elizabeth was right about the spitting. I am becoming so bitter I'll turn the milk sour even though it's instant in the hot black water. I'll stir and stir, but flecks of white swim to the surface and the spoon is yellow with scum.

"I saw the man who raped me yesterday," I said suddenly and I could not bury the pleading in my voice. Oh please believe me and have sympathy for me. "I knew it was him. How could I forget those eyes and the way his hair flamed from a white head.?"

"And where was this?" asked Elizabeth, her voice doubtful, but she could be relied upon to give attention to pain.

"I can't say," I said, not wanting to admit to the pub. "But I can do without his sort. He does need putting away, putting down. He's mad, madder than me." Elizabeth did not know what to say and so she turned on the TV leaving me to think about the day to come.

I shall bus to the suburbs and walk along the river until the houses pass away and the green gloom folds over my head in its delicate sad array. I shall sit on the bank and sketch in sharp black lines Brunel's suspension bridge and then surround the whole structure with the haze of early morning sunshine so that it shimmers, insubstantial, holding a temporary lease on this rich land. The willows will kiss the water's edge and the mallard, with its strong underwater tow, will forge ripples over the still river and, when I look into my reflection, my face will jump and change, crack and stretch like a clown's in a hall of mirrors. And then I shall rise and inspect the shrubbery, the dancing trees for butterflies and shake the branches until the peacocks, tortoiseshells and red admirals fly, for I love the darting, inconsequential fluttering of these painted creatures. They know how not to fly and they do it with consummate ease. Robert Graves saw how they did it. I know how not to live, but I have much practice in the art still to do, now I've rejected the rules. In such a reverie and such a summer's day I shall lose my bitterness.

Jane's arrival broke into my dream. She was carrying two shopping bags, which she hoisted on the table from her hips like a coal man with sacks.

"I could do with a donkey," she said brightly, cheerily, "but Peter's still in bed." Then she laughed noisily in her throat as if gargling.

"I'm only a pig," I said.

"He's a pig," agreed Elsie, shifting her hams so hard I worried about the cane chair that was taking her weight.

"Now now kiddly-winks," said Jane. "We can't have you trading insults. Try putting this lot in the cupboard will you Elsie?" Slowly she rose. I could smell her sweat mingling with the baby powdered body from the other side of the room where I had gone for sanctuary. Her legs were mighty rolls of fat rubbing against each other. "Sugar in the top, flour in the bottom, a pot of plum next to the old one and will you put the spuds out in the tray?"

Easy does it, Elsie, I thought, as, with face furrowed to hold the instructions tight inside her head, she lifted the bags from the table and waddled from the room.

"She'll do anything for you," said Elizabeth, shaking her head with wonder. "You have a way with you."

"Just a big kid really," Jane said, whisking away the cereal boxes. She sat down and flicked a cigarette to her mouth. "But it's more that medication she's on, you know – keeps her quiet and down in the dumps, but it's the devil own job to get her to the hospital."

"She's turning into a blancmange," I said. "And all because fat is thought a more serious complaint than jeopardising a sane brain."

"Don't try to talk medicine at me, John. You don't know the half of it. Besides what do you care about Elsie?" Jane smiled to take the sting from the words, but they hurt.

"My fags," said Elizabeth, "I can't seem to find my fags. Could you spare one dear?"

84

Jane laughed pleasantly as I knew she would.

"Remember," she said, looking at me, "don't give her fags, whatever you do. She has money enough of her own."

I nodded pleasantly back and then smiled all empty eyes at the old sparrow.

"Except when he nicks 'em – goes off to the pub with my money," she said, twisting her hands because the blue twirling smoke was driving her mad with craving.

"Don't tell whoppers and don't moan," I chipped in, still grinning and rocking my head backwards and forwards at her.

"Oh but he did you know." Elizabeth's eyes saucered and gleamed with fury. "He does you know." She was right, of course. I nick and run like the rabbit out the hutch. I looked all injured pride, but slowly reached into my pocket and pulled out a packet of L.and B.

"I only bought you these first thing this morning and still you accuse me. It's hardly fair," I said. Oh you bitch, you person, you human fright, I think. Lowest of the low, but not restricted in growth, I can twist and turn, find the sunshine and bask. I preened and purred in Jane's praise.

"Here you are accusing him of nicking your fags and he's bought them for you all along. He's a good man, deserves better of you Elizabeth."

Elsie came back into the room and stood, feet apart, clamped to the carpet, peering round as if sniffing the air. She plunged forward and picked up her knitting from the wall shelf with suddenly purposeful hands.

"What are you knitting?" said Jane, all bright and keen.

"Abadoty," said Elsie firmly.

85

"And what's that when it's at home?" I asked, still cocksure and happy in my landlady's smiles.

"Pig! Pig! Pig!" shrieked Elsie and her hands flew to her head, knitting dropping to the floor and Jane leaped up to fuss her into hush. I stood, palms flat towards the shaking jelly mould.

"He is a pig, a fucking pig!" Elizabeth agreed.

"I know. I know," I said. "I'm a pig. It's the way I'm made. Nobody would have me any other way."

"A baby's coaty," mouthed Jane severely, "and it's beautiful," she continued switching a beatific smile to the unhappy Elsie. Elizabeth arrived with yet more tissue for her eyes and the three women looked at me as if I were the torturer, the destroyer of their dreams.

"Very nice too," I shuffled past them out of the back door into the garden where I could sit and think.

It is only in dreams that there is a soft woman with smoothing gentle hands and open thighs. It is only in a dream that her eyes are moist and wide, her tongue gentle on my tongue. She mingles in a dream, but even then there are interruptions, coitus interruptus – a dog barking suddenly, ferociously, three doors away, a spasm of coughing that hunches her to a ball, a reference to an earlier time when the flowers had been honeysuckle, so much sweeter than everlastings, so much more redolent of love.

I have painted many women stretched out on wanton beds, their lovers just out of sight, their hands hovering over their vaginas ready to bring flames to life, eyes following their lovers as they turn to the door. She is receptive, warm and inviting, but she is a dream, a pre-Raphaelite fantasy and her bed is, in fact, the river by Frenchay with her hair entering the reeds like willow strands on waves where she is drowned.

That tiny smile is no longer an invitation because the smooth silvered fish have long since enjoyed her secret meal and turned her eyes to goggling sequins. Those are pearls that were her eyes and her limbs are twisted branches now. Come live with me and be my cold love, mermaid of Avon.

I can not rid myself of this dream. Even though I could hear the three women inside the kitchen talking of ketchup and how Home and Away had been a let down the other night, their voices cried for romance even in the most cynical old bastard that ever lied. It is the need for tenderness that infants may have experienced from their mother's breasts once, long ago, when the world was young and there were no shrivelled drought dry dugs, when innocence was haloed and hallowed like love in the mist.

Was it so bad to hold this dream as a reminder of what might have been? Perhaps women now were all composed of work and shopping, work and ironing, work and things. Perhaps children now were all composed of hard-bitten dollars and cents, screens and self. Perhaps men were reduced to a body and a wallet. Wouldn't such materialism lead to Cromwell Road, paedophile rings, childhood prostitution and the death of compassion?

This sort of thought sitting on the hot metal chair on the crazy Peter patio led me to my ex-wife, almost inevitably, but there was a strange hiatus in my brain, so much having happened since the break up. At times I was not even certain of her name. Years ago she had come and now she was no longer in my life. Monica or Muriel? What the hell was her name and who was to blame? Doctor Rhodes told me she now wished to visit, to bring the two children, no longer children. She would be coming by train. I would not want her to meet Elizabeth or Elsie. I would not want to be seen with the dwarf. That was the sort of woman she was: she made me worried about status, ready to pass judgements on the weak and the poor. The palms of my hands were hot on the chair's arms. I could feel the sweat bead on my lip. It was going to be a scorcher again.

There were flowers in great buckets by the door, along the nave and at the altar: spring flowers in pale pinks, yellows and blues. Her dress was icing sugar, petticoated with rice paper. Her veil held by a silver coronet. I knew she was wearing her grandmother's bracelet; she had borrowed exquisite pearls from Aunt Louise. Beneath her skirts, there was a garter in blue. Tricked out in finery, all details in place to marry an eligible man. The presents fitted the painstakingly created list. The music dovetailed the waltz down the aisle and off I was led, my eyes in blinkers, to follow the ritual until I was dead. Her father had warned me.

"Likes her own way, does Monica; likes everything nice. You'll have your hands full." But all I could think of was how full my hands would be of her rich flesh, her glorious pulsing body with my body, the slow delirious days of painting each delicate fold of each delicate part of her. Dream on Dodo! What a fool I had been and what an insult to ask of any fellow creature to waive the right to develop, change, find other means of expression than the acquiescence to lust. I was the raw one. I was the fool. She had come to me quite calm, collected and cool, knowing what she wanted, seeing in me a chance to create the little nest and to lead her little dance. I was the betrayer of her artifice. This man was not what he seemed.

Dear Monica, if you could have born two point four children, you would have done so. Instead you found two children growing inside you almost by accident for sex was a rare and generally sterile event. I think you looked on me as part of another whole, for you had to have your patterns neatly etched. I am inclined to believe that superficiality and underdone steaks are similar. Both are bloody and speak of rawness, scarcely covered pain. I don't eat steak, of course. Have you bought any for the Pekinese recently? Well you know the cost and the consequences for the brain. But when I open the trap-door in my head I can hear the prices reeling from the butcher's purple lips as if all our yesterdays were long shopping lists bought from the small salary of a small-time teacher. £9.34 pence, I'm afraid, Mrs. Comefriendly-On.

Outside the home so pleasant and smiley, inside the home so harsh and crisp. My father used to stiffen his elbow on the bar at the Slag and Gravel, having fought for his country to no great effect. But Muriel, you never fought for anything but the right to have a freezer, microwave and the CD player that finally broke me down. Christ, music should have fluff on it for God's sake. How dare you sanitise my soul, my heroes in vinyl?

My eyes open blearily back in the garden. I am sitting in a cloud of weed flakes as they pour on the boiling breeze over from next door. There will be rose-bay willow herb in every cranny of Peter's yard unless somebody does something about it. A few pigeons lift on dry staccato wings and settle over the toast crumbs, peck pecking at grit and bread. Blod, the large grey rabbit, sits like stone behind wire. He has been known to chew through to reach the carrots, but I shall watch him from my burning chair and he shall watch me. Any move he makes I will scotch. Any move I make, he will flick his long ears and sneer, before hip-hop-hoppety into the shade. The great white cat slinks over the wall, slides between rhubarb leaves and then, becoming domesticated after the long night, trit trots past me, rubbing my legs, claiming me as territory. His pink mouth opens and a snarling plea mews out for milk.

"Here you are Splodge," said Jane, bending down with the jug and bowl so that I could see the roundness that Peter enjoys. The pigeons up and fly.

"It is good to have a pet, a creature to care for," Doctor Rhodes had said. "It teaches responsibility."

It is good to hear Blod's filing teeth on his bars. It is good to know his doe is waiting for him four gardens away. It is good to reduce the days to escape, to fuck and run. Blod gives me a voyeur's satisfaction and teaches irresponsibility.

"And how was Home and Away? Score draws or did you draw a blank?"

"Elizabeth does rabbit on," Jane said. "But it's good to talk."

"Pays BT's bills," I grunted, suddenly suspicious of all this goodness. She did not hear, just whisked inches past my chair with washing for hanging. I love watching women peg wet clothes on lines. They bend unselfconsciously, their thighs flexing, and then with a flick and a stretch their torsos twist and they breast forward to the line, holding the pose for the pegs to clip into place. Their faces are intent, each movement focussed.

"I love watching you hang washing. You are so beautiful," I called out and then blushed at the corny comment, but Jane did not seem to mind, just turned her head, smiled and told me there was life in the old dog yet. Monica would never have spoken so casually. She would have frowned because there was no connection in her mind between the chores and beauty; they did not fit the pattern of contrived effects. I thought about the importance of having a home, a simple language for everyday living. I spent so much time reading meanings into trivial comment that a place where a common language could live and grow without worry, without tension and fear was greatly to be desired. But the peddler to Eyam brought a common language. He was a creature coming from away to home, carrying the accoutrements of recognised lives and codes of behaviour. He had been trusted as a wholesome entertainer. What a plague he had unleashed! What an inheritance of fear, mistrust

91

and hatred! Was there any wonder that I had become so passive? Any initiative leads to misunderstanding, but how I admire the buck rabbit as he tries to bite through wire. I can even sympathise with the smashing of pub windows, the white obscenities scrawled on black walls and even the bomb blaster on a bus. I had become the fearful dead creature with the frozen brain and hand.

"Why did you marry me Muriel Monica?" I had asked her that in bed one night when the big freeze was on. Although her face was in shadow, I could hear her answer.

"I just hoped to have children with you and give them the start to help make the world a little better. Each generation should try to improve for the next so that we spread a little happiness."

"And you thought I was the one to help you?"

"You were too clever by half, John. Always there with a quick word and I could never reach you, never touch your feelings, but I had thought you were the one for me." Even as I recognised the truth in her words I could not help sneering at her cliched words.

"I admire your regenerative gift, your initial spark, but optimism is a dead duck for me," I said. I was under the doctor for depression and he had talked about maintaining an even keel, keeping steady, running to stand still, not biting off more than I could chew, while the tumbling vortex into oblivion loomed at my feet. The rot was in the brain. The more the rot within, the greater the chaos without, however ribboned and bowed the quilting, however polished and tidy the house. And which came first? The chicken or the egg? The mother or the child? But I had been a creature of habit and obedience. I bowed to higher authority. The top people spoke and I huddled in my camp awaiting the broken bottle in my face.

"You always did exaggerate," Monica had said at our last meeting through the grille in the prison, "and you never explain what you mean, just hide away inside your head with the weeks floating by. I don't believe there's anything left in there worth bothering with. You won't talk until suddenly bang, you do something stupid."

"Just pap," I'd said. "Inside the crust there's pap and inside my head there's no joke, I tell you." I remember leaning forward to grasp her wrist. It had been incredibly small in my hand and I had caught her grandmother's bracelet with my forefinger. "I had to escape you see," I had said, but she had not seen and could not have seen beyond my howling mouth and the pain on her arm. She had pulled away, breaking the clasp and had gone.

Chapter 7

The garden at the back of the house is well sheltered from the road so that the traffic roar is a low mushing sound like water in the ears after swimming. I sat, head close to my chest, and I conjured the element of water to lap around me. It was cool, soft, capable of soothing my dried up brain, although the heat was rising. When I peered through screwed up eyes the darting sunlight seemed to be cracking the Peter patio stones and knifing the clump of blood-red fuschias in the walled corner. They were beginning to wilt, flopping away from the central stem on the search for water. By carefully sliding my eyeballs to the left I could see the shed lean crazily like a gypsy's caravan and on the other side of the wall the circular tower rose in early morning orange brick.

It was there that my gaze stopped: red against blue, green tufting from the black unpointed joins. The tower had no visible means of entry, no windows and no doors. I recalled what Peter and Jane had said about it when I'd come to the house on my first visit.

"It's Napoleonic," Peter had said proudly.

"One of the reasons we bought the house," Jane chimed in.

"Standing up for fine weather," Peter had grinned and winked at me.

"Oh get away with you," she'd said happily. "You men!"

"What is it then?" I'd asked because its bulk and roundness, the darknesses in its side, its whole original purpose seemed a mystery. It had been a cool misty day on my first visit. The circular tower had seemed to be standing alone, out of all context, stuck in a white and grey sky with shadowed buildings beyond. For an instant I had been irritated to hear Peter's casual explanation until I realised his words left so much unresolved and undiscovered.

"It could not have been part of a defence system this far round the coast. It's not like a martello tower: no turrets, no arrow-slits, no entrances," I had said.

"Napoleonic – used for defence. That's what the estate agent said – a pleasing feature, but I'm not so sure." Peter had seemed quite sure and I had not argued against him, leaving the mystery to swill around my head a little, liking the feel of uncertainty from the past, the physical challenge of its presence. It would be a search, I had thought.

"So that's why you called the house, Tower House," I'd said, accepting the explanation at face value.

"It was called that before we moved in," Jane had said. "But it's a good name."

I remembered the way she had looked at her husband, shifting her hand down her right leg so that her shirt tugged and her breasts had strained towards him. I had known that they had made love before my arrival and I had imagined them – she, a little plump and sturdy in the

95

thighs, her high-coloured face and wet full lips; he, stocky with black hairs sprouting from his chest and the mole on his shoulder lifting and falling. I had not known about the mole and hairs, of course, until I'd seen him painting, torso bare, on the stairs, but pictures accumulate over time, building up their texture and truth. I had definitely sensed the love between them, the sweet muskiness of their mingling only minutes before I had come. It had made me sad then to think of my exclusion, to recognise that my presence would be just a convenience for money, an inconvenience for their lives. Surely they would have preferred their house together, their lives together, their confident seeking after each other's deepest joy without the advent of the emotionally lame, the broken-hearted and the bad.

"You could do without somebody like me cluttering your place up," I had said. "I'm famous for being in the way."

"Have to find you something to do, won't we?" Jane had answered brightly. "Besides it's what it's for, this house: too big by half for just Pete and me and you'll bring in some income, don't you fret. It says you're a painter on this form. Why don't you paint the tower? It would look nice in the entrance hall." It had seemed to be another joke or maybe all their conversation was watered by an undercurrent of shared and secret smiles.

I had smiled gently, distracted from the vision of their bodies to the image she had found "nice". She had goggled a little and nudged Peter with her elbow so that he had over-reacted, lurching in his chair as if he'd been pushed.

"Go easy love," he'd said. "I'm not made of metal."

That had been a joke too connected with the tower, with Peter's body, his strength. They had been thirty year old children playing with the phallic, fresh in their relationship, able to welcome me and other damaged goods into their home from the warmth of the love they had shared. They had shown me my room, promising its decoration from bottle green to any light colours of my choosing, although Peter did have a nice supply of light pink and gloss white to use up, if that was all right.

"What do you do?" I had asked Peter. "Are you a painter decorator?"

"Was in the navy," he had replied. "Built up a few resources, can turn my hand to most things," and he'd looked at his wife with undisguised admiration.

"I'm one of your things, I suppose," Jane had said with ill-concealed excitement.

They had made me feel tired: middle aged and past it, but I had taken the room. Doctor Rhodes had made it clear there was no choice in the matter.

Now, as I sat in the sweltering garden, my eyes closed, I decided to investigate the tower over the wall. I had been passive for too long; it was time to assert my self. Unbidden words entered my head. "The people that walk in darkness have seen a great light. Yeah, they that live in the shadow of the valley of death, upon them has the light shined." There was no doubting the light. The sun burned like a steel furnace and the shadow lay on the tower. And so, in order to escape burning, I hurried my mind into the tower's shelter, forcing a way between a narrow rift in the brick. How silent it felt, how deeply close and holding. Peering up, I could see nothing but a turning, turning staircase leading on and on to nothing but more darkness.

For a moment the sun outside beckoned for my return, but I shunned the fire and started upon the first tread. As I did so I heard a faint cry above as of a child, as of my son James, when he was first home and did not sleep.

I took the treads steadily and saw on each splashes of yellow, dribbles of wetness. There was the smell of baby's sickness in the air and I carefully leaned forward to wipe away each little patch of vomit with my sleeve. I had forgotten my handkerchief again. It took so long to rise and still the cries beckoned me. My back ached with the bending and cleaning, the leaving no trace behind. My legs hurt with the lifting, the climbing, but I soldiered on for was this not a place of defence, a wartime retreat?

Eventually, after long travelling through semi-darkness, I reached a place where there was a cool wind and above me there seemed to be night sky stretching on towards eternity, but there were no more stairs. I looked round for my child and saw him, a stocky pale child of crawling age and eyes like a cat's, blue and round in the moonlight. But his body was hunched and his eyes were filled with tears. I moved towards him, but then was stilled for suddenly he stretched out, brought up his mouth and retched, his face reddening. For a moment he seemed to be bringing his whole heart out into the world, but then a great ball extruded from his yawning snake mouth and rolled to my feet.

I was so used to the routine of bend and clean that I automatically stooped as if to clear the ball away, but I found myself holding a large orange fruit, a fire of richness. At last he had produced his heart's desire and I was holding it. It was perfect: round and whole, firm and strong, brilliantly coloured and scented. It demanded to be noticed and so I rolled it in my hands, held it to the dark sky so that the sun appeared there again. But then I observed one small flaw, one piece the size of fifty pence, which was brown, flaccid to touch, bruised from all his efforts to gurgitate and regurgitate. And yet it had seemed an easy enough birth at the height of the dark tower and the blemish would be noticed only by me. The child's eyes were now clear and his tears had dried. He was no longer crouched over his belly incubating his pain, but lay on his back, feet kicking in the air and his eyes sparking.

"I have journeyed many miles," I said, "to see this sight and have walked alone through this great house of darkness to find this orange a little bruised in its skin. I should celebrate, bring in friends and relations, to join me for what is a child if not the evidence of shared creativity? Where are my fellow companions? Who will drink the wine with me?" But the landing on which I stood stayed dim. From far below there came a hissing whisper to leave the child alone, not to give him ideas, to keep him sensible and sleeping soundly. Darkness again intruded and all that shone was the child's eyes and the golden orb of fire in the darkest velvet night.

"Oh what can make it whole again?" I cried for it was monstrous that this child's innocence should be so early abused, that the stain of living without hope should be placed so firmly on creation so soon.

"He'll be perfect as long as you don't mess him around." I recognised Monica's voice curling up the stairs. "Just got a bit of tummy ache, that's all." But I plucked my son up and held his white face next to mine, rocking him and telling him the story of the mighty Gog and Magog, their battles on the hills. Suddenly I was surrounded by angry shouts, a fierce shadowed shape rushed upon me and my child was borne away from me, his small body ripped from my hands. "Just needs his nappy changing – can't you even see that?"

I awoke outside the tower with the sun still beating down, my eyelids sticky, my head whirling. In the kitchen window stood the hulk of Elsie and she was pointing directly at me with a knitting needle, her mouth opening and closing, and Jane was back at the line, pegging up smalls. Bend and lift, bend and lift, her torso twisted in the sun like a silvered fish. She was beautiful; her hair swung like gold and her hips were rich with promise. I ached to hold her, but the world reeled in black and gold flashes.

"No chance, old son," I muttered in my beard. Her brisk quick competence denied all approach. "You'll be up to your neck if you tried – past it – old before your time. In the catalogue you may go for a man as semi-dog is dog, but there's no point in yearning for the moon when the sun's in eclipse. Old Percy himself knows it. There's been no flicker for days and if the heart's dried, can procreation thrive?"

Three women and two men in one house! Peter and

Jane were our keepers; we were emotionally deprived, hurt and capable of hurting others. I was of all three kinds and had to keep in the darkness, light denied. Elsie was standing in the doorway now poking her needle like a gun.

"Needatat! Pig! Needatat." Her voice cracked like a machine gun.

"Sit there much longer and you'll be fried," said Jane. I opened my eyes wider, squinted up at the landlady bright in her blue cotton dress in the white sun. "You's already caught it," she said and touched my left temple with her palm. It was like ice on me and I recoiled. "Feel cold does it?" She laughed. "You'd better get inside, splash some cold water on your bonce. It overheats enough without cooking it."

Slowly I stood, the sky darkening round me and the stars flickering in their orbs.

"Whoopsadaisy!" said Jane, putting her arm under my arm, propping my shaky leg with her firm thigh. "Come on old man. Where's the do and die gone to then?"

Slowly the fainting passed.

"A touch of sun," I grunted and released myself, making my way towards the comparative coolness of the house. She tracked me. I had been startled by the touch of her body on mine, the sight of her full breasts as she leaned to support me, the sturdy confidentiality of her leg against mine. I am her patient, I thought, and must not think of her rich sex. I have renounced being a man long ago. But I paused by the step into the kitchen, wondering where Elsie may have gone and what she had been doing, machine gun rattling me. I turned towards Jane to say something of my past misdeeds, the reasons for my nasty, hasty actions and the cause of the slow poison within, but she just patted my back and urged me in.

Slowly I tottered into the dark house, my pupils failing to adjust quickly enough. I banged against the table and smelt Elsie's fury from the chair in the corner, but I shook my brain a little clearer and negotiated the door. The whole of my head was singing with the previous day's beer and the morning sun. Blindly I found the stairs and reached the bathroom with its long wall mirror. Time for the body check, I thought, now the sun had scorched through my shirt and my back was on fire. Dr. Rhodes would be pleased. He had told me my body was an object to be inspected dispassionately. It carried clues to my experience, but flesh was just a temporary vehicle for the soul. Any damage should not afflict the central core of being for ever.

I paused by the mirror, frightened by the prospect. I had been a good looking young man. What if, under the clothes now, there was only an ugly shell? The image of my youth was far from me. Besides I knew what I looked like, for God's sake. It was stupid to go through with it on the whim of a doctor. I could not even remember what he'd said to justify a slow and thorough inspection. I sat on the edge of the loo seat trying to recall the purpose of such an examination, but there were bright flecks still in my eyes and the room was swimming. I remembered the need for water and quickly turned on the shower, pulled off my clothes and winced under the fierce jet, biting back the scream of pain as the cold struck me.

Ye gods and little fishes, how the spray shot needles in my flesh and the goose pimples rose. Soon I was shivering by the river, sheltered by the strong willow and shaded from the bright sun. Rub and down. Rub and down. Bring back the sparkling into the yellowed skin. Where was the blush of invigoration? Gingerly I avoided the wound in my side. Then I was still, naked, and back in front of the mirror.

What was the purpose of the bodycheck again, Doctor? Was it to remind me of the physical presence, the here and now, this is what you are. Prick me and I bleed. Pinch me and I bruise. Abuse me and the shell of flesh is split down to the marrow. Perhaps the purpose was to force me beyond the body for I gained no joy in seeing the sag-bag rag-bag withering on the vine. Was there more glory teasing away the strands of flesh to the presence within, the Blakean assertion of human redemption, angelic youth, in the deep-down seed of divine man? I recalled the etching of Blake's death bed with the wonderful Adam of all our youth shining above the broken shell of his body, the old man's eyes gazing upwards into ineffable bliss. How could you keep such untainted visions when the blood of infants ran down the castle walls?

I put thin fingers out towards my reflection and tried to touch each nipple, but the whirled fingerprint intervened on each occasion. I turned my fingers back towards my own skin, but the sensation was that of smoothing glass. I could not feel the shiver of human contact, when the touching was all my own. I supposed that if another came and anointed my shell with deft and gentle fingers, smoothed the thinning hair from my face and whispered of eternal love, I might be soothed as a child is soothed after nightmares. But Monica's hands, for all the creams and unguents, all the rubber gloves and careful manicures, had always touched like cardboard, packaging my body into a restricted frame. And since the Redhead's vicious attacks, the sore on my side had often scabbed over and I'd waited for the pink skin to mend. But there had been too much betrayal and the poison pus had built up and oozed through.

"I wish you were more romantic," Monica used to say, but she had meant, "Why don't you bring me chocolates? Where are the flowers? When was the last time you took me somewhere nice?" I had been too romantic, searching for love's connections in the tiniest detail, ignoring the material in search of the grail.

"What sort of consolation do you need?" I spoke to the mirror quite angrily for I was beginning to feel surprisingly chilly under this scrutiny. "There's not a lot of chance of young girls catering to your needs with your grey, wrinkled scrotum, your pot-belly and patchy scab, your thin grey hairs, million moles and empty pockets."

"It doesn't stop you looking at the girls though, does it?" My reflection answered.

"I search for sweet faces and eager eyes, but all I find is the twist of cynicism on thin lips, the deadness of hurt in defeated shoulders."

"Male menopause," Doctor Rhodes had said with sudden vigour when I'd mentioned my feelings.

"Oh you've been there too, have you?" I had asked because he is much older than I am.

"It is natural for the old and ugly to worship youth and beauty, even as it hates its joie-de-vivre."

"The eye of the beholder," I'd said pompously, "can change ugliness into beauty and beauty to ugliness in a moment."

"You are an unregenerate romantic," the doctor had said and it was good to be recognised at last. It is possible to be vulnerable and male even in the twentieth century.

"I must be lovely to myself," I'd said, tears springing in my eyes. "Even when I am most hateful, there must be some small worth."

Doctor Rhodes had shrugged and patted my shoulder awkwardly. This was out of character for him. He'd seemed at sea for once as if I'd touched a chord within him which had not been played for years.

"Look on your last for all things lovely," I had misquoted wildly, "but my last has no redemption."

"Are you telling me that beauty is transient, that it only lives in the last experience of it?" He had resumed the mantle of counsellor and I nodded. "Are you also suggesting that the last lovely thing you have experienced has also destroyed your chance of happiness?" This time I had shaken my head because I had been playing silly buggers with words again. The last "last" was the shoemaker's last, the grindstone of work, my work as a painter but not a decorator. It had been too much hassle to explain that my painting no longer seemed to help me see a way through into understanding and so the dialogue had lapsed and here I was by the mirror thinking about hypocrisy, two-faces and the eye of beauty.

It was all very well to talk of the outward show hiding the inner man, but what beauty lay in the last look at Elsie with her encrusted chins, her gland-swollen limbs? In every fat person, there's a thin person screaming for release, preached weight-watchers anonymous. You too can be slimmer of the year and be reduced to a wisp of mist moving wraithlike up the estuary waiting for the flush of sun to burn the last fat away. Was I alone in thinking it cruel for Elsie to be shown pictures of emaciated fashion models from Somalia?

Now I remembered the purpose of the bodycheck. I was to try to bring my thought of worth to the body of shame and make them one, to remind me that abuse stems from the inability to accept the reality of flesh and bone. I made myself gaze at the reflection of me again. I was still nauseated by the loose folds and the scourge marks, but the scabs from the thorns had peeled from my head and were pale threads of healing. I could touch the scars without wincing away from the memory of ugliness they brought. "It is in the eye of the beholder," I mouthed to the mirror and then thought a little more. "No, it is behind the eye, but how shall we know what lies behind the unseen and unknowable?" I became silent, caught in the net like a small roach I had plucked from the river with the hook deep in its throat. "They are like tiny fish scales," I said, leaning towards the reflection and touching my forehead where the thin skin shone. No, great water lover, ducker and diver, see what you want to see and hide from the rest. I made myself face myself. These marks are like the dried seeds of honesty, the silver moons that spread their truth biennially and I am caught in an off year! The most, I concluded, was that my body was an image and I had grown introverted, annoyed with my introspection, annoyed with Doctor Rhodes who had counselled such thought and what was worst of all, insufferably boring to myself and all who sailed in her.

"Here and now! Here and now!" I chanted loudly. "Living for ever in the Bull and Cow." No such pub, just rhyming words, (No, don't start investigating the relationship and reasons for the nomenclature – accept chance collisions) but time to jolt out and cover up. I decided to go to the station to meet my wife, Monica, Joanna, my daughter, and James, my son. I decided to wear my old grey suit and a clean shirt. I would hold up my head and speak kindness. It was time to cast the slough of passivity and become action man at last.

Chapter 8

"John! ... I'm sorry about this ... that bloody man (sotto voce) ... John, will you come down? You've visitors." It was Jane shouting up the stairs. I was holding the letter from Monica. I had cleaned my black shoes and borrowed the house iron to bring some order to a creased white shirt. I had tied my maroon tie with small yellow crescents on it round my neck and straightened the collar around it. I was dressed as I had promised in the grey suit. I was shaved and had plucked grey hairs from both nostrils. I had acted. I had forced myself out of the receiving end into the delivery mode, but, when the time to catch the bus to the railway station had come, I had let it pass. Now I could hear footsteps clumping up the stairs, but I could not respond either to push down the lock or to fling the door open in greeting. "I knew he was to meet you, but didn't know the time, otherwise I'd have sorted him out for you."

Oh do not make me a piece of jumble and don't sound so apologetic, Jane. Monica Muriel has ways of making everyone apologise for no reason. I shall apologise, I thought, when the door is opened and they stand on the threshold uncertain of their greeting, uncertain of their entry. I did not ask them to come, did I?

"He could have said he didn't want a visit and then we wouldn't have put ourselves out, would we?" I heard the breath gasping from the woman outside the door, but I did not recognise her voice at all and this was astonishing to me. I had heard it in so many dreams since her last departure from Dartmoor that I could not believe it had changed. She had explained in her letter that she had unfinished business to settle, but I could not imagine of what kind. But why else this journey, tracking me to where I was scarcely alive in a fragile shell of the state's devising? I'd sent back the papers for quicky divorce. I admitted my incompatibility, my criminal tendencies.

"You are their father, John," she'd put in the letter. "It is right they should have concern for you, want to know you just a little." But this was not the unfinished business. She had other fish to fry. She was walking up the stairs with the pan in her hands. The fat was sizzling hot and I was the mere sprat for her heat, the smackerel for her hunger. She needed to be confirmed in her rectitude and perfection; she needed to see me as the sole cause of failure. Bitter? Yes bitter like lemon juice on mouth sores and I had let her come. Mad, I am. Past redemption.

I stood in the centre of my room, my space, with the Redhead buggering me on the wall behind two coats of emulsion, holding her letter to my chest, rocking, rocking, heel and toe, listening to their trudge up the long stairs, listening to their furrowed-brow voices, listening to the knock, knock, knock on the door and I was scared. She had tracked me down, cut through the layers of prison

109

and hospital to thrust our children into my face and say, "Take note. Here is the progeny of our limbs. You owe them duty and service." I closed my eyes because I could give them nothing. When with them, passing through the grey days of neat semi-detached, workaday blues' days and chore, chore, chore, I had merely given pretence and the monthly money. Now I had nothing to give. I should be a terrible disappointment to my children.

"Now don't expect too much," Jane spoke outside my door and the knocking stopped for a moment. "He is better than he was, but it will be a shock to see you. I just wish more families would keep in touch. Most of my tenants are very lonely."

I turned to face the door, stretching a smile over my face like a rubber mask. The panic ran through my gut like fire and I squinted down at her letter for her name, but it was a blur. I'd cut her out of my thinking and still she haunted me. The anger burned me, but I would restrain it for my children's sake. I managed to reach the handle and to swing the door open.

"I'm sorry I did not come to meet the train," I said. "I fell asleep on the patio in the sun and the time ran on." They were not to know my heatstroke had been two weeks earlier. The weather had not broken.

"You always did drop off when the going got tough," the woman at the door said. "May we come in?"

No chairs, no room, bed only roughly made, a wet towel on the floor, my baggy trousers crumpled by the wall, the ashtray full and the old mural coming into sight through the slapped emulsion if you knew how to look for it …

"Perhaps we'd be more comfortable downstairs," I said, but I did not want them to meet Elizabeth or Elsie. I had my pride. I would not be lumped together with the old and the fat.

"Nonsense," said Jane and ushered in the crowd.

It had been a distortion of the stairs that had produced an alien echo in her voice. Now Monica was here, perched on the bed, with her neat suit neatly smoothed under her neat hands, she had the same voice as ever, but she had changed. She had managed to arrest the encroaching wrinkles round her eyes and send them back twenty years to when we'd first met. Her dark hair was shingled with highlights artfully placed: no silver strands left. In my mind, she'd been an overripe pear in floral clothes, but she was trim in a dark high-shouldered business suit. But her voice could not be disguised. It remained flat, tuneless. Even when she spoke soft thoughts, her lips moved on metal flanges.

"It's been some time," she said and nodded towards me. "You'll hardly know Joanne and James."

"Three years is not so long," I said.

"Depends what's packed into them," she said.

The strangers stood on either side of their mother at the bedside and I darted guilty looks at both, but could not meet their eyes, for they were looking at their mother with embarrassment. It would make a good sculpture, I thought, pushing the experience away into an art form, where it could be encompassed, redirected and moulded into acceptability. James had grown through puberty to be tall and lean. He had a flush of pinprick spots beneath his cheeks and a darkening on his upper lip. His eyes were deep-set and there were hollows at his temples. He was clutching a plastic bag and his knuckles were white.

"Does he eat?" I asked, trying to smile in his direction.

"Like a horse," said Monica. "Never stops."

"Hi Dad," he said, transferring bag to bed and nodding towards me like a grandfather.

"Hi Dad," said Joanne, shifting from one foot to the other.

"Hello," I said, a yard away, and my bottom lip trembled. If either looks up now, I'm lost, I thought. Then Joanne did, as I knew she would, because James had always claimed I favoured her and he was right. Her eyes were troubled, dark and fearful. She should not fear her father, they seemed to say, and yet she did. I could not take her fear on top of mine and turned my back abruptly tears flooding my eyes. She was my child, but she was also a woman.

"There's not much of a view," I said, unable to see anything, refusing to brush away the tears that ran down my cheeks like rain. "But if you crane up you can see the tops of the houses on the other side of Fishponds." Slowly I gained control of my voice. "It was called Fishponds because there used to be a religious foundation very close and the monks kept a large stew pond teeming with carp. From the other side of the house," I was now able to turn to point vaguely towards the back of the house. " You can see the tower – a construction built in Napoleonic times to make lead shot, like a marble run for lead. It's quite a rarity, I'm told. It was highly unlikely old Boney would invade so far round the coast. Most constructions were on the South and there are some who argue it was made for different purposes. Who is to tell?"

"They've come to see you," laughed Jane. "Not have a

tourist guide from your bedroom. I'll bring a cup of tea."

While she clattered out the door I drew deep breaths to hold myself together and wondered how to talk to strangers who could yet bring such an emotional charge upon my heart that the tears scalded and the eyes pricked with needlepoint pain.

"I sounded like a teacher, I'm afraid," I said apologetically. "It's seeing you both so big and grown-up. I did not know what to say."

Joanne smiled and she nodded to me as James had done, as if conferring benediction. I know I nodded back in doll-like response.

"Landlady seems efficient," said Monica crisply. "Are you looked after well?" I nodded yet again. "I thought we might find a place to eat for lunch."

"There's not much round here," I said. "The fish and chippy is still closed, but there's a cafe round in Weldon Road."

"In the city," Monica continued as if I had not spoken. "I've already booked a table at Monique's." I did not know the place, but it sounded too expensive for my pocket. My face must have shown doubt because she followed up almost curtly. "Don't worry John. The food is on me. You'll not have to dip into your pocket. It's recommended in the good food guide."

This time I did not recognise her voice. There was an iron confidence in her that troubled me and where would this money be coming from? When I was inside, the single parent benefit hardly covered for the upkeep. She used to berate me with her poverty.

"Won the lottery?" I asked, feigning a joke. She'd explained in her letter that she had returned to nursing now the children were older, but nurses were not well paid, I thought.

"Working woman," she answered crisply. "And some more news that will wait."

Monica avoided drinking the tea. She thanked Jane, but left her standing in the hall carrying the tray. I wanted to stay behind because Jane had made an effort. There were cups and saucers, not a chipped Mickey Mouse eared mug in sight, and chocolate biscuits on a doily on a flowery plate.

"We should drink the tea," I said. "Jane's been to some trouble." But Jane herself was behind me, pushing me out of the door into the midday sunshine.

"See you later!" She called. "And have fun."

There was a taxi waiting. It must have been standing there, clocking up the fare, for twenty minutes. Monica gave instructions while we clambered inside. Joanne to my right and Jamie to the left and me stuck in the middle. It was a long time since I had been in a car, but when I told my children they looked at me with disbelieving eyes.

"You may find it hard to imagine," I said. "But there are millions of buggers like me without immediate recourse to four wheels on a bubble." I pushed back against the rest and Jamie helped me shove the safety belt into place. "I don't like feeling closed in," I said. "But it won't be for long, will it?"

My last car journey had been in a police car. I could recall the soap smell of the large officer at my side: a huge man with great thighs which pinned me to the seat and made me feel like a schoolboy caught scrumping.

114

"Little boys should not play with matches," he'd said. "They always get burned."

I remembered craning my head round to look out of the back where the redness warmed the darkness and the spitting flame flecks sparked through the swirling smoke cloud. There had been a stench of burning drifting on the pall from the school roof. It had seeped into my clothes, into my nostrils and my hair and yet I had smelt the cleanliness of the officer in his hard smart uniform as an enemy to what I had become.

"Cars are like that." I turned to Joanne trying to smile away the memory. "They appear neat and tidy, clean and crisp, following routes to inevitable conclusions, but underneath they stink of carbons and leads." Monica settled in to the front seat, smoothing the back of her hair. The taxi drew slowly into the stream of traffic, the trundling queue to the city centre.

"Mum's got a car now," said James. "A new Peugeot."

"You surprise me," I said. Monica looked round from the front seat.

"There's been a few changes recently." Her head moved up and down like a doll's and her grin was pasted into place.

I spent the rest of the journey looking past my children through the windows and realised that car dwellers and drivers see very little of the world they pass through.

"You could almost believe this place was clean and thriving," I said once, whisking down Park Street. "That's the dossers' spot, beneath the archway." But we'd passed it by together with the squatters' house and the alley where kiddies hang out switching from Ecstasy to Rave to LSD to the grave.

She's managed to creep into my life again, I thought, and it had reached a sort of stasis without her that I could manage, despite suffering the latent threats of the Redhead behind every turning. At least today there would be no chance of him spotting me. He would not recognise me in this company, trailing up the gangplank into the riverside restaurant, being greeted as fully paid up members of the human race, being escorted over plush carpet to a mahogany black veneered table and gazing with largely unseeing eyes at the hand-written menu inside leather-backed card. Even when I was working for the family, we had never afforded this sort of joint. A teacher's salary would not run to it as well as funding Joanne's trip to France and James' mountain bike.

"Now we will not talk about anything but nice things during the meal," Monica said, adjusting her napkin and firmly breaking her bread roll with a manicured fingernail. "It has been a long time since breakfast."

I tried to smile, but there was more than a hint of bad to come and I did not want to wait for it. Do you want the good news or the bad news first? I always opted for the bad, but Monica never would. In fact she'd always rejected unhappiness as an unnecessary encumbrance. Very sensible too, I thought, if you could manage that way. It had been desperately hard for her married to the perennial depressive. One sign of the lobster crawling out of the pot and my claws would be out dragging the escapologist back into the same world as the rest of us. Escape? There was no real escape from the drab and confined, the little and manipulated. For every one "successful" person I could show a million pretending a

116

vestige of happiness in the daily trap of poverty of mind and body. But Monica? Oh no. Hers was a different ethos. Even as a man lay dying on the hospital death bed, she'd be there singing always look on the bright side of life. The last thing she needed was the whining tones of my twisted vision picking away at every scab until the wounds showed raw. Now, without me, she was bright, vibrant, clear and totally in control of the happiness she was born with, but from where had the readies come? Monica could never be happy on single person's benefit. Not many people could be.

"Still your trim figure, Monica," I said. "I never could understand how you could pack so much food away and stay slim."

"Hollow legs you used to say," said James.

"Did I?" I didn't remember that as one of my hackneyed phrases. My father used to use the term, but I had tried so hard not to send his tired words into the next generation. I bent my head over the food.

"It is imaginative," Monica said, "to make a restaurant from a canal boat. But why the name, Monique's?"

"Kindred spirits," I ventured and was gratified to see a small tight smile of gratification. I could still play the right notes and hide behind them. Personally the taste of the place left me cold with its dim lighting, mock candelabra and silver-threaded black and purple carpet. The music was also recherché – bruised and mushy mellifluousness, but I could tell Monica liked the ambience and she was paying.

My belly churned with the feeding. I had oysters sluiced down with white wine, a rolled shoulder of lamb with onion sauce, roast potatoes and asparagus shoots, apple pie with ice cream and cream and the cheese platter. I gorged and the waiter ducked and wove. Eventually the coffee in tiny little bone china cups was placed in front of us and the business side of lunch was heralded with Monica placing her napkin briefly to her lips and looking across at me for the first time.

"Bread landed butter side up?" I said immediately, jumping in.

"I've had to look after myself and the children after what you did."

"No man's a meal ticket for life," I said. "Too unreliable."

"I'm not relying on a man. I'm administrative secretary for the hospital trust. I work for the directorate." Oh how she shone when she rolled out the words administrative secretary! And which director directed her to open her legs for him? I wondered, but I would not say anything then. There was wine in my brain and I had to concentrate across the table to keep focused. I did not want to talk about our marriage with James and Joanne alongside, with the divorce papers reaching their inevitable conclusion.

"Men are far too unreliable," Monica agreed and rummaged through your bag. "I could have sent these back through the solicitor, perhaps I should have, but I thought it best to see you myself." She opened up the forms to show me what I'd done.

"You know I hate forms," I said defensively. "And I did not like the way I'm described. I'm not a dangerous criminal. I've never threatened violence. It was my first offence."

"There's your dignity to think about," she continued,

"and your children's self respect. They do love you, you know."

"Isn't this out of all proportion?" I asked. "Decree nisis are given without so much as a sidelong glance. If Charlie and Diana can manage to split, surely we can manage without my having to sign on the dotted line. On second thoughts, perhaps that's not such a good comparison, bringing death in its wake. Besides," I continued, "I've only drawn Pooh, Piglet and Eeyore on the form. They were your favourites."

"Don't be naive, John," she said, her lips pursing. "I don't want to say any more in front of the children, but I do need your proper signature on this replacement form. Otherwise how will it look to the judge?"

"That's the unfinished business," I said flatly. "How do my children feel?" I looked at Joanna and realised that she had eaten very little.

"We're not children."

"No, of course not – just what your Mother said, not me. You're old enough to make up your own minds." How I resented the way Monica had brought them along to be a protective front for her, to prevent ugliness being spoken. "Perhaps you'd like to have a stroll along the old dockside while your Mother and I finish here?"

"Don't be patronising, Dad," sparked James. "I came to look after Mum."

"Oh she is in no danger from me, rather the reverse I fancy." I tried to speak dryly but there were tears behind my eyes again. "There's a small gallery a hundred yards towards the SS Great Britain. Maybe, one day, you'll see some paintings of mine in there."

I did not know whether they were pleased or reluctant

119

to go, but both stood and left, Joanne turning at the gangway to wave a few fingers at us. Then we were alone and I wanted to tell her how despicable it was to try to buy my unnecessary signature with a meal and still my tongue with the children's presence. I wanted to tell her that she had to be desperate to use Joanne and James as a shield. But I said nothing, just waited for her salvo. It came.

"You've scrawled "I refuse you garbage" between the lines and "Je t'accuse" at the end. I didn't have to bring this here, John. I hope you are ashamed."

"Who is he?" I asked and the cliché rolled sullenly like a lead cannonball. "He's got to be very up-market," I continued. "Very conscious of his position to make you file for divorce in such a nasty way, making me out to be the archetypal wife battering bastard and you, the innocent deceived. Why waste your time like this? You can have a divorce no strings attached. How terribly deceived is he?"

"Just sign it and I'll go," she said, leaning over and picking out a mint chocolate with manicured nails.

"You didn't have to send me a form at all," I answered. "Just go ahead without me, but perhaps it wouldn't look so good for you that way. Poor old John, suffering from depression, is deserted by his wife for another man. I am right," I said. "There is another man."

"You just don't see what you've done, do you?" Monica asked and I still couldn't tell what she was feeling or thinking. Her mask seemed impermeable. "I'm trying to save your face. If I sent in this paper, you'd be answering a charge of gross obscenity."

"It was meant to be funny," I said lamely. "He has no

sense of humour?"

"Not where A.A.Milne is concerned," she said very primly and I had to laugh.

"Donkeys do have long ones," I snorted and seized the form to have another look. "It's bloody clever," I said.

"It's not clever. It's stupid. I shouldn't have come."

"Up yours with knobs on!" I tried to laugh again, to jolly some flicker from her, but she would not budge.

"Just sign the paper John or ignore it, one or the other," she said wearily. "I've had enough. I'm doing it for you."

"Sanctimonious bitch! Frigid stick! You never did anything for me!" That reached her. Oh I still had the power, I thought, as her cheek paled, but then the waiter was at my side, murmuring in my ear about the rest of the clientele. I flapped my hand at him. Get off my back. There was business to be settled and I was getting into stride.

"Give me the bloody form. You wanted it all quiet, hushed up in this posh little joint, well you can have it with bells ringing and sirens blaring. You can have your pathetic little divorce so you can marry your pathetic little man. Why it can't be like any other divorce – mutual separation and on our separate ways, I don't know! But somewhere along the line you have to be justified. It has to be officially recognised that I was the bastard, that I was in the wrong lest your halo be rocked, lest your sanctity be questioned. Little wronged woman whom nobody loved, why do you drag my name in the mud?" I scrawled my name across the page and flung it back at her so that it knocked a cup and sent it to the floor.

The waiter was lifting on my arm. Another was circling to close in. You stood; your face now exposed, at last, all its protection creams and make-ups could not hide the haggard despair. Yes, I thought. I did that. I made you face yourself. I made you cut away the plastic flesh to find Muriel beneath the Monica, the unhappy person beneath the plastic paradise doll.

"It's bad news from beginning to end," I snarled at her. "You might think there is a moment of happiness just waiting to be plucked from the tree, but there is none. Just scrabble, scrabble scrabble among the rats in the sewers."

"I shouldn't have come," Monica mouthed. "He told me to stay away, but the children wanted to see you. I wanted to part in a friendly way – no hard feelings. You're ill, John, just ill."

"Sod off!" I shouted over the strewn table. "I'm not ill. I'm seeing it as it is – you money-grubbing blood sucking bitch."

Their arms were on me now even as I screamed at her. I was hoisted out and away. I had no argument with them and kept my vengeance spewing out at Monica Muriel until I hurtled down the plank, landed on the walkway and crawled to a bench.

She'll pick up the pieces, I thought. She'll marry her new man, see the children through university, be respectable and suburban.

"I am for the under-class!" I shouted at the green leaves above me. "I am for the poor and lonely!" The waiters returned up the gangplank rubbing their hands. Bouncers always rub their hands after doing the bouncing. I've noticed that. It's automatic and instinctive, wiping away responsibility for the dirty sod lying outside.

Meanwhile there would be money to change hands, the quiet covering placed over the unfortunate incident and, of course, what a conversation piece for customers later.

"Won't do your trade any harm," I called after their backs. "People like a bit of excitement." They did not look back and I was suddenly filled with fury that she had got away with it again. "She's got what she wanted. She always gets what she wants!"

I leaned back against the tree behind the bench to feel the air about me. Away from the claustrophobia of air conditioning and hushed corners I could breathe. The plane tree whispered and the water washed the stone. Solid feet trod on the solid walkway and the good old sol shone down through silver clouds. You've cocked it up again, I thought, and closed my eyes. In a short while, James and Joanne would return; Monica would trit trot down the plank and I would apologise. They exacted apologies like regular road tolls, but I thought I had managed to leave the road, break into open country and hurdle the barbed wire fences.

"Well my old cock – pissed again." That's all I need, I thought, looking up to see Martin looking down at me from his low height.

"Too right fart features," I said, closing my eyes again to avoid him, to signal that there was no conversation required, no money to be given.

"I've never been thrown out of there – won't let me in," he said confidentially, a hint of congratulation in his voice.

"You should wear a suit and have three smart tailors' dummies round you – never fails."

"I could try it I suppose," he said, asking me to dare him on. "There's eccentrics dressed like tramps but loaded with cash. How would they know I couldn't pay the bill?"

"Because you smell," I said. "It's the smell that does it every time, not the looks." I paused waiting for him to shuffle on, but he did not move. "Look," I said, "I am waiting for people to arrive. I can't be seen with you."

"Not good enough for you then?"

"That's right," I said.

"I'll stay," he said. "It's a free country."

"You must be joking," I said.

I looked up urgently: right towards the gallery – no sign of the children. I looked towards the restaurant – no sign of the ex. I scrabbled in my pocket for a pencil and paper. There was a grubby piece of a notebook I could use. Quickly I scrawled,

"I love you and have lost you. You know where I live. I am your father and you are yourselves. Be happy. A separate message for your Mother." I marked an arrow and turned over the page, whetted the pencil stub and block capitalled "Go forth and multiply!"

There was a stone on the ground and I weighed down the paper with it on the bench by my side. Then I stood and shuffled, head bent, along the dockside to where the bulldozers were gravelling the ground. I ducked between the hoardings and followed the dwarf to his hutch. I had leaped over the fences and would not be found again.

Chapter 9

Martin tracked over the rubble-strewn site. I followed. He wavered by a broken down brick wall and then turned towards me.

"Nobody's to know this place," he whispered urgently, big lips flapping spittle, eyes shining like a kid with a secret. "I don't know why I'm fucking doing this: trusting a bugger like you at my age. I must be mad."

"Just a few minutes," I said. "Until the coast is clear."

"You're an adult. Could just walk away. Tell them you're going and go. Be free inside your head and you'll be free of them for ever."

"You don't know, do you? Cradle to the grave you're trapped and still you pat the bloody leg irons and say it's good to be free. I tell you this," I said, warming to the theme, "one step from you outside the accepted, the lawful, the code of the powerful and you're done for. Ton of bricks, load of shit and no more peeking above the parapet."

"I saw them, you know," he said as if I hadn't spoken. "Good looking woman, fine youngsters – you don't know what you're giving up. And all for what?"

I shrugged. Ask no questions, be told no lies. There

was no time to explain the burning in my head that said conformity was death, that every sodding robot in every sodding place of work had lost the right to claim individual humanity unless she systematically and continually eroded every bureaucratic regulation, every unnecessary law and even most supposedly necessary ones. With every year that passed the drive to sameness, little ticky tacky boxed living, became greater and the opportunity to fringe it, to live on the edge of possibilities became less. Yes, it would be more comfortable to try to quench the burning, to try to resume the mantle of social respectability, but there were enough people doing that job already, thank you very much. Now I just smiled at Martin and said, "Please help me out, mate."

He succumbed to the flattery of it: to be asked for shelter from a member of the human race, to have something that another wanted, needed. The power flashed in his eyes like a firework.

"Don't say I didn't warn you," he muttered and then ducked around the wall corner and beneath a grey tarpaulin into home. I squeezed in after him and doubled up in the dim stench of the hideaway. Slowly my eyes stopped juicing and I could see. Under piled soiled blankets, his camp bed looked new. Along one short wall ran a plank held up by bricks where his personal possessions were lined – nothing worth nicking – a mug, an empty bottle with candle stub, a large demolition hammer, a Gideon's Bible engraved with the Imperial Hotel crest, a brown check cap so big its peak hung over the shelf ledge and a couple of biros with blue oozing from their rears. On the rough ground were hessian sacks. The roof was made from floor timbers covered with blue plastic sheeting. I crouched in an area not much bigger than a great dane's kennel. Just by the makeshift door was a rusty primus stove. I sat with my back to it and my knees at my chin.

Martin loosened his neck scarf and brushed fat fingers down his swollen misshapen jumper as if removing crumbs. Suddenly the sneering words in me shrivelled and died. I wanted to praise his wonderful survival and to thank him for his shelter.

"It is not in the looks of a man that true worth may be counted," I said. "You could have passed me by like the Levite. Good Samaritans assume strange shapes."

"Fuck off you pompous prat." Martin's head wedged down on his shoulders and his hands continued to work on his clothes. I could not see his eyes in the dark.

"It's not easy to help somebody else regardless of the cost," I continued, trying to reassure.

"Oh it'll cost you," he said, beginning to rock on his bed, his hands now flat on his knees, his shadowed face turned towards me so that I could feel his breath.

"What do you mean?"

"Ten minutes at the outside and then you can get out. This is my place."

"I can understand that," I smiled. "Your patch. It'll stay that way."

"Yes, my patch," he said, rocking more violently. "I should never have let you in. You're just a fart-arsed queen, full of fancy words and stinking air. It'll cost yer. Got a tenner? Can you spare a measly tenner for this old dwarf?"

"A tenner?" I tried to keep the smile, but he was

getting to me now. "I'm in the same boat as you," I said. "Benefits don't get me far."

"Benefits? What fucking benefits? You taking the piss?"

"Not me mate," I grinned pacifically at the shadow on the bed.

"I've to move now. I can't stay here."

"Yes," I said. "Bulldozers are on the way."

"Not bulldozers," he sneered. "You're fucking here. It's the least you can do for me – a tenner – removals' expenses."

I began to laugh, thinking he was joking, hoping he was joking. He shoved his thumb into his mouth, worked it to his cheek and then spat it out, gobbing on the ground at my foot. I had no room to retract.

"Don't fucking laugh at me." His head loomed forward like a great nodding balloon face and his hand scrabbled out to the shelf. I stopped laughing when he seized the hammer. "Nobody fuckin laughs at me in my own home."

"I wasn't laughing at you," I said, but he pulled the hammer off the shelf.

"Now don't be stupid," I mouthed.

"Nobody laughs at me here," he said and his eyes disappeared into his face like black worms. I had to act. I could try to wriggle through the tarpaulin flap like an eel with the hammer squelching down on my back or I could fight and so I shoved my foot up and into his stomach, grabbed the hammer arm and pulled. The flesh gave in front of me. I launched backwards and out of the hutch. There was a dreadful wheezing from behind me and then the dwarf's voice:

"Only a joke!" He gasped out at me. It was followed by

a long gurgle of phlegm. "Just didn't want to be taken for granted." And then his head appeared through the flap. "I shouldn't've done it. I was scared." He looked up at me from the ground and his face was absolutely round with a flat nose and no eyebrows; it was smooth, skin stretched taut over his anxiety to make amends, the enlarged face of a little boy. "At least you talk to me," Martin said. "At least you give me the time of day. I shouldn't've kicked you in the teeth like that." Slowly his shoulders began to emerge like a fat caterpillar through a leaf. "Just give me my hammer back. There's not much protection round here." "Oh I'll give it to you in my own sweet time. Once bitten twice shy, me." The head twisted and upside down eyes stared straight into mine and his shoulders squirmed towards my shoes.

"I'm sorry. It was all too much, seeing you inside my house. Nobody's been in here with me before. It was like an invasion. I know you didn't mean any harm." He gathered his knees beneath him and began to push himself up.

I backed away, shoving the hammer under my jacket, turned and ran to the hoardings. I peered through but could see no sign of the family and so I began the long trek back to the Tower House. There were six sets of benches along the way, away from the mooring posts, with about fifty metres between each bench. I kept my head down, not wanting any attention lest Monica was still on the hunt and so I did not see the man on the last bench until I was almost upon him and then my heart frogged into my throat and my legs jellied. The red-haired bastard was lying flat out, his feet propped on the arm rest, his hand flung out and round his carrot hair. He was wearing just

129

a pair of white shorts and his whole white body sprouted with stubbly red. I may have caught the sun in Jane's back garden, but he was lying back quite deliberately, daring it to cook him on its griddle like pork. I would have known his bulk, enclosed in cheese rind, anywhere. I couldn't help it. I had to stop with the shock of seeing him again, but then I desperately wanted to move on past him, but if I did so, I feared his eyes opening suddenly, the lashless lights piercing into me, recognising me. I forced myself to remember that the sun would be bright in his face and he would not be able to focus immediately. I made myself remember that there were other pedestrians about, that I was quite safe out in the open by the newspaper kiosk and the gift shop. But the shivers ran down my spine like flames, like ice.

What level of inferno do you inhabit, you bastard? I thought. It is an insult to bastards to call you so. Now gods stand up for poor bastards like me because this creature is born of monsters. He has no saving grace. My hand clenched on the hammer handle like a vice.

With an involuntary forward stumble I managed to move on past the last mooring post and out to the road, but all the way to the corner I imagined my torturer opening his eyes, seeing me, following me up the hill towards Fishponds. There were small alleys, quiet corners where I would be vulnerable to attack. I could hardly bear to walk alone, but I did, and only at the multi-storey car park did I turn my head to check I was not followed. There was no sign of the beast.

The hall was silent, cool and shaded. The stairs up and up to my eyrie were deserted: no sudden quavering voiced Elizabeth, no cheerful enquiring Jane, no Peter chipping out old wallpaper, just staircarpet blue and the feel of my palm against the smooth wall as I mounted. Back in my cocoon, my attic room, that was my place now. I could flee the pain, pull in the walls around me like huge muffling quilts, stuff cotton wool plugs in my ears and rock gently to the beat of a heart. I sat on the edge of the bed and slid the hammer out of sight underneath the fringed coverlet. Then hands between my thighs and head on my chest, I closed my eyes. I was trembling and could not still the twitching, my nerves tense and twanging. Deep breathing was needed, but I could only snatch shallow saucers of air and let them out in a rush. Slowly now, slowly, find the equilibrium, stop the horizons swimming, focus on security. I was home, unseen, unfollowed. I was totally safe and could begin to think again.

Dr. Rhodes was a fool to think by facing evil I might overcome it. Far more likely was the succumbing, the welcoming of tiny sucking incubi upon my dead flesh until my cowardly blood was transmuted into the dribble of scorn, the self-hatred that loathed all others because it loathed me. I wept for my loss; let others weep for theirs. I suffered my life; let others suffer theirs. It was another division to acknowledge: body and mind; my suffering and others'. To pull them all inside the one mortal frame of me was beyond me. I had to fight to keep them separate, identifiable, capable of analysis and rejection, even analysis and acceptance.

There were times when I was sucked into other people's situations so strongly that I ceased to have a mind of my own and took on all the feelings of hurt or elation that others experienced. It is a strange feeling to be losing one's own personality and finding oneself wincing at another's pain, smiling at another's joy. Inside there is a void. Outside there is the huge pretence, but that pretence is others' realities.

But at the back of my head there was a chiming sound of full words. They were bells ringing out from old churches over churning seas. They were speaking of green meadows, clean hills and purer lives. Theirs was the sound of simplicity and innocence. When the heaving lump of Elsie pounded the stairs and Elizabeth clutched at her cigarettes with frantic claws, when Martin heft a hammer at my head and Monica Muriel passed divorce papers like confetti, the bells rang out that these were all distortions magnified by my fear, that these were all creatures to be pitied, that I had to learn to pity myself just a little. Yes I could accept all that. It seemed intrinsically sane to recognise that others created images behind which they could shelter. I was a past master of the art. But when I tried to introduce the Redhead into the canon of humanity I could not do so. A wave of revulsion surged over and through me so that bile swam into my mouth and every pore of my body oozed ice.

Slowly now my room ceased to whirl and my hands came away from my legs and began to rub up and down on the old suit trousers.

"Please doctor, what should I do now?" I asked the

mirror image of Doctor Rhodes.

"Make instant and full confession of your past so that it attains an objective reality that may be shared."

"Whom may I trust?"

"You may only trust yourself and in so doing you learn to trust others according to each person's capacity for compassion."

"It is insufficient to confess to myself."

"It may be a step in the right direction."

"You're stitching me up with the verbals, doctor. There are too many eager for power. Just giving my name is enough for the abuse to start."

"Emotional insecurity leads to excessive self-absorption."

"You're calling me immature are you doctor?"

"If your feelings are hurt, they can not grow normally. Immaturity is not a term of insult or abuse. It acknowledges early damage in an adult."

"Too easy to blame upbringing," I crowed. "I do not bring my parents into this identity parade."

"And nor did I. Who did?"

"More trapping words, doctor. Don't lead the witness."

"You're not on trial you know."

"We are all on trial, doctor," I said, pleased with the fencing ploy, the play. But I could see you doctor sitting in the chair you normally used when visiting, shaking your head, your thin fingers arching over your narrow chin, seeing the way I played games to stay safe within.

"A trial demands a sharing of values, an agreed awareness of good and bad so that conclusions may be reached. Do we share any values, doctor?"

The problem with my imaginary conversations with

Doctor Rhodes was that when I met him next time at the hospital I would be confused about what he had said and what I imagined him to have said. In addition, I had to invent so much about him: family, attitudes, activities and morality. He gave away so little of himself, but always appeared to be giving so much of himself that I longed to invite him home as a friend, not a professional counsellor.

Last time at the hospital he had told me that he should be allowed to speak his own thoughts, not be invaded by my spirit. People had the inalienable right to be themselves. Even assuming another's name was a violation of identity. But I could not stop the process in the privacy of my own room and in my dreams. And, although I was confused about many things, I was clear that the doctor wanted the best for me. I would not abuse his faith by abusing his spirit in my imaginary dialogues. Now I decided to continue the conversation because it had genuinely calmed me down.

"You see doctor," I said, picking up my pipe and packing it gently, "there is no order or schemata left for me, just disparate images that float and spread nimbus for a moment. Occasionally they generate a connection, a shared impulse, but these connections are not bound to communicate further than from one cell to another and they do not comprise a system of values at all, although they may sometimes be dignified with that term. Even among people who espouse the power of conscience to distinguish right from wrong, their lives are in schism and fraught with contradictions. The vortex towards chaos works in a kaleidoscopic helix of continual movement. I search desperately for stability, some raison d'être, a structure and apply increasingly draconian laws to a disintegrating world, demanding order, but I can not pack all the coloured scarves back up my sleeve and my juggling balls bounce to the ground."

"Take it gently from day to day." I imagined the doctor saying, but I answered that the time for gentleness had long passed and only the brutal seemed to survive.

"Do you recall I told you about a girl at the entrance to the station with a baby on her hip and her boyfriend snorting on a mouth organ while she danced?"

The doctor nodded. "You wanted to paint them," he said, "but could not bring yourself to do so."

"She'll not be half so hippy hoppy happy in winter when the frost is down and her bare feet are chilblain sore," I said. "She won't carry her baby like a peace offering and jump in the way of passers by with an eager new age grin and the wide eyes of a practised tart and beggar. I could not show what she would become in what she was."

"Arrogant of you to try perhaps."

"Oh you don't need a magic orb to see she'll be pulling all the benefits she can like a sensible girl and holing up with the squatters at Coronation Row. If she goes on taking it gently from day to day, her baby will become diseased, her body will become racked and her home will be the street or prison."

"How many times before you hear me say that you can't carry others' lives as well as your own. You have all to do to cope with your own."

"We have a clash of values, doctor. I was brought up to put others first, but the others have beaten me down."

"Too easy to blame other people," said the doctor,

but I suddenly knew he would not have said that. He had jumped out of character and I wanted to push him away back into the hospital, being tired of the circular conversation suddenly.

"Not all others – there must be good where the dunes stretch away, where the children lie on the warm sand and there are cheese and tomato sandwiches with warm salt-in-the-mouth orange squash."

"No. I will not be fobbed off so easily," he said. "You jump into a childhood memory whenever the going gets tough. You create a sentimental picture and the picture protects you. It is no answer. I, for one, do not like cheese and tomato sandwiches. It is a mirage."

"You must leave me now." I could feel my blood rising against the intrusion. I would not accept people in my head unless I agreed to their presence. It was bad enough having my personal space invaded outside my room, but sitting on my bed I had to keep control over my visitors. "Go away," I shouted. "I'm tired and want to rest."

Doctor Rhodes disappeared. He had been right, of course, and may be he had also known how the gentle image had the habit of transforming itself into horror, how the Portuguese men-o-war would creep from the waves, fasten on the legs of the child and drag him into the drowning sea. The doctor was an intrinsically decent man, a little staid and stolid, but steady enough and I could be as patronising a patient as any Duchess.

When he had quite gone, I rummaged under the bed again, pulled out the hammer and inspected it minutely. The shaft was fissured, but not split. The head was secure with the wood jammed through its head like a spiked head of white hair and banged in firmly so that there was no movement between head and shaft. They were as one. The gleaming face was clean, not a mark upon it anywhere, but I rubbed it with my sleeve and then kneeled by my bed and shoved it all the way under until it nestled behind my box of books up against the wall. Out of sight and out of mind; a foolish mantra, but one to parrot until it might feel righter than the opposite.

Chapter 10

It is time to explain about this Redhead. I used to think Redhead equals woman equals beautiful equals exciting equals shiver down my spine and noli me tangere for Caesar's I am, but just see me walk away and watch how my body sways. There was a girl once with just such redness in her lips and the slight flush of her blood under the thin translucent skin of freckled beauty and she had walked with me inside the park, let me carry her bag while she played needle words with my heart until each small smile was an invitation to explore further and yet she had always reached her father's doorway just too soon for me. I cherished her memory once, but now all that is ruined.

This Redhead, and I find it hard even to think it, let alone write it, dates back to after Dartmoor and before hospital. There's a film called Alcatraz and a filthy bastard called Wolf who wants the hero, Clint Eastwood. He won't get him because Clint is too good for him and so he gets mad and tries to kill him, but Clint just isn't there anymore. I could never be Clint and had to be there when the giant slug with bristles of fire came towards me, but in prison there was some respite, some means of hiding. I used to slide through the canteen with my back to the wall and then pull away, assume a shining face and swagger past the screw: no point in troubling the warders. I would wait until the last minute to whip in the shower and my eyes would flicker like an adder's tongue questing the steam every second lest the Redhead pushed in.

But after prison I thought I had won release. The half way house was a flat in a council block known locally as the rabbit warren. Long walkways, concrete stairs smelling of urine and a play area reduced to a dumping ground for old tyres, cars and mattresses. There was always a skip due next week. The warren had been built in the sixties high rise boom and was on the demolition list when the tenants had all been allocated alternative housing elsewhere. Those people hardest to move stayed to the bitter end, and, of course, the council used a few flats for temporary accommodation for strays such as me, straight out of prison, no other place to go and in need of rehabilitation.

A social worker took me there by bus from the train station. He introduced himself as Eric and showed me his card.

"Is that all you've got?" He said, taking one of my two bags and trotting away from me with it. I eased my two pictures up under my free arm and lugged after him. The wind breezing up to Temple Meads carried freedom's voice and, standing under the bus shelter as others hurtled by without a second glance temporarily convinced me that I could assume an effective disguise as a normal human being out in the big brave world.

"You'll be sharing I'm afraid," Eric said putting my bag down with a flourish. He traced a finger along the bus timetable and scanned his wrist watch. "Ten minutes if a miracle happens and the 19 is on time."

"Sharing?" I asked. "They said nothing about sharing when I talked with the community liaison."

"Well it's all muck in together when there's no alternative, John." I'd only met him off the train and already he'd assumed first name familiarity. "A couple of lads for a short while – they'll be finding their feet like you. It'll be good to compare notes and help each other along."

"My own room?" I questioned unable to hide the anxiety in my voice. There's always this strange belief that company improves people. Having other people around creates the environment for unhappiness.

"Oh yes, your own room," he said. "It's a three bedroom flat – shared amenities. That's all."

I nodded, having no alternative, although I had cherished the thought of having a place to myself, however small. When you've shared a cell for two years the idea of privacy increases its attraction.

Eric lapsed into silence as we waited for the bus. He was short, wore a trench coat, had thinning grey hair and a round face with little eyes which blinked a lot. His words, when they came, were staccato, full of what I felt was false cheerfulness with a hint of ex-army officer pretence that all was under control. He was the first social worker I'd met outside the prison, but he carried

140

the hallmark: low confidence behind big image. Who was I to criticise? I'd lived that lie as a teacher, husband and father for years.

"What are they like these others?" I asked.

"Oh they're all right," Eric replied and my heart sank at the doubtful intonation on the 'right' as it moved up stealthily towards a 'but'.

"What are they like, these others?" I asked again.

"Had their troubles, but well on the mend: on the way up and out, like you." I loathe comparisons, the strange belief that it is reassuring to be told that other people are as unhappy and twisted as I was and am. All the more reason to be afraid, but I thought I had become used to fear and failure.

"Names?" I asked, wondering whether these had achieved the dignity of family names.

"Keith and Steve," Eric answered rapidly.

"And what's your name again?"

"Oh I'm just Eric," he said, picking up a bag with a struggle as the bus pulled in.

When we arrived at the Warren it was growing dark and I did not see much of the squalor. It felt good to be approaching my own front door with my own key. And when I walked in there was nobody else there, just a slight smell of damp. The hall light did not work, but the living room had a table, chairs, television and sidelight, all quite tidy.

"That's good," said Eric. "Give you a chance to get settled in." He showed me my bedroom: a cell size room in dark blue and yellow, clean and cold.

"Do they know I'm coming?" I asked when Eric

seemed ready to be gone. Territory in a prison is a major conflict zone. The more overcrowded a place, the fiercer the battlegrounds. The men with a big pull over others were also in the big cells and carried a large space around with them. I'd quickly learned to slip like a shadow and only move towards other prisoners at an unthreatening angle. "Is this bedroom the smallest?" It was important that it was.

"They're all much of a muchness," said Eric, thinking I was about to complain, ask for more space. It wasn't worth explaining and he had answered my question. My room was the third bedroom, the tiny hole for the second child. I shrugged and followed him into the rest of the flat, my eyes flickering over the amenities, checking there was three of everything – no chance. Three piece suite – two broken armchairs and one sofa – potential conflict. Two hard back chairs at the kitchen table and one stool – the stool would be mine. Lots of mugs standing by the sink, unwashed, waiting for me. No ashtraysunusual – I already needed a fag.

"Do they smoke?" I asked and my voice must have risen a pitch or two because Eric stopped short explaining that the television rental was shared three ways and looked puzzled for a moment.

"I don't think so," he said, his face clearing, as if this were good news. "Steve's a bit of a fitness fanatic." My heart sank.

"Can I smoke in my bedroom?"

"It's your room, John," he half answered and I knew that I was in for trouble. It was the clean living bastards that gave most grief in prison. They kept their noses snot free with the warders and gave squalid little men like me

142

hell as if they had to turn their scouring pad self hatred on a weak target and I was weak, as riddled with the terror worms as the leg of a desk my father had given me when I'd studied for college and he'd slowly turned his eyes away from the Daily Mirror, the beer and his everyday appetites to see me with a book.

"What did Steve do then?" I asked flatly, but I did not expect a reply. "What about Keith?" I asked, plugging away for any information I might use for protection. Eric seemed happy enough to tell me that Keith was an older man, was going steadier and wanted a quiet life. I realised that Eric was worse than useless. There are two sorts of reality in prison: their reality and mine. They never matched. It was guaranteed that a prisoner with the best credentials turned out the nastiest, that the warder with the bad reputation was without doubt the fairest to all. Eric was a soft touch, a natural idiot, the sort of well meaning cretin that finds excuses for granny fuckers and pours a load of shit on the heads of remand innocents. If he said Steve and Keith were all right, he was totally wrong. I had very sensitive antennae from prison living.

"I'm not staying here," I said suddenly. "It's not what I was promised."

"Oh dear," Eric said, his face screwing up and his mouth tunnelling. He shook his head. "I thought there might be trouble. I told them, but would they listen? You know how it is. It's the only place we've got and beggars can't be choosers. That's what they said."

"I was promised my own place, a chance to find my feet. This isn't it." I could hear the pleading in my voice and couldn't stop it. I knew it was unhelpful to sound like a whinging con. Eric took strength from my weakness.

"I know it's not right yet, but I'll keep an eye and we'll arrange to have you out shortly." "Like right now," I said, going back to the bedroom for my bags, stomach shivering.

"Oh no sunshine." Eric followed me. "You'll be perfectly fine here for a couple of weeks, but I'll pass on your request for a transfer immediately. Trust me."

I'd sooner trust a rattlesnake, I thought. At least a rattlesnake does what it threatens. "You'll stay till the other two get back?" I asked, pleading with him.

"Don't get in a state – no need. They're good enough lads and they know you're coming. Probably gone out to get in a few beers. They know what it's like to be just out. I don't know when they'll be back and you've unpacking to do. Don't see you need me around to hold your hand. Don't want to look softer than you are, do you?"

"You're fucking staying to introduce me," I said, scared witless.

And so he did, making a great show of doing me a favour, but it didn't make any difference. When the two of them stalked through the half open door, I knew I was in trouble. The Redhead's role was macho show-off to the older man's kid gloves. There were cats' claws inside leather sheaths. Neither of them could be doing with me and they sensed the fear in my blood as soon as they spotted me, huddled small on the stool behind Eric, in their territory.

"Who's this then, Eric?" asked Keith, all sweetness and light.

"New tenant," said Eric. "Just on the outside – needs a safe place and a couple of mates to help him along for a very short time. He'll be off and out on a new life before you know it. I did tell you he was coming."

"I'll be no trouble – off to another flat as soon as possible," I said.

"Oh don't mind us," said Keith. "Always pleased to help out, aren't we Steve?"

Steve laughed, a short hard cough of sound that scoffed at me.

Have you ever considered what it does to a man to be given a bunk bed in a cell for his territory, to have his walks curtailed and the walls around him barbed? It makes each patch of free ground, his. It makes him go out as hunter, predator and controller of any patch he can claim his own. Steve and Keith had made this dark flat their own, but Eric would not have noticed the signs if they'd been shoved up his nostrils on an electrified pole.

"He's called John," he said. "He'll only be staying a week or two."

"I'll be gone before you know it," I said, trying again to reassure, smiling ingratiatingly. Keith moved over to the sink, pushing past me. He wore heavy duty jeans and a black T shirt with a silver scimitar emblazoned across its chest.

"Two's company; three's a crowd" he said softly, between clenched teeth, but his handshake was immediate and Eric did not hear because Steve had clattered up to the table and dumped a bag of shopping there. "My name's Keith," said the older man, "and this is Steve."

I want you to know that when Steve swung round from the table and looked down on me I recognised him as the Redhead immediately. He was six foot four, four square strong and his face was white, round and blank with small fixed eyes. Ginger hair sprouted from his nostrils and he exuded hatred from every pore.

"Yeah, that's me," he said. "Don't I know you from way back?"

I pretended I had never met him, trusting to my civilian clothes, but he knew me, every inch of me because I screamed victim at him even as I tried to appear relaxed and confident in my words and body.

After introductions there wasn't much left to say. I tried to keep Eric back, but he told me that the boys would show me the ropes. As soon as he was out the front door, I scuttled to my room, dreading the next move. I could hear Steve stomping down the corridor,

"John'll be gone. Long gone John! So long gone, John!" Keith chanted and then there was laughter.

I will not say what happened yet awhile. At least there is some background to the painting on the wall. I've managed to colour in the landscape as Gladys would have me do and I've put down quite unequivocally the fear I had. It is fear that conjures pictures: fear and fantasy fused.

There are many times when I can not be convinced of any sort of reality. Jane told me yesterday that I had eaten the last orange in the cut glass bowl on the sideboard in the kitchen, but I could not recall doing so.

Oranges normally stay with me a long time. First there is the careful rubbing and rolling between my nicotined fingers to ease the skin from the flesh below; then there is either the careful insertion of the fingernail or the use of a knife point. Either way, the hiss of fine, specked tang and the sudden odour are so idiosyncratic as to be memorable every time. Perhaps you've blotted out the orange with the red, the doctor might have said. Perhaps it was a blood orange, I thought. "But yes you ate it, every piece," said Jane, "And rubbed your sticky hands down your shirt front like a small schoolboy, the juice dribbling from the corner of your mouth because you'd stuffed it in like a giant gobstopper. You even said it would keep you regular before you walked out the door."

I can not remember either the eating or the departure. It is even conceivable that Monica never arrived with Joanne and James, that the journey to the restaurant was in never land and that Martin Beverall's hide-away was hidden away from all comers because it did not exist at all. Most of the time now I can distinguish between what counts for reality in most people's observations and I fully realise that their reality does not coincide with mine, but I can live with that, can adjust my lens to fit their ways of seeing. I know they see with more rational eyes than I have ever managed to do. It is intensely appropriate that I should blind my own eyes with cataracts of the doctor's and drugs' making so that I can imagine how other people might grasp the world in a more cogent useful way. I have never minded pretending and it doesn't bother me to be told that a precious memory was a falsehood and another actuality existed all the time, but I have to record that in matters of the direct senses of taste and smell and touch I have normally been spot on. If once I start to question these fundamental tools of an artist's observations I am likely to find all my art to be derivative, based on what Jane might wish to see and hear.

And so, I have decided, that having supposedly eaten the fruit, albeit unknowingly and without the proper dispensation of the landlady, who had cherished the last orange for her husband, I have decided that I must defer this telling of my great Redhead fear for just a little longer. I know it to be true and I know myself to be truly afraid, but what if all that is said is nothing, is just a blank emptiness peopled by other people's minds, which in themselves are empty too? It is all so fragile, what is and what is not.

I am currently peering out of the window in my attic room, standing on tiptoe to catch a glimpse of the evening sky and all that comes to my eyes is the orange glow from the street light; all that reaches my nose and tongue is the day's leaden fume. The colours are grey, orange and metallic blue and the taste is acrid, but it is perfectly feasible that my body is in another place in another's reality and that reality is trying to invade my present senses through the nastiness of the traffic fumes. And if I had to name that nastiness in another's reality, it would be the small bedroom in the half way house with Steve leaning against the wall, his foot down on my chest and his great fist pulping in my side or even the tiny gap between two buildings along West Street where the meths heads hang out. But I said no more of that reality for now.

And so, having eaten the fruit and met with Monica again, I would cry you mercy, dear sisterhood of mercy. It is in living in the Tower House with Jane, Elsie and Elisabeth that I can hope to find a route to cope. I have always imagined the sisters have a quick desire for oneness, a united policy of being at one with one another. Even as I splinter and break, the sisterhood surely possesses healing agents to produce new wholenesses, new lives.

Jane convinces me utterly of her regenerative powers. She manages to stay direct to the path of every day and all her impulses seem to say there is worth here. If all the world were covered in deepest muck and the final trump were sounding out that apocalypse was upon us, it would be Jane to lean forward and find a sequin to carry with her through the darkness into death. But Elsie and Elisabeth do not convince me of their shared capacity for renewal. Distortions on the way have brought them into my sphere of sorrow. Perhaps their wombs have shrivelled with the hatred of their pasts. Perhaps men have inserted destruction and no longer can the amoebas in their bellies duplicate and reunite with harmony. And yet, even so sad, they find singular ways to state themselves. It is Elizabeth who brings the tea, who holds the routine of tea and biscuit to be sacred and healing for others. Unlike me, with my automatic do it for myself and nobody else, she forces the brew upon all and sundry and even in the telling of the dead child, she asserts that there is precious kinship between mother and daughter, between yesterday, today and tomorrow. And even Elsie picks up knitting needles in her surprisingly slim hands to mould abadoty for another birthday or carefully apportions mounds of shopping to various places in the larder, following orders and reaching an ordering in her troubled head. In the calling of me pig she has right on her side. I know because all I see is her fatness and all I smell is her leaking flesh.

Oh give me mercy sisterhood for having abused your trust, so should all men say. We have thrust our stiffened lust into your secret lives and burned away your wombs, your sweet regenerative bed of love. You have lived, sisters, glorying in your ability to reach wholeness in harmony with self and others. It is the great service of trust you do to open yourselves to the scarcely known, to achieve your own oneness and to translate it to the mother of all symbols, the creator of feelings' truth, the moonlight that reveals the best of self even in the worst of darkness.

Only child of an abused Mother and a savage Father would keep these idealisms close. When, women, and I include the incubi of men in women – we are there, deep inside you – you look at my ravings, will you see the craving or the craven? Will you offer home or order me to roam footloose, the wandering Jew, the homeless Palestinian, the whole exiled crew plucked from their groves of sanctity and safety, nurtured through their cultures of ages to stand now on bare hillsides, in barren high rise flats, on corners of litter-strewn estates, their heads filled with flickering dreams and their bodies shrivelling into dried kernels of bitterness? I once thought of Monica as bright idea and warm home, but I made a bonsai of her brain and bruised her heart into a stone.

As I moved into half sleep, I remembered the tower and the way the orange had rolled clean and whole, except for the bruise, to my feet. It all should be simple. There should be no need for anaesthesia in the brain, no need to seek escape routes. If I could stay inside the tower walls in simple meditation I would achieve goodness by denying evil its entry. I would find solace in the communion of souls and forgiveness from and for the sisterhood of mercy and brotherhood of cruelty. But, without the evil, I can not define the worth in me. When now I reach for the simplicity of a dream there is a sardonic head beyond me nodding and sneering, saying he understands what that's all about and surely I should too, being an educated man. What purpose does the dream serve except as more arrogant posturing to hide the fear? The orange, he crows, is the heartfelt desire to create an impression. The impression is a flawed bubble of orange fire. There are no applauding crowds, just the stillborn vomit of the baby at its birth. The travail was for nothing so let the flames of bitterness reach high into the dark night.

"It's a round-shot tower," Peter said, "for making cannon balls in case Napoleon decided to drop in on us little Englanders for a knees-up: not likely here at the Avon facing West, but the powers were scared shitless enough to set up watch systems right up to here!" He motioned with a confident hand to a place above his head.

"You're having me on," I said, picking at the tip of my

nose as I do when uncertain whether a leg – pull is being made, but Peter smiled and I believed him.

"Straight up," he said. "It's truth. The poor buggers had to pour molten lead down the funnel into a chute. Gravity pulled the lead down at a rate of knots and how's your father out the other end rolled rough round cannonballs. Later a sieve was put in to split up the molten lead into lead shot."

I poured her down, I dreamed, seated at the kitchen table with her voice beating my brain. I heaved her to the top and poured her molten passion down into hard cold rocks of leaden hearts. The sun god burned red blisters on my back as I laboured up the ladder to the top, holding the steaming weight of slopping silken metal and then I twisted and down it flowed rolling into a massive ball to plop out at the end of the ramp and on to a barrow. You may see on the pitted ground mounds of cannon balls never blasted out, never removing limbs, green with mould and oxidisation like giants' marbles waiting for a game.

There is a small opening at the corner of West Street past which I roll some days. Even in sunshine the gap between wall and wall is dark and there is graffiti of silver grey on black, a space ship, a saucer bristling with antennae and a name in chunked handwriting, SLIME. The pavement seems to swing towards the gap and then straightens back. It would only take a small barrier to turn me through the hole into an alternative marble alley where there was neither building nor pavement, neither garden nor yard. It is part of the dark country, knock down ginger and rapist country. Brutality lurks there and when I pass I flick sideways glances lest the urine-sodden stench leaps out in the shape of a silver-slimed red beast wielding a club.

I wrote to the council suggesting a filling in of bricks, a clean passage from block to block, but the council had other priorities – cleaning the golden unicorns on the heavenly towered Town Hall, making out lottery bids for a gladiators' stadium and reassuring the wealthy that their cables would be underground in two shakes of a lamb's tail and a Murdoch stitch up.

One day, in the interests of health and safety, acting as any man should to protect the tribe, I blocked off the opening with a plank of wood taken from the back garden when Jane was out shopping and her husband upstairs was laying the purple carpet on the landing outside Elsie's door. Now at least the dark place was marked for others. I daubed Beware of the Beast on the wood and warned the household to avoid that way to the bus station.

The alternative route was a mile longer. In hot weather it might be tempting to take the dangerous short cut down Corporation Street into King's Square, but, given the wrong speed and hitting the camber at the difficult angle, it would be possible to breach the plank and find oneself careering through the minotaur maze, rolling and crashing along the giant chute into the monster's maw. Besides, as I explained carefully to all and sundry, the new route took them by Queen's Buildings where they could see how clean the grass was, each blade shining because rain fairies had been at work all night caressing the leaves with their tears.

I could tell Peter was humouring me when he said he'd think about it, but would use the Audi as usual, but Jane seemed troubled.

"Ever since you came back from seeing your family you've come out with this sort of warning, John. There's nothing to be scared of, is there? You can always tell the doctor. Just don't make mountains out of mole hills."

Is there? I would hate to undermine Jane's confidence. I rely on her straightforward vision, but did I sense a qualm of worry in her?

"Is there aught to frighten, aught to fear in the hidden pathways and public screaming headlines of murder?" I asked, recognising that there was significant exaggeration of the dangers inherent in living in Bristol at this time of history. No press gangs, just wandering killers smashing through the shop grills at night and selecting bottles of wine and vodka for drinking and stabbing. No, Jane wouldn't go marching past there with her shining hair flicking in the wind and her peach-bum swaying without wondering, without hastening that tiny bit faster. I was pleased to have warned her for she is my friend, but I regret having frightened her.

"It's probably all in my mind, Jane," I said very seriously. "Most of what I say has only the slightest hold on other people's reality. Don't pay the smallest attention to what I say. It doesn't pay."

She seemed much happier then but told me I shouldn't play games with other people's fears if inside I knew that what I said was untrue. I let her believe I was aware of the distinctions between true and false, but suggested her route was better beyond Corporation Street and she told me she never went that way anyway, so both of us were reassured.

There were workmen next door hammering through walls, beating sheets of metal into thunder while the traffic roared outside like anaesthesia. It was morning again already and I conjectured that the polluting fumes were carried up with the eleven o'clock heat through the high window into my room at an intensity of nine parts out of ten. I peered through blueness and the haze thickened my brain. Others might claim it was pipe smoke, but I knew otherwise.

Chapter 11

Ten days ago I returned from the city centre, haunted by Monica and the red-haired beast. For ten days I have not ventured from the home and Jane, my infinitely competent landlady with a dust scarf on her head, wants to know the reason why. I told her that I needed time to pause, time to reach the core of my unhappiness, but she told me to pull my finger out and stop moping like an old moggy Tom who has lost his pull on the she-cats.

"Time to pause?" she said, patting me on the back as if I'd gripe. "More like menopause. There are more fish in the sea."

"Don't want her back," I said. "Just need time for myself."

"Who's feeling sorry for himself then?" Jane smiled and patted my cheek. I was a schoolboy again. But Elsie had shifted on the twanging springs of her huge armchair, being jealous of Jane, and the Woman's Weekly landed in the cat litter.

"He's a pig," Elise said.

"Now come on Else," said Jane, rescuing the mag, and patting the chair's arm, inviting her to slump back again. "He's not all bad."

But I was in tears again. I had not mentioned how my eye ducts fill at the drop of a hat. I was ashamed.

"He's not a man. He's a mouse," said Elizabeth, queening it by the chest of drawers, dragging in her Lambert and Butler and puffing it airily away over all our heads. "I always said it's not worth crying over spilt milk. What's done is done."

"You're a bloody hypocrite," I spluttered. "Fifty years on you still blubber about a bloody baby."

"That'll do," said Jane.

"I meant," said Elisabeth with great dignity, "that it's different for a man. He has to learn to tough things out or where's the protection for us poor girls, eh?" And she smiled round in a frightful mockery of gaucheness. I stumbled out.

Was it any wonder I was happier inside my room even though Monica had invaded my head when I had begun to think I was strong enough to repel all boarders?

"You should not have hit me," she'd said the evening of the great little fire. "I always said no man, and I say no man, shall ever lay a finger on me in anger. I'm going. I tell you straight and you can lump it. Who'll do your washing and your socks?"

"It was only a love pat," I had squeaked petulantly, scared of what I'd done, seeing her eye swelling, red veins in the white leaking. "You walked into it. You turned just as I was patting you on the back, a love pat." "Like hell!" She'd said, "You meant it. Don't give me that."

"Bristol is a lovely old city," I should have said ten days ago. "We could visit the docks area – so much is changing there. But the church of St Mary Redcliffe still soars above the water, its tower a delicate tracery, its spire a silver needle. It stays resolutely the same through the eternity of beauty and the spear of its tiny cross injects ideas of God's love. The cross was originally meant as a love pat. He did not mean to use it as a bludgeon. He was merely bringing it to our attention then suddenly there we all were tacking our friends and enemies up on the cross like rows of Christmas cards on the wall, like butterflies in boxes, like litter on parky poles. We'll take you down; we'll ease you off the point of it all when you've agreed to become like us, when you've accepted the inevitability of being in the wrong. I saw a picture of a man trussed and bound sitting on top of a bamboo cane – ancient torture of the Chinese gods. There is the spire. There is the cane. There is the anal penetration.

"Don't try to squirm out of it, bastard," she'd said. "That's always the answer. Hit and run, you yellow coward, you bastard.." and she'd ended up dabbing her eye with cottonwool dipped in cool water. "What'll I say at the hospital?" She'd said. "Walked into a lamppost?"

"And why not? You could have noticed an advertisement on the other side of the road and collided through inattention," I could have said, but she did not have to go to the hospital anyway and so that was a red herring. Instead I could have pointed out the place where pirates were hanged until the tide crept in and covered their last cries, but she would not listen then and she would not listen now, just jangle jangle in my brain refusing to go away.

"You women," I'd said when she'd refused my third apology. "You ask for a nest; you ask that the nest be made; be feathered; you ask the nest be left by the maker whenever it pleases you. We men are merely appendages, extras, unnecessary after the only active verb. I have furnished your nest with babies and now I may go."

"Are you jealous of your own children?" She'd sneered as if asking an impossible question and I had nodded slowly and certainly before lighting yet another fag. "You make me sick," she'd said and I had left the house because I'd wanted to hit her again just as I'd wanted to hit her the first time when she'd turned her back on me and I'd looped my fist into her face.

So much had happened since I last thought of the marriage breakdown, but the small of my back was aching and sweating and my hands trembled as if the shock had been today. Downstairs the women were barbing their hooks to pull me from the water gasping and hopeless. In my room, Monica was slitting me to the back bone, ready to fillet me for mackerel tea. I lay back on my bed and crammed the last of the cherry cake in my mouth. I'd bought it ten days before as a treat for the children, but it had stayed on the green leafed plate by my bed. It was important I removed all traces of their visit lest they crept back through the door on the back of a crumb. And there was the plastic bag James had brought with him. I picked it up cautiously and scrabbled a paw inside. There was a book: A Guide to Welsh Mountain Walking and a card with Dad on it. Hope you like the book, Dad. Perhaps you can get to walk around the place now you've time to be out and about. He'd signed it with love. More tears, such dark and wincing tears.

Somebody was scratching at my door. It was not Elisabeth's nervy little paws, but neither was it the confident beat of Jane.

"Come in," I wanted to call out, but my lips were super glue stuck. The noise continued like a migraine and there were dancing spots on the window pane. I quickly wiped my face with the bed sheet and called again. But the door stayed shut. Soon there would be shuffling feet outside and crinkly crumpling paper shoved in smelling of paraffin. There would be blue acrid smoke and the sudden spurt of flame up into the blistering gloss. The smog outside would invade and I could either remain lying on this bed like a large shop dummy or heave myself up and through the burning window to the roof where I would cling in the cool of the burning sun, my face a beacon and my body riddled with degrees of burns. It would be a gamble. How long could I leave it before the monster crackled through flesh and there was no escape but the climb to the roof and the joyous leap into the arms of the tarmac?

The door swung open. I flinched, knocked out my pipe on the plate, but it was Peter, only Peter, with his tattooed arms and his fists holding brush and paint tray.

"Come to touch up you know where," he crowed. "Needs another coat to do it justice." And he swaggered across the carpet. "You've been up to your old tricks again, haven't you?" He said, stopping and sniffing the air like a connoisseur of wine. "We can't be having smoke in the boudoirs you know. You'll be crusting my nice ceiling with nicotine before you know it." He picked up

160

my pipe and tucked it in his pocket. "Get it back later," he grinned. "Keep it downstairs eh?"

"No cats neither," I muttered.

"What?"

"No pets, no fags, no pipe, no nothing," I said. "Just this empty landscape."

"Who rattled your cage?" Peter squatted by the window and began to stroke emulsion over the shadows. I managed not to spit. The room was better than Dartmoor, far better than the Warren.

"To tell you the truth," said Peter, leaning back away from the wall to admire the handiwork of destruction, "I'm here 'cos Jane is worried about you locked away up here, not eating, not passing the time of day. She thought seeing the old woman would be a help, but it's knocked you back. Anything we can do?"

He meant well. I recognised good intentions, but I had reached the brick wall and had no faith in moving forward, no reason to believe in discovery through thought or action. There he was smearing paint over the truth and here I was trying to face what I had done, understand where I might go. "Besides," said Peter, "we've a little problem of our own needs sorting out ... thought maybe you could help."

"I just keep papering over the cracks," I said. "But wallpaper's no protection from earthquakes."

"What is?" He said with a grin to encourage me to speak. "If you talk about it it might help."

"Talking's no therapy," I said. "It winds me up."

"Please yourself. I can but ask. Don't you want to know our little problem?"

"You took away my picture," I said and brushed at my

161

eyes angrily.

"Common decency mate," Peter smiled. "Can't have obscenities on the wall, can we?"

"Oh piss off," I said.

"Please yourself," he said again, refusing to be riled. "Don't want to know about Elsie and her hospital visit, do you?"

"No I don't," I said. He carefully propped the paint brush in his tray and walked back towards me on the bed, leaned over me to the chest of drawers and took my fags and matches. "You can have them later too," he said. "Downstairs. Better safe than sorry is my motto."

I chose to ignore him and he left without another word. Thought he was safe he did. But my lighter was still in the drawer.

If denied definition through art, should I achieve definition through action? Were art and action different? There were still those who looked for purpose, characterisation, stylistic belonging, continuity and recognisable structures – the nest of security. They were running the elitist show as if the chaos was a temporary blip on the consciousness to be soothed away with predictable soft soap and mollycoddling lies. I scratched my pot belly round the navel near, but not touching, the scar. How many times had I been here before lying on a bed, wondering what act could be a catalyst for change and, if change was to occur, what change and whose change and where change and, hardest of all, was there such a thing as change anyway? It was conceivable, but barely so, that there was an essence called existence just as there might be its reverse, negistence. It was tempting to believe that change could move between these states, but it was more likely that the two states were the same state seen from different angles. In which case, the only change was the change of perception not of the essential state. Hence a holiday was just another pair of spectacles with the old blindness hiding behind them. Change and action were pretence, the third essence. Existence, negistence and pretence and what came before all other essentials had to be pretence, but to pretend was to fabricate an outward show, a Hollywood set and puppet figures. It was not possible for me to walk among the creatures of any essence and even my pretences became obliterated on the wall.

As the outward show crumbles and breaks like frozen clods of earth on the vegetable patch, so the search for Mills and Boon secure worlds gathers momentum. When existence and negistence are one, pretence becomes ever more desperate. Where was the pattern leading to happiness, cried the heroine, looking at the craggy features of the blue eyed man? But he turned away from her, loaded his machine gun and fired into the thickest part of the crowd where the children huddled, where Elizabeth's improbable baby offered an easy target. The only pattern lies in acts of blind faith and the rejection of easy notions of redemption. It was time to assume the high ground and bring sniper fire to bear on all targets of cosy indifference. I had to harden myself against feelings of sympathy because humanity was in my hands and my task was to drive the lemmings on to self feeding disaster – their disaster, not a human disaster – before the essence of existence was lost in drivelling trivial negistence waving flags and spouting advertising jingles.

There would be wailing in the ruins of Sarajevo; there would be the crushing of spirit in Azerbaijan; from crevices in Kurdistan the rotting limbs of starving men would crawl to martyrdom and on and on the death call would sound, echoing over the mountains of Iraq, the plains of Cambodia, the valleys of Bosnia, the valleys of Lebanon, the shantytowns of South Africa and even into the fortresses of plenty in America. I had to be the forerunner, the contaminator, the one who showed ugliness to people who lived in ugliness, but did not see it, barbarity to the barbarians, who did not know it and hatred to the haters who did not feel it. Only then could there be a craving for the peace of virtue, tolerance and acceptance.

Stay, therefore, people of gentle principles out of the force field, out of the fire power. Your time might return when the killing fields are sated, when the revolving helix brings new perspectives. Even Monica Muriel might be needed when the nations call for order through mutual respect. But not yet, not now, when the apocalypses of destruction are upon us and the dark places are opening wide their jaws of bombed brickwork and their judgements bring mind and spirit into the negation of existence, far worse than death.

How I needed a cigarette already, but the nicotine was downstairs and so were the preying mantises waiting to pounce.

I recognise that I am but one creature among many millions, but my reality is shared surely by many in the scrabble for living. My mind is a necessary part of the disintegration. In fact I am conscious that I do not exist in my own flesh, in my own right, any more. I have become a conduit for the chaos beyond me that pretends it is not a chaos, but an essential order. Doctors no longer make up their own diagnoses; teachers no longer decide their own lessons; politicians no longer follow their own creeds; we all follow the black hole of prescribed living and fascist language and, therefore, I no longer need to take responsibility for my own actions, such actions being the natural result of prescription and loss of freedom.

When existence is ruled by the ordered pursuit of power through chaos, my actions are informed by chaos. It is a relieving thought that I am at one with the social mores of the time, no longer an exile in ideas, but still I am desperate for a cigarette and they wait for me downstairs like cheese in a mousetrap.

For example, I think, poking my big toe through the hole in the bedspread and enlarging its scope, when the old crone who is Elizabeth comes to knock on my door I should react on the spur of the moment, with no consideration of weighed judgements and behaviour. If I then give her love and time and generosity, it is because the thoughts of society are golden and harmonious leading towards the glory of happiness. If, however, I drag her into the room, strip her from her musty clothes and strangle her in the cord of my ceiling light while knifing her skeletal body, then that is a reflection of the chaos around me. Either action is totally beyond my power to condition and change because there is no such thing as change just different perceptions of the essence.

"What has she ever done to you to be treated so terribly?" I asked the mirror, pretending to wave a cigarette towards my image and realising its absence with a pang. The image had to be treated with contempt. It carried outmoded concepts of conscience. I wished for her arrival to test my theory and soon she came hobbling up the stairs to find out from the horse's mouth how my day with my family had gone, whether I would be going back to Luton with my children – mad as hatters in Luton the lot of them, she laughed – whether divorce was final. How her voice grated and then she said how sorry she was when she heard of break downs when people had so much to live for.

"Look at the royals," she said, her head nodding on the puppet strings of her neck. "If they'd suffered like I've suffered, I might be able to understand it, but they're educated people with lovely children and a home – they shouldn't be throwing them things away and nor should you with your family. A lovely girl that Joanne of yours."

I should not have put the photographs on the mantelpiece. She kept poking her yellow-stained finger at them. She was like a desecration to my family, but then I remembered the doctor I'd seen after leaving hospital the first time, the one who had called me lowest of the low. This man who called himself a doctor would applaud the killing of the low, the unimportant, the shabby old woman who climbed the stairs and often bleated about wanting to commit, what do you call it, euthanasia. That doctor saved Elizabeth's life today even though she had not brought me any cigarettes because I would not subscribe to his ideas of ethnic cleansing. The pattern of chaos demands I inflict pain on the wealthy and the deadened, not the tired old woman who kept clambering up to see me.

"Elizabeth, you know deep down you were but a child yourself when the blitz happened. You couldn't have been the Mother of a baby. Which baby are you thinking of all the time?"

I lay flat out, easing my big toe through the hole. She cried then, not answering my question, and spoke about her arthritic knees and the way men used to look at her when young, but at least she could get around the house, not like poor old Else who needed hospital treatment so bad, but couldn't get there. We cried together about the passing of the years and I pecked her cheek and patted her shrivelled leg, saying she was still a beauty. It was all in the eye of the beholder and Elizabeth said that I was a good man under all my nastiness. Eventually she told me there was a cup of tea downstairs and maybe I'd fancy a nice pipe to go with it and then, stopping at the door she said, "Ask Jane." And she'd gone away.

My main concern was tea and nicotine by now and so I found my way downstairs, knowing that both Peter and Elizabeth had been sent to induce my return to the living room. They had an ulterior motive and I needed my drugs.

"I don't see any alternative," Jane said. "It's just one of those things. Elsie has been waiting for this appointment

167

for god knows how long and there's nobody else to see her safe there." Elizabeth cringed in her chair, her fingernails scratching away at the reddened skin.

"You know I would," she said. "If I could, I would, but I'm not up to it and it's not as if I should, in a way. She's my friend, but I can't be going out. The door's shut and it's best kept that way."

Jane tut-tutted and shook her head because she could do without this sort of worry being a busy busty woman with so much more to do than ferry tenants to and from the hospital.

"She'll miss her appointment and there won't be another for years. You know how she's been fighting to lose enough weight for the operation to work, and Pete and I can't help this time and that's flat."

Elizabeth tried to sit tall and all her heart was in it when she said she would try, but tears were bursting out from her lashless eyes.

"It's my agoraphobia," she said. "I put on my coat and I freeze, but if you try to make me, I suppose I'll have to go."

There was Elsie stuck in a chair going nowhere. There was Jane at the last chance saloon because Peter's sister was getting wed on the Thursday afternoon down at the registry office in Bristol centre and there was the appointment slip for Elsie to attend at last for the operation to restrict her food intake and she'd missed an earlier appointment because Jane had not intercepted the mail for her and now what was to be done?

"Is there a hospital ambulance to pick her up?" I asked

and they looked at me as if they had never expected any sort of sense from my lips ever again.

"Tried that," said Jane. "No chance this time."

"Hospital visitor car?" I asked.

"Maybe. It's worth a try, I suppose."

"Couldn't you drop her off and pick her up after the wedding?" Even as I said it I knew it was wrong. Why should Jane's life be ruined by Elsie? She'd be dressed in her best, smelling of Apercu, a fragrance she used on Saturday nights. There'd be Peter tucked in his smart suit, button-holed and ready for the family do. How could they stuff the giantess in the back of the Peugeot and dump her at the hospital like left luggage? Didn't they have the right to a life of their own?

"Can you take her then?" Jane said. "You're so full of ideas."

Oh you bitch, I thought. Slowly, carefully, over the days since my return from the abortive Monica visit, she had been moving in on me. Interference on the radio, imposition of domestic tasks, interruptions to my mind time and again. "Just lend a hand with this paint pot, John. Have you sent in the form, John? Shake out the cloth, John.. it won't take a mo." All I had wanted was to browse through my head, continue this process of divulge and despair, but the sisterhood was conspiring against me with daily tasks of mindless do and die.

"You've been leading up to this all along, but I won't be trapped so easily," I said coldly, pushing the small of my back into the hard rung at the back of the armchair to stop it aching. It was tension, the doctor said, made my back go wibbly wobbly, until I was forced to lock it tightly

169

at the base and ramrod straight strut around. I forced my self to think of my own woes and tribulations. It was all very well for Elsie to make demands, but I was the frozen one, my own victim with the skewer of inaction thrust up the rectum refusing me leeway to move on anyone's behalf, except for myself, and then with extreme reluctance. "If the bus comes, it comes and waits for no man," I said. "She could do what you would do: bus it or leg it and all by herself."

"I'd go with her," Elizabeth cried caught between sorrow, frustration and anger, "but I'm just not up to it and you know it. Mind you, you can't trust him, you know," she said, an evil light gleaming at the back of her head like a neon, "not even to buy me fags."

"It's a put up job," I wailed. "You're the same as all women all over the world. If everybody just gets on and does without thinking about it, you think it would be happier place. No point in moaning, no point in sitting around holding your head and aching all over to understand why the moss grows more slowly than the dandelion, why the black hole in your head leads to an alternative existence … it's just shopping, mending, ironing, driving, cleaning and working all hours with the occasional sniff at the sun and an ave maria for luck, a stab at the lottery and a current bun on Sundays with an extra cup of coffee and a chocolate for a treat: that's it with you lot."

"Damn sight more than you get out of life as far as I can see, John," said Jane.

"You're only interested in what you can see and hear and taste and feel. There is more to life, you know," I bleated and knew I had moved into very deep water indeed and the underlying tow had seized me already by the knees and was preparing to pull me into the Severn bore. Hadn't I only just before been clinging to the here and now in the bull and cow, the identity through body building, through sense transaction? If I were to strip away the skin and say the bare flesh was unfeeling because thinking ergo I am and my thinking was a sham, what else was left but the butcher's block or Prometheus' rock? In the microscopic analysis, there is no sense, but there is a grim determination to survive.

"This little pig won't go to market," I tried to grin at Jane, but she was looking straight through me and out the other side with a face so serious that it would have fetched a lump in the throat of a murderer. "I'm not the one to be lugging Elsie across the city," I continued. "She hates me; she wouldn't go along." To survive might ask more of me than I could manage, might demand more of Elsie than she could give, might feed my selfishness more than her survival. I turned to look at the woman and all I could see were her frightened eyes flickering backwards and forwards from face to face, unable to make out what was happening, knowing the conversation was all about her and not knowing why or what or how.

"You've been spending too much time with your own thoughts lately John," said Jane with the crisp certainty of an executioner whetting the blade. "It'll be a useful exercise to escort Elsie to the hospital. We'll get a taxi. It'll just be a question of putting her aboard, paying off the driver and making sure she reaches the ward for three o'clock – not much to ask."

"It might be too much," I said. Responsibility is such a huge noun. To act is such a definite verb. For somebody afraid of taking on his own life, afraid to break out from the cocoon of inaction, it was a monstrous request to ask, but Jane meant it, every word. "What does Elsie think?" I asked desperate for her to scream abuse at me, reject any thought that I might be her guide and companion. I wanted her to scream that I was a pig, an unfit unkosher companion.

"John here will take you to the hospital on Thursday," said Jane. "He'll look after you."

I caught Elsie's spasm of sheer panic as if Jane had dashed a cup of scalding tea across her face. The woman's mouth began to work, her lips goldfishing and no sound coming. Then she began to shake her head so the pendulous chins could not catch up and tears began to squeeze out of the eyes. Elizabeth convulsively clutched her friend's hand and began to pat it and Jane sighed heavily, looked up at the brown ceiling and brought her right palm down on the table with a slap.

"It won't do, will it?" She said and looked at me as if I were a worm. "I should've known better than even think it. Don't worry Elsie. We'll come up with something. God knows what, but we will. We normally do."

I crossed over to the other side of Elsie's chair and forced myself to crouch next to her. The small of my back protested, but I managed to kneel awkwardly.

"It's all right, Elsie," I said. "Well it's not all right, but it'll be all right, you'll see."

What was I doing? Why was I there? What sort of torture had made me offer help when the only help I had to offer would lead to misery? Fooled again, I thought, and Elsie will be the final fool. In another moment the smell of her would drive me from her side, but strange are the senses at times of emotion. There was a smell, but it was of years before when Joanne had lain in my arms with a wet dirty nappy to change and eyes like saucers. "We'll have you right in three ticks," I used to say and flicked out the nappy changing gear like a professional. Warm water, cotton wool, zinc and caster oil, baby powder, terry towelling, central pin not through the navel, cosy and tucked, sweet smelling and pink. There weren't many Dads who handled the rough with the smooth, but I loved the turning round of dark into light, but now knew that such reversals were no longer in my power. It would be a pretence to believe so, but Jane was still looking at me with her eyebrows raised and her mouth half open to say I was a bastard and so I beat her to it.

"All right I'm a bastard," I said. "But if it'll make any difference, I'll take Elsie to the hospital." Quickly I turned back to the fat woman. Her mouth, small in her wide white face, was open. "You'll be right as rain with me and we can't have you missing your chance after you've tried so hard to lose weight," I said and patted her hand. The mouth snapped shut like a trap and I left the living room desperate for sanctuary in my attic.

Chapter 12

The hot stormy weather broke last night. I awoke at two in the morning to hear the thunder machine mashing the sky and then rain smashed through the skylight with a wind-shriek. I had been running through dust filled alleys, choking and stumbling, looking through blind red eyes for the tower. There might be refuge there. It was simple to scoff and hide behind literary Childe Roland illusions. I should have hurtled from the bed to save my art therapy paintings, all four of which were lined up on chipboard under the window where the light was reasonable, but I stayed under the blanket. Strange how my brain was able to think dispassionately and without fear, yet it refused to send urgent messages for movement. I remembered we were held in the vice of the moving vortex and if rain fell then what could man do about it but be drenched? I remembered Charlie and the "wevver" and gave up the pictures to his ghost. A dark voice tried to creep through the worm channels of my brain saying that fatalism was a lame excuse for inaction, a sign of impotence, that I should fight, swear and kick my flyblown body out from the spider's web, but I lay back, mixing metaphors in water colours.

"Can't do nuffin about the wevver thank Gawd." And the rain hissed.

The road was rarely hushed, but at two in the morning only the occasional rushing vehicle swished past and I quickly relaxed against the suddenly cool pillow. Freshness spilled into the room with the scent of water on earth and hot stone. I shivered and pulled the cover over my bare shoulder, turned on my side and slept.

In the morning, mind your eyes dear, cup of tea-time, I deeply regretted not having closed the window. My pictures were threaded with pale streaks where water had run, mingled with the paint and trickled to the carpet. It was not so much the physical destruction that concerned me as I squatted grimacing over the ruined tower, but the challenge the rain had levelled at my theory of haphazard creation. By recognising that water had damaged my scrawling work and by not intervening in its actions, I had evinced awareness of some values and beliefs about the worth of my creations. If these values could be observed in their absence – oh shit the green had smudged with the orange fruit, turned it to a lime, bitter to the taste oh bitter beautiful – then the presence of worth could also be observed. That orange had been so round, so full of mature pith; the zest had lived in its rich colour. I had genuinely believed that a purity of expression could only be achieved by ignoring the values intrinsic to design and content and concentrating solely on the conduit theory of education. If the refined consciousness and creation combined, then art could occur through even the worthless medium of me.

I flung my head back to stare at the window and wondered at the precise angle of wind that had forced the rain through the skylight in such a direction to cause maximum damage. The malevolent coincidence and the fresh breeze were sufficient to goad me up and out of the room, through the front door and down to the art therapy. I explained the dilemma to the therapist, Gladys Mitchell, but she was unhelpful being full of summer cold and the fact her pet cat had been to the vets for the jabs and found to have ear mites and a small infestation of fleas.

" I thought infestation was bound to be big," I said to her snuffly nose and kleenex.

"They are only small fleas," she answered without a trace of a smile.

"You can puff powder on the cat and all will be well," I reassured.

"I felt so ashamed," she said. "I asked what caused them because she's ever so clean." "And what did the vet say?"

"He said it was common in cats. Hot wet summers encourage fleas and I was not to worry."

Gladys did not like the common streak. She was no snob, but her cat was a sophisticated companion. I nodded sympathetically.

"And then he asked me whether she'd been wormed recently. Well I ask you! She only has the Whiskas Luxury Meat and never goes outside. She's a house cat, not a mouser.

'Better be safe. She looks a little thin,' he said as cool as a sodding cucumber. ' That's the Siamese in her,' I said, nose in the air. You know what he said? 'How many

176

generations removed?' Cheeky bastard and me with my nose streaming like a gargoyle. I couldn't keep up the snooty bit at all, sneezed like a geyser and left paying over more cash than this bleedin' twopenny ha'penny job can afford."

I knew there was a good reason for staying inside my own cell. Venturing outside was to run the gauntlet of everybody else's troubles, but I muttered how sorry I was and how cats could be a real source of solace in times of need. I parrotted good old Doctor Rhodes in time of others' problems.

"Oh I don't take it to heart, John," she said. "Quite funny really – not like that bloody copper. Did I tell you about him?"

I hastened in with my worry.

"But what about my pictures?" I whined.

"Rain's cocked 'em up," she said.

"Ten out of ten for observation," I said sarcastically. "But I wanted to explore the relationship of the artist with the experience of the natural world. Strictly speaking the water should have enhanced the artist's work in subtle ways, not made a mess. I did not want it to be a mess. I wanted to show that the finished article was bound to be greater after fate's intervention than before when the boards only carried my feeble attempts to capture a dream."

"Load of cock," Gladys said, having no inhibitions about being common in her language. "Just use the brush and paint what's in the system. Practise a few techniques and stop being bloody wet. You're not pickarso yet, you know. Don't worry so much. There aint no such thing as the great artist; they were all great fartists. Let other people build the bloody pedestals."

From the corner came a wailing cry and Gladys' face crumpled into sympathy for her cat, closed in its basket. "It's all right diddums," she called across the room. "Mumsy's here." She turned back to me. "I didn't have time to take her home and get back here for the first knockings, but I don't like to let her out in a strange place. Perhaps she'll have a run round at lunchtime. I've brought the litter. But she'd be better off at home."

There was an itch on my forearm. I scratched.

"Well are you staying or going?" Gladys asked. "Because if you're here, I can run the cat home. Take twenty minutes at the outside and you know your way around. Better than having her in a box, unless you want to draw her." I peered into the basket and shook my head. She was no tiger for a jungle drawing and moving moggies were too hard for me. Of course I agreed to stay, but I knew Gladys would have gone home anyway, if she'd wanted to. We were used to her wandering in and out. If she was there in her orange smock, then she was there. If not, fair enough, she'd turn up. The hospital wanted her more organised, more to time, but then she would not have been Gladys.

"You're a darling," she said. "Here, have the paper while I'm gone – in case the painting doesn't come." She plucked the Bristol local rag from her shopping bag and threw it on a bench. She left, carrying the cat basket like a bomb, looking left and right out of the door, pretending to steal away, and then clattered down the corridor at a hundred miles an hour.

She'd been right to sense I was not ready to paint. The room with its chipped easels, the dry smell of turpentine, the window ledges crammed with potted plants and still life objects was suddenly quiet and still. I wandered round, picking up a boot with its sole flapping and placing it next to a frayed and dingy yellow tutu. Too obvious a contrast, I decided, and moved over to the wall where charcoal drawings of a fox head were displayed. The stuffed model stood beneath the pictures and he was right to look displeased. The charcoal did no justice to his snarling gums and mottled, patchy fur.

And so I returned to the table and picked up the paper, turning over the pages in a desultory way, from back to front, through the sport, the letters complaining about too many cars on pavements, the Council proceedings and a new arts' policy. I was headline scanning and nothing caught my eye until inside the front page – a small column telling a story of death under mysterious circumstances.

Initially, as I skimmed the article, I did not feel it carried any relationship with me. It was in the paper, a different world from mine. "A vagrant found on a building site by a labourer had been battered and then burned to death, claimed a police spokesperson." And then the name began to ring a bell. "Martin Beverall, a man of restricted growth, was of no fixed address but well known in the area. He had lived in a makeshift shelter behind advertising hoardings near the Lloyds Bank new complex, off the Watershed. Police are anxious to speak to anybody seeing the deceased during the last week or so."

I flicked hurriedly to the front page, but the information exploded in my head and I had to return to the tiny patch of newsprint. So much was unsaid. When had he died? Who had wanted him dead? What should I do? The last week or so? Had he recently been found? Had he been dead for long? I had been in my home, hiding away. I had nothing to say – best leave it alone. But Martin's head invaded the room. When I looked at the plants, he was there nodding in the midst of a cactus. What friends did he have to help him now? Had he seen some crime he shouldn't have seen? Were drugs involved? Soon Gladys would return and joke about my lack of work as if I were a schoolchild again and I would have to pretend normality. I shoved the paper away from me and quickly arranged some paper and paints. It would be an instant painting of definite colour blocks, unconnected, dark, letting the light speak through the narrow gaps between the brooding shapes. I could see it. I would paint it.

But when I held the brush it froze in my fingers and I could not decide where or for what or how to use it. I did not hear Gladys return, but when she came behind me and touched my shoulder I almost screamed aloud. She joked about needing a sauna and massage to free me up, but I told her my ex wife saw me the other week and that silenced her. I sat in front of a dead square and could not make a mark. I told myself to lift the lid of my skull, take the pleats from my heart, but self-instruction is a poor instrument and I could not teach myself to view calmly the dwarf's death. There were tears running from the eyes of the red haired man I had painted on the wall. They had not been there before. It was the face of the man who had attacked me and he had not then been crying. How could he have shown remorse for his rage was dry and full of fire? How could the rain betray me?

Eventually, with tiny scratches, in the bottom left hand corner, where I normally placed a signature mark, I drew in stiff hard lines so small they could hardly be seen, the dwarf's demolition hammer. I had carried it off, leaving him without protection and the man with red hair had been lying on a bench just a hundred yards away.

I racked my brain back to the building site just before I had left Martin, scrabbling from his tarpaulin. Had wisps of smoke been oozing behind him or just dust? Had the primus toppled and burned in my haste to escape? 'You are the man for burning,' I said to myself and, in extremis, could I have killed Martin? But I remembered the round, apologetic red face shining up at me as I backed away. I recalled nodding back at it, flapping my hands in a fitful apology of my own that I should have intruded on his space. I could not have been guilty of this arson because I had resolved to protect the weak, my kindred. If I were to unleash the anger in me now, it would be levelled against the self-satisfied power people, not the downtrodden and poor. Yet, by taking Martin's hammer, I had left him defenceless. I could imagine the Redhead bastard seeing me slip through the gap in the hoardings, deciding not to follow me, but back-tracking to where the dwarf was lying. I could hear him jeering at his round head, kicking at his small ribs, huffing and puffing his straw house down, setting it aflame with his hot breath.

When Eric, the social worker after Dartmoor, had asked me man to man, confidentially, hoping I would shrink away and not add to his case-load with a court case, whether I wished to prefer charges against the Redhead, I had hidden his crimes. I was frightened of the consequences. Brush it all under the carpet and start a new life away from the evil was an understandable intention, but now the dwarf was dead. At what stage was it right to draw the line, to blow the whistle, to demand justice against the violent?

"I must face my fears," I suddenly blurted out to Gladys.

"You do that thing," she smiled, showing the big gap between her front teeth. "They say these fears disappear like snow in August when you stand in front of them and call them home."

I nodded, knotting my jaw, grinding my teeth and setting my chins.

"This Martin Beverall," I said, "I knew him. He was all right. He was a friend." I poked at the paper with my brush. "Some bastard's knocked him off and I think I know who."

"Who you going to tell?"

No evidence to hold up and no more than the terror of my history to adduce stopped me in my tracks, but I would tell. I needed to explain how murder happened without cause and without compunction.

"The doctor," I said. "I'll tell Doctor Rhodes first of all."

"Now that's sensible," said Gladys. "You don't want to make a fool of yourself, do you?" She did not believe me. I could tell, but the doctor knew my history and would understand that the Redhead was the obvious culprit. He would advise. I was pleased to have reached a decision. I was yet more pleased to pass the responsibility to the doctor. Although I was afraid of the Redhead, I was also afraid of taking any responsibility. Responsibility placed importance on my shoulders like a judge's gown. The doctor had often told me that I should not take on more than I could manage and what I could manage was all too little, not even a packet of Lambert and Butlers for Elizabeth. Nevertheless, the idea of confiding in the doctor gave me the lift I needed. Marjorie Daw's see-saw was my mental state. When it was up it was very very up as light as miracles conjured from seed drift, and when it was down it scraped holes deep into the earth like huge cratering bulldozers.

"Thank you Gladys. I can leave here happy now," I said, putting on my coat and marching off.

Chapter 13

I must now tell what happened at the half way house. In memory of Martin Beverall and for the honesty of my story, it must be told. I told it to Doctor Rhodes and he believed me. He, in turn, told the police. It became public property, official, part of existence after so long being negistence.

In prison I had been alone, but always controlled, under others' eyes, not expected to go beyond the terrifying walls of thought and concrete that surrounded me. I had experienced security there and, when I had looked out over the huge and unforgiving moors, I could appreciate the close control within the fortress. I had renounced all responsibility for myself and what I had done to bring me inside the stone walls. There was a comradeship of enforced solitude. Although I had loathed the restrictions, I had come to depend on the screws' authority, the pecking order of man above man. Dartmoor had come to feel like a Victorian father to me, a huge and frightening tower in which I cowered, a frightened child but knowing my place. I had been promised support on release, a half way house, a hostel as temporary haven, but this could not serve such a turn.

I am a gentle man and when I resort to violence against places I have never threatened people directly. When I burned the school I notified police and fire brigade so that the caretaker could be rescued. I had not known about the technician in the craft block doing some double glazing on the side, but he had managed to crawl out with only minor burns.

"Remember son," the young officer had said to my middle aged frame, "matches are for ciggies or for a pipe and nothing else. Take the medication and stay a simple good lad. You don't belong inside." And every fortnight in the prison I had walked to the medical room and received the jab in my arm that took away the poison from the tree of knowledge. Was all that routine to be thrown away so soon?

Eric would not listen and I was fool enough to stay in the unsafe safe house. I should have walked out there and then, demanded another hole for the night, but even as I knew I could not trust this social worker I also recognised that I was in no position to argue.

There had been days of anger in prison when I had wanted to pull on iron tipped boots, pick up a long walking stick, whistle the dog and walk the moors for miles. I would have returned with pictures in my brain to daub, but Dartmoor held me in thrall. I had written to James, telling him of my desire to be out walking the high moors and now he sends me a book about walking, showing he took to heart the escape words of his father. There had been all that countryside to patrol and all I did was shuffle in the exercise yard with the East wind blowing over the high wall. I had promised myself walks in Bristol – no dog to go with me. Monica had him in her new place together with the children, the proceeds from the sale of the house and the new man. I was left with my tobacco, pictures and the thought of freedom. Already the thought was turning to fear, but I would hold my son to walking together. He would stroll along beside me while I panted up the hills and scurried along muddy lanes. His easy teenage pace would outstrip my steps. It would be a treat to feel his presence by me because being a father gives dignity, although that had been stripped out of me like a leg bone from a boiled chicken.

I smiled vacantly when the two were introduced to me, withdrawing into my skull, trying to build a rigid armour of protection around me. I would freeze intruders with my baleful eye, but the small pink worm of me was full of fear. I recognised them both you see and Steve was the known nightmare I told you about before. Short of grabbing hold of Eric's arm and refusing to be left I had no alternative and scuttled to my room dreading the next move. When I had left Dartmoor that morning I had not been so naive to believe that all would be well for me, but I had hoped for a short reprieve from feeling bullied. But no such luck. Steve and Keith did not need a fearful man, just any unhappy bastard in their way and they had already sensed my fear in the silent shell I carried round with me.

Keith took to banging on my door at night screaming that I had no right to freedom if I did not wash the pots or run the hoover down the passage in my turn. It was always my turn. He took to coming up behind me and shoving a scouring pad into my mouth. "Wash your mouth out, bastard!" He bellowed in my ear and then laughed as I tried to pull away from his asphyxiating arm across my neck. Steve brought back cans of lager and the two became pissed each night, often heaving up and blaming it on me. "Can't take a joke, can you, you bastard!" Steve would crow. "Get it cleared up."

"You're bloody mad," I said one morning when they had stolen my pants and trousers, shoved them down the loo. I stood leg naked in the kitchen while Steve squealed at me, pointing poker fingers at my limp old rag and pretending to bounce on the end like an ecstatic flea.

"I just want my trousers," I said, backing off, hands folded over my private parts.

"Wants shoving down the loo to find them, I'd say. Put the John in the john," said Keith casually, flicking over the pages of his newspaper. Steve needed no further invitation. His hair blazed as he leaped towards me. I rushed out of the kitchen, but he caught me, dragged me back to the toilet and shoved my head down into the bowl.

"I'll flush it while you hold him." I heard Keith's voice, still relaxed as if working through MFI instructions. There was a roaring round my head and I was dunked down until I thought my cranium would be sucked through the bowl into the pipes. Then I was gasping for

187

air, swallowing filth. A hand clutched between my legs grabbing my testicles. I tried to twist away, but there was no escape. My head came up and I spat out scum and tried to shout. Then my head was down again and one of them was on my back, riding me, pushing me down and down.

I was saved on that occasion by Eric, the social worker. They must have heard his yale key in the lock because they left me gasping, retching on the mat in the loo. Then I heard their voices, cold, calm and studied.

"He's a weirdo – sticks inside his room … " said Keith.

"Never does no work unless we tell him to … " said Steve and I could imagine his pursed prim lips in his red face.

I pulled myself to the door handle, managed to stagger out to make my complaint, but Eric was not listening.

"You'll have to mend your ways, old son," he said, trying to placate them, ignoring my streaming hair and naked legs. "People don't like shirkers – can't blame them really. Just pull up your jolly old socks and do the decent thing."

"They stole my clothes and shoved me down the loo," I wailed.

"Bit of a joke," said Keith. "Needed sobering up – came back canned again last night and Steve here had to clear up his mess."

"It was the other way round," I claimed, but I knew I sounded weak and unconvincing. It is easier and more comfortable to believe the bully than the victim.

"Nobody's saying it's easy," explained Eric, shaking his head slowly from side to side like an elephant, "but it's the only new start you'll get. You don't want to go back inside now, do you?"

I remembered Animal Farm and said I didn't want Jones back either, but Eric was no Blair, while Keith screwed his temple and Steve gave a great stretch of his upper body, flexed his arm muscles and said, "See what rubbish we have to put up with. Just how long is this creep staying here?"

"Just tell them to get off my back, will you," I told the social worker. "And I mean that literally." But I did not turn and show him my anus, ripped sore and so Eric smiled his pathetic let's all be chums' grin and pushed his fingers through his wisps of hair.

"Bygones be bygones," he said. "It won't be for long." And he was gone.

Keith and Steve, fortunately, threw their coats on and left the flat as well. I should have packed what was left of my things and got out when the going was good, but I was a trapped animal and could only envisage a cell or pain. I seemed to have lost the ability to act independently.

I tried to lock my door against Steve that night, but he rammed his foot through the board and blamed the damage on me. I had to pay in cash and body. Every night after that he rapped on my door and poked his head round saying, "Where's the fuck then?" And I would have to suffer. Oh Monica Muriel where were you then with the quiet coupling of gentle lovers and the breeze? His sweat was smoke and his talons were flames on my back. I could not fight and every move I made excited him the more. It was a coward's act to lie still and acquiesce, but at least it gave me a little more peace during the days. It was Keith then who orchestrated the torture with his tongue.

I became obsessed with fear of AIDs.

One of the terms of my discharge was that I should attend a doctor's clinic for a fortnightly jab and medication. I tried to tell the doctor of my fear, but my notes held details of fantasies, self-delusion and self-abuse. Whatever I said, he looked at my nicotine-stained claws as evidence of self-inflicted wounds. Whatever I said, he talked of paranoia.

"I know when I am dreaming and when I wake," I said desperately. "And I can not sleep for fear. I want to bring a charge against this man for assault, for buggery, for rape, and all you do is smile and call me mad. If I were mad, you would lock me away where I can be safe. Please take me into protection." But out came the ampoule, out came the syringe and in came peace. Perhaps it would be better in time.

I began to light matches again and scorched the sheets where he had been. I put rings of fire under door handles and wondered where the tin of regulation dark green paint was stored. In the lock up where the caretaker was supposed to be based? The padlock was strong and the kitchen knife I used could only splinter small strands. Keith called in Eric to look at the damage I had caused. It strengthened the social worker's belief that I was to blame. He gave me an official warning and I pleaded that he should take me away from the warren. I was desperate to escape, but could not move without official sanction. I was a pirate hanging on the tidal wall with the water creeping up my body like freezing slime.

I lost weight. The doctor put it down to more exercise

than when inside. I was haggard and did not wash, feeling such shame. I decided to become so shabby, dirty and unappealing that even in his alcoholic lust, he would wince away and vomit out the encrusted dirt of me. But the two men barricaded me in the bathroom, stripped me and shoved me under the shower. They shoved the hose inside me and lathered me until I slipped and slithered from their grasp and ran for my room, but there was no escape, just momentary respite from abuse and their laughter chilled me. I huddled in a blanket and wept, but each tear was weakness and made them crow.

"He's lighting piles of bloody newspapers now," said Keith to the officer at the weekly meeting. "I caught him in the kitchen last night blowing on the flames. Can't you do something about him? It's not safe in our beds at night with a nutter like him."

"If you don't sort him, I will," said Steve and his anger was palpable. It screamed out of his mouth like cobra spit. Why couldn't Eric hear it? Why could nobody stop my pain? I had made all the signals of despair and I was said to be an articulate man. Why could I not make myself understood?

"I'll have to forward a written complaint, old son," Eric said regretfully. "Your probation officer won't be chuffed."

"You've put me in here with a murderer," I said, jabbing my finger at Steve. "I'm an ex-con, but so is he, but will you fucking listen to me?"

And the two bastards looked holy, raised their eyes as if I had the screaming adjabs.

"Now don't be abusive," Eric said. "Steve is trying to

mend his ways. He wants a new start. His room is as neat as a pin."

Steve smiled, but I could see the clenched fist by his side kneading at the rubber ball he used to develop his muscles every evening as he sat watching television, downing beer, waiting for the madness to possess him.

He came with a cosh that night and beat me on the shoulders, on the arms and legs. I covered my head and brought my knees to my chest, and then he beat my ribs. Suddenly he stopped and I waited for worse, but I heard him rummaging through my cupboard, but I did not dare move lest I unleashed another bout of fury. He slammed from the room and then, trembling and so terribly bruised that every step was fire, I took my coat from the floor, avoided the excreta he had left and tiptoed from my room, down the corridor past the living room with its blaring television out of the front door.

I stumbled down the stairs, through the grounds and along the road like a drunkard. It was raining. I arrived at the general hospital and propped myself on a chair in casualty, feeling the blood on my back caking, a numbness in my arm and a sword sticking in my side. I did not report to the reception. There would be no point. I was in the right place, but nobody would believe me. I was inhabiting the wrong body of another man waiting for oblivion. I tried to think of good things but there was none. Even when a nurse came to me, I refused to speak. Her nose turned up in disgust and distaste, thinking me a tramp off the streets looking for refuge. She was not far off, but to her credit she noticed the blood and suddenly I was part of the hospital process. I belonged to the routine of care, but I still refused to speak.

I did not want to explain all that stuff about my pain. It does not pay to hurt others with my own hurt. Eric did not want to know. Jane and Peter didn't want to know even through a picture on an attic bedroom wall. Nobody wanted to know and I could not blame them because I did not want to know. A man should not be raped. He should be in control of his own body. It was shameful, a weakness, to be abused. Bad taste was never part of my background and Mother would not have approved of public shouting. She always kept her husband's treatment of her like a guilty secret. I should have learned by now that unwelcome news should stay unspoken. Deaths-heads are shoved aside or assumed to be lying. It merely diminished me to speak it. It made me more the victim and less to be pitied. Not that I wanted pity. I did not deserve pity. If I were convinced of a moral purpose in this world, if this world exists at all, and if I believed in divine retribution, if there were a god, I would only talk of justice, not pity. I would only talk of the primacy of beauty beyond the soul that may only be reached as through a glass darkly through the compassion of justice, not the pity of the powerful. I have no power. It demeans me to feel another's pity. Semantics? Feel with me if you can. His dotage now, do not begin to pity. I pity a dog, a rat, a cat or mouse. I pity the frozen corpse of a dead rabbit in its cage. I have compassion on man and woman. I have compassion on Elsie with her glandular size and simplicity. I have compassion on the dwarf, the Martin Beverall, found dead in his own home. By reading of his murder he has given me power to relate my terror and my pain. It was crammed away inside my brain and all I could do was play word and picture games round the reality. Martin's death placed me with him and I knew the feelings of the victim without wishing to take the power to pity him.

Too late for pity or compassion! Pity is trivial. Compassion assumes another is suffering with you. Martin was beyond suffering. All that is left is passion for justice.

Farewell pretence, I thought on the way back to my safe house. I had done with finding wrongs where there were none. There would be no more self-induced crises to hide behind: the drinking, the wet paintings, even the mural under the emulsion. I had followed the newspapers and others' stories as if they were to be viewed through a glass darkly, never face to face. But this dwarf's death hit me hard, made me explain what had happened after Dartmoor, cut away all the frills and fol-de-rols. Jane would not like it. It would have to remain secret except in the closed files of Doctor Rhodes' accounts, inside a brown paper cover. I did not want it leaping out brandishing a hammer to crush my brain like a beetle under a boot. I was pleased now that Martin's death had been recognized in the newspaper. Perhaps the police would follow it up with the passion for justice that the murdered deserve. I had no absolute faith that this pursuit would be prosecuted wholeheartedly, but I knew the Redhead's name and divulged it, not for personal revenge but for the memory of Martin Beverall.

Chapter 14

"Oh I'm so pleased to see you up and about," said Jane, meeting me at the door, ushering me in like a welcome guest. "You've been stuck in your room with a face like a wet weekend for so long that when I found you had gone out today I couldn't help but worry about you. You are feeling happier I can tell. It's the change in the weather. That's what it is. One moment we're all down in the dumps with the leaves frying on the trees and the smog enough to clog the nostrils of King Kong, the next it's all cool and showery, with the grass greening up again. Peter said to me, just this morning, that it would only take a barometrical shift to have you as right as rain. Besides, Elsie came back yesterday and you did so well taking her to the hospital all in your suit as well – the proper gent I know you are. The operation went well and her heart held up. That is the big problem – so much pressure on it."

"If only it were that simple, old fruit," I said, pulling off my shower proof, stacking the ruined pictures and smiling at her.

"Less of the old from you," she said, smiling back. "And why can't it be simple, eh? Just answer me that."

"Where's Elizabeth?" I named a possible complications.

"In her room," said Jane promptly, but returned to Elsie. "And Elsie seems so much better. She didn't know how to accept your offer to take her to the hospital, but it made a difference. She said so when I brought her home yesterday"

"How could you tell?" I said. "She just absorbs the slings and arrows, the brickbats and the compliments into the jelly of her being."

"Don't sound so cruel," said Jane. "You don't mean it. Why say it?" I shrugged. The quick sharp words were easier to find than the positive ones. "Besides," said Jane, "I heard her singing this morning. Have you ever heard her sing?" I shook my head.

"Elsie has a beautiful voice," continued Jane. "I couldn't believe it was her in her room, but it was. Elisabeth told me that Elsie used to sing once."

"Believe it when I hear it,"

"What about your better half?"

"Visiting the bank – business," said Jane.

"Keeping you in shekels, is he? Doing what a good man ought for his good woman?"

"Talking about what we're to do with his lump sum now he's out of the navy."

"And so it is all simple after all," I grinned. "All sea-shape and Bristol fashion!" I found a tune to match a feeling. "All the best girls love a sailor. All the best girls love the sea! All the best girls carry bristols! All the best girls fancy me!" I sang, taking Jane in my arms with old-fashioned courtesy and waltzing in the hall. "It's the hanky panky upsidaisy. Pinch of salt to drive her crazy. Come to bed then. Come with me."

196

My God, she was strong in my arms; she was firm and rich; she was butterscotch meringue; she was melting moments and the after taste was glorious, resonant and sweet. My hand cupped her buttock and percy quivered and jerked. There was life in the old dog, after all. And then she was gone. Her hands pushed me away from the fruit of her breasts; her face was flushed.

"Now that's more than enough of that," she said, brushing her hands down her apron in a fluster. "Whatever next!"

"Whatever takes your fancy, honey-bun," I said. "Simple desire, that's me."

"Don't be dirty," she said. "You men are all the same."

"Had one, had them all," I said with mock seriousness.

"You're so up and down," Jane said, becoming more severe. The colour had ebbed from her cheeks and her lips were thin.

"Rarely up; too often down," I said. "Don't begrudge it me, Jane. It was not meanly meant."

"You can keep your hands to yourself. Pete'd kill you."

"Forbidden fruit tastes sweet."

"You'll be finding another room in another house. And that's not easy with your track record."

I stepped back then, swallowing the bubbling words. I nodded at her, feeling the threat.

"Didn't mean any harm, Jane," I said. "I just came over full of love and you seemed so open, so welcoming. I wanted to show how much you're appreciated. Didn't manage it too well. Sorry. It's not so simple after all, is it?" I said. "There's always the down side."

Then Jane folded her arms and looked daggers at me. I'd really gone too far, she told me. There was more to

197

human relationships than grabbing a woman because she seems friendly. It was possible to be friends without jumping into bed. It was possible to have affection without needing a condom. I apologized again, suddenly wanting to cry because she had taken my happiness in holding her all wrong. She hadn't needed to be so angry.

"Can I change the subject?" I asked. "Can I show you the mess of this picture?"

I turned to the wall by the coat pegs, knelt down, leafed through and found the picture of the tower spoilt by rain. It gave a few seconds to return to normal relationships. "It would have gone in the hall here," I said. "But it's all to cock."

"Can't you cover the splodges?" Jane asked, moving to my side to see the picture more clearly.

Not a prayer, I thought. The precise, thread-thin brush strokes in exact colours fissuring the brickwork with moss green, gold and silver were merged into greyness. The clarity had been washed away and an outline form remained.

"It'd be nice to have a picture of it before it's pulled down," she said. "It's very good, John."

"Who is going to pull it down?" I asked. "Is it dangerous? Will it tumble in the next great storm?" I walked through to the kitchen and peered out from the window at the squat ugly tower. It seemed beautiful to me and I wanted it to stay exactly where it was for a hundred years more. There had been too much destruction.

"Unlike your picture, it's a bit of an eyesore now," Jane said from behind me. "The great thing about good pictures is that they make things look better than they are. You've even managed to make the bricks shine where the sun catches them. It looks like silver after the rain."

"Are good pictures the ones you like then, Jane?" I asked.

"They need to make me feel happy. That's not to say that they have to be of happy things, but that the artist has managed to show that happiness is possible. I like strong shapes and rich colours. I can't be doing with artists who push their own unhappiness on the rest of us. That's why I like this picture. The colours are a bit thin in places because of the rain, but the shape is just right. It's what it is, only better."

"What it is made me paint it like this," I said. "We need the tower as well as the picture."

"Things wear out," Jane said.

"Although I am a creature of whims, moods and fancies, structureless and whirling in chaotic and self-indulgent feelings," I said, concentrating on the tower as hard as I could, "it seems important for one or two man-made artefacts to defy the general decay. Why not this napoleonic tower at the end of a Bristol garden?"

"Not important enough, I suppose. Not as if Napoleon was ever going to come right round here on his travels," Jane said. She put down the painting and ferreted at the sideboard. She found a leaflet and brought it to me. "It was on the lamp-post outside," she said. It was details of a planning application to demolish the tower and build luxury flats.

"There should be a preservation order on it," I said, barely able to contain my anger. "Is there a local history society to protect it? Isn't it a bloody listed building? Who owns it?"

"It does attract the rats," said Jane calmly. "And it's

hardly pretty – keeps the sun off the dahlias too."

"And a block of flats wouldn't?" I asked. "All those tenants peering out on your private back garden."

"It'd be a blank wall facing this way," she said. "Pete says it'd be good for the area, more up market."

"So that's where the toast's buttered, the cookie crumbles. It's Pete's property, eh? He's put his little nest egg into property now he's out of the navy lark, eh?"

She sat down at the kitchen table and put her head in her hands.

"I don't really like the idea," she said. "But Pete says there'd be a good return on the development. It's just a mucky old tower with nothing happening to it, just crumbling away and attracting vandals and rats."

"Pete Speak," I said. "And you want a pretty picture of it for your hallway to salve your conscience – a picture done on the cheap by your cheapskate tenant."

"There's nothing definite yet," Jane said all dithery, nothing like the competent landlady I knew.

"It should be cleaned up with a plaque on its side," I said.

"And lots of visitors trooping through our garden at a quid a time – I'd rather not, thank you," she said, rallying a smile.

"It's a little bit of the past. It needs respect," I said.

"Just paint over the smudges for me. I'll pay you fifty quid," she said. That was not to be sneezed at. I'd picked up an old wooden surround for nothing from a skip in Barry Street. With work from the fretsaw, some unobtrusive pegging and a coat or two of varnish, it would serve a turn. But I resolved to write to the Council at Unicorn House and raise a stink with the local press. I picked up the leaflet from the table and shoved it in my pocket.

"It will give you a focus," said Jane.

"I'm the opposition party," I said.

"I meant getting the picture in place."

"What about a slogan? We need a sound bite, a quick setting concrete solution to stick in the belly." I was caught by a sudden enthusiasm for using the advertising medium of mild hysteria to generate concern for the important. "'Tunnel for the Tower' – could undermine our efforts."

"I don't think you'll beat Pete," said Jane. "Once he's set his mind on something, it's as good as done."

"We'll see," I said and nodded my head, scratched my nose and winked my left eye significantly. It was a gesture from a silent film comedian and the doing of it always created a solution of sorts. "Can we have a party? A midsummer barbeque?"

"That sounds a lovely idea," Jane smiled, back in her landlady role.

"First thing to do is get lots of people in the garden looking at the tower. A party would fit the bill."

"Pete likes parties, but there'll be no change in him." She rose from her chair and went to the pets' calendar on the wall. We set the date for a fortnight ahead and I bit my lower lip to stop myself grinning at the complicity. Then I carried the pictures back up the stairs to safety. I sat on the edge of the bed and thought of mounting the campaign to save the tower and artistic considerations did not enter the equation. Action was its own therapy, its own art. Sod the dwarf! Sod to buggeration the complications of a battered skull! I would shove it all

201

away back into the bin of my brain – no thinking – total selfishness – that had to be me. "When times are bad," Doctor Rhodes had said, "try to treat yourself a little. A little molly coddling never came amiss." It would be a treat to enter the fray, having been sidelined for so long.

"Now don't get carried away, old son," I said to my reflection. "She's only doing it to keep you dangling, to keep you amused and out of trouble. She's told me there's only one winner and that's not you."

I pulled writing paper to me and smoothed out the leaflet. I copied the planning office address and then trembled at my daring. I had never challenged authority in the seat of its power. I had never dared question the takers and doers. I steadied my nerve and my pen licked across the page. 'I wish to draw attention to the fact that the tower adjacent to Tower House is of significant historical interest. You might wish to enquire at the archive within Bristol Central library about its provenance and importance. Certainly, it ill behoves a council concerned to preserve the heritage of Bristol to countenance the allocation of planning permission for flats rather than sensitive renovation of this Napoleonic cannon ball tower.'

The words trickled across the page in dark blue and reassured me that I was doing the right thing. There wasn't another soul who could write with such assurance. Even if they discovered my instability over the immediate past, it was clear I was an educated person, able to make the case fluently and effectively. I looked at the wall for further inspiration, but Martin's head gazed at me.

There was a large hole in the wide pimpled surface of his forehead and his eyeballs were on stalks like obscene toadstool heads.

"Trying to forget me then? Didn't take long, but what else did I expect? Police won't be bothered, not with a runty vagrant. Why should you be troubled? A few pints in a few pubs don't forge any obligations." His mouth opened just where the mirror joined the wall and words of dribbled blood trickled down the wallpaper.

"Following doctor's orders," I said. "It's displacement theory."

"You'll have to face me sometime," Martin said. "Why not now?"

"No. It's not to do with me. I've told Doctor Rhodes. The police know and then it will be over and done with."

I returned to the letter to explain that local residents looked to the tower as a barometer for the weather. It would take just a few moments for Elisabeth to be convinced that the tower was an extended thermometer stuck in the mouth of the sky. 'If dark with velvet green patches oozing silver liquid in the small hours, it is about to rain insistently for at least three hours around noon. The tower has stood up for fine weather for over two hundred years and its every pore is redolent of past history. How can a sudden whim to build flats overcome the warlike verity of past glory?' The weatherman would say all sorts of banal showers of words gathering in the west on the television and receive his forecaster prophecy salary without giving recognition to small fry like this fry reading the weather tower for himself and finding it closer to the truth of Bristol weather. By now persuasion dripped from every pen stroke. My writing too often was ridiculed for extravagance, the unreal mingling of dream and truth. This letter, however, was the epitome of taciturn incisive language. But even as I wrote, I recognised the new constraints for what they were. All very well to be fluently in charge of one's mind and sentence construction, but the case could only be answered in the British Imperial War Museum with a careful reconstruction of a model cannonball chute. There was no direct evidence that the tower was as described by Pete and he would be pleased to change his story in order to demolish and build flats. Worse still, Martin continued to peer at me. His face would always return like all previous nightmares. He saw through my threadbare argument for protection because we were kindred spirits clad in different bodies. "You will be a witness," said Martin. "Stand and deliver the truth."

"No!" I screamed. "That won't be necessary."

With the formal letter of protest written, enveloped and awaiting a stamp, I deliberately turned to thinking about Jane. It had been good to feel the urge and my brain pictured her ripe round bum with my fingers sliding down the trouser elastic. Monica Muriel always wore striped dungarees like Andy Pandy trousers and tights underneath – double dyed defences. She used to tell me to get off her, made me feel I was a filthy little toad. Even when she gave herself, she'd sigh like a disgruntled dog. I wondered whether her new man managed to flick her switch, whether it had been all my clumsy oafish fault.

"Come on Percy!" I muttered at my flies, but the flicker of life had died.

I had been Gyges, the first peeping Tom, I decided. I used to peer round the bathroom door when Monica was slipping into something casual like her skin. She once told me she hated men who undressed women with their eyes and I was becoming one of them. Dream on, clothes stripper, paint stripper, layer under layer, until all the accretions of day to day were scraped clean and the true flesh glowed under the new sun. If Jane was to be believed then Elsie had an essential core deep within the folds of fat, but how was I to know? Outward show must attract inward exploration. I used to garner the top shelf in newsagents for exterior come-ons. I used to sing for pussy, puss willow, and imagine silken thighs, soft breasts and hard nipples. My daubs held frantic purple flesh colours on a dark palette and I called them art, shoved them on a wall and drooled over tonality, composition and form. Tom cat, sleaze cat slinking round the she cat, wailing for the oyster, wailing for the moon! No wonder, as my legs grew thinner and my belly thicker, as my toenails yellowed and my nostrils whiskered, that women should wince away. There was no dignity delving into bodies when old percy penis was flaccid in my jeans. I had never learned a sensitive way to a woman's heart, the private part of her. Perhaps there was no such route. Sex is urge; sex is young; sex is babies and bye-bye Daddy.

"No more cannon shot for you, old pal," I sighed. "Percy is due for demolition, each tidy brick hacked out until the thin trunking is revealed and then a stick of dynamite! They don't like it up 'em and I can't make 'em see that the older and uglier something is, the more necessary that it should be cossetted and loved."

Such a conclusion is easy for self lovers. My weeping abscess does not revolt me. Elsie's hugeness filled my head again. Just thinking of her made my fingers itch as if contagious thought had introduced scabs between my knuckles, but, nevertheless, she was able to conjure music from the mountainous clay. Not that I'd heard her. Her music was mere hearsay, but Jane spoke straight. There was a stark chance for me to achieve redemption from this blackness, but it would involve considerable courage. I shelved the thought for my own voice, my own art.

I turned over the chipboard to examine the tower. No. It would never do, not even with scraping and bodging. It deserved better. The tower would have a fitting memorial and the frame required a better picture. I would not be seduced by the artist's dream. There was the tower with its crustaceans scuttling through the fissures in the brick and here was I, the holder of chaos, the observer of destruction. Light the blue touch paper and retire should be my creed, wanting to freeze the tower, trap its waving grass hair and scrabbling moss into stillness. It was a contradictory impulse because my normal instincts were to explode the static into violent flame.

There was neither rhyme nor reason. A man either did nothing and saw himself fall into the abyss or he did anything, called it worthwhile, and walked into the abyss without noticing. One death was continuous and lifelong; the other was suddenly upon him. Was it better to see where I was going or to hide in the mists of important deeds like cleaning the windows, painting the

Sistine Chapel or, what Dr Rhodes had helped me do, giving a statement to the police?

Inside me the curled shrimp, plucked bare and cold like a dead man in a dead newspaper, winced in the ice. Even if I pulled on a new skin and inserted plastic antennae, the shrimp would lurk within.

"But you could be a fine pretender to life," said Doctor Rhodes, sidling in through the back door. I did not want his presence. He was too good a man to be true, attended churches, gave food parcels to the Armenians and spent spare time with his grandchildren. He was satisfied with small contributions. I preferred the grand gesture – always was an old ham. Working in miniature was a precious and meticulous skill that I did not possess.

"Sorry doc. It's not your time and place. I need my pipe." I wandered to the downstairs loo to find the pipe on the cistern top. Back up the stairs I began to climb when I heard Elsie's door close and slow steps approached the landing. I refused to be daunted. Assertiveness was the right of every cringing little bastard like me. I walked up to meet Elsie coming down and then stopped, turned back and tiptoed into the alcove by the front door for Elsie was singing and her voice filled the house – no words just glorious vowels working the scales and then silence followed by slow shuffling steps and I moved back up the stairs to meet her, for movement was tough after such an operation. Jane had told me Elsie had to keep moving. "She sings to cover the pain," she had said.

"It's all right, Else," I said. "Give me your hand. I'll help you down."

"She don't need help. She just needs you out of the

bloody roadway!" shrieked Elisabeth, pushing up behind Elsie's bum like a weasel. Gently and slowly I reached out to the hand on her skirt and tugged her finger into my palm.

"Come along then," I murmured. "Nobody's going to bite you, least of all me." For a moment I thought she was going to pull back; the hand over her eyes flashed away and her body trembled. "No, don't fall backwards," I said with as much reassurance as I could muster. "You'll land on Elisabeth and she'd not thank you for it."

"If you just got out of the way, there'd be no problem," continued Elisabeth, but she sounded far away, disconnected from the immediate task. I looked down at Elsie's feet and realised how small they were to balance such trunks of legs. I braced my arms and held her by the elbows as slowly, ginger step by ginger step, Elsie delicately touched tread after tread like a ballet dancer and I held her weight so that she could feel the feather of her spirit and not the lead of her bulk.

She reached the hallway.

"You would be a fine dancer," I said. "At our party, will you dance with me?" She did not answer, but heaved herself round towards the hall away from my face. I managed to squeeze past and escorted her down the corridor with Jane backing away into the kitchen. I presented Elsie to the kitchen. "The queen is in her parlour and all is right with the world," I crowed. Elsie stood in the doorway, her mouth goldfishing, and then, suddenly, words tumbled out.

"You're a pig," she said, but there was a new note in the sound, a sort of puzzlement.

"Pigs are highly intelligent and sensitive beasties," I

replied. "I shall take that as a compliment." Elsie pushed on into the room and found her normal seat near the television.

"And what have you been up to now?" asked Jane, arms akimbo.

"Good deed for the day," I said.

"He got in the way!" Elisabeth accused me, wheezing down the corridor.

"Petty, petty considerations!" I laughed. "Seen my baccy?"

"I'll give you baccy!" Jane smiled, unable to resist my sudden fine spirits.

"I left it somewhere round here," I said peering round the table short-sightedly. Jane leaned over to the chest of drawers and lifted some magazines, but there was no sign. I crouched down by the coffee table next to Elsie. "Have you seen it, Elsie?" I asked and picked up her knitting. Suddenly I could feel the sulphur of her burning and she grabbed down, pulling the wool from my grasp, but there was my tobacco.

"It's all right Elsie. This is what I'm looking for," I said, standing up quickly so that my eyes saw sparks. I did not want a knitting needle in my eye. "Ah! Condor ready rubbed, wings astride the vaulting azure sky – enough for a squeeze and a puff, a wheeze and a ruff of silver blue smoke, a halo of perfect snuff."

"And you can keep it out of the house," said Jane. "No call to contaminate all our lungs." But I was off on another scent. Jane was just joking. Didn't Elisabeth fag away every day? Sometimes it was necessary to create a new world and a new joy.

"The bridal way was strewn with fresh herbs; the

bridal bed was festooned with rich fruits: apricocks, damsons and the sweetest of ripe pears. Naked putti Pucks surrounded the frieze of flowers, their dimpled navels like sweetmeats, and, as the luscious maiden in her rich array approached the night-time bower, their tiny hands reached out, clutched her silken dresses so that one by one her royal fruits of tinted flesh lay bare. With one crooked finger, she beckoned to her paramour and said, "May your volcanic ashes choke your throat; may your hacking smoke blow cancer in your gut. Leave our royal presence to the approach of pure things."

"Stupid idiot!" said Jane and stomped to the kitchen. Elsie squeezed down on the floor with tender and reluctant feet, making the floorboards wince with her involuntary weight. Jane picked up her feet and brought them cracking down in ship shape marching order.

"The ground she walked on!" I chanted after her. "It is the reality of your body that announces a place on this wretched earth – no winsome piece of light-footed gossamer nothing, you!"

I struck a match and frantically inhaled the barbs of Raleigh's smoke. I was intoxicated with excess of nothing, the exuberance of marshmallow, of candyfloss, of a tiny act of contrition blown into a whirling doughnut of jammy sweetness, but to hell with it! Living in sullen, solemn trains of dire and dirty underpants and shirts had to be challenged.

"He doesn't know whether he's coming or going," muttered Elisabeth and she left. I twisted round towards Elsie and gave her an extravagant wink, nodding towards the sink where Jane was sluicing water, shifting crockery. I crouched in the doorway, poking my pipe through the door jamb and began to laugh. I was like a dance. Up and down, up and down! The smoke puffed and belched in little clouds with every giggle.

"Put that pipe out, you dunce-head clown!" Jane shouted, her eyes bright, arms sudded to the elbow.

"Just you try and make me, it being the year of the goat and the freedom tree."

"You'll regret it if I have to chase you." She pushed a red hand down into the water, her forearm gathered whiteness. "Says who?"

"Says me."

"You and whose army?"

"Bring your army and start bashing! I don't need an army."

"I can believe it. Got a rolling pin?"

Suddenly she was after me and soap suds landed on my hair, but she missed my pipe and still the smoke oozed out. I smoked the baccy under the automatic sprinkler alarm, laughing at warnings, but she rushed me with a milk bottle full of water, pouring it down my neck, sending me staggering into the garden where the clouds scudded without rudders and the parched flowers lifted their heads to the wet wind sucking juices into their multi-coloured trumpets and the great whirring dumble dum bumble hums lurched drunkenly round the side of the house and tried to straightline it to the inviting roses. Oh it was action day in sprogland too because over the fence I heard the shrieks of children. I went to peer over at two boys belly down on skate boards whisking past the tower round the back of the garden and landing splat in the long grass.

Scrooge-time had gone wrong, the very merry rouge-time had flushed with pleasure, when birds do sing, heigh dingaling ling – heather musk and toast without crusts. I was happy and needed no cause. Up, up and away on my beautiful balloon, sang the croaking baritone and I could see them as I saw them on the day with the dwarf, no the little man, no the little person. Och no, for today we have naming of parts and I'd call him whatever he liked. 'I like to be called Martin.' His round mouth dribbled round a blue comforter and I nodded at the balloon as it spoke. I'd even acquiesce to the language manipulators for there was recognisable life beyond the alphabet. Why bring further hurt to the memory of the titchy nitchy man with the large head with a deep cavity stuck in it? Why bring hurt to the moon mountain woman as she sloughed her obesity?

Their balloons were tugged by the fierce wind, their trail ropes flicking the heads of trees like whips, their baskets bucketing. It was escape time, the ignore the dog dirt time; there were more things inevven'ninnerf time. It was Save the Tower time – a picture, a party, an article in the paper, an argument with Peter and even, quietly say it now lest the boys were improbable skateboarding innocents, a stripping and a nestling, a stroking and connection with a fellow creature, a woman, the better half of the ugly world. 'Will you come now I know you? Will my sun bud your flower?' I sang raucously and then blew on my pipe until the spittle spattle crackled and cleared and the smoke drew strongly through.

Suddenly I was shivering and giddy. The wetness on

my neck was chilly. I held part of my mind at a distance. The rotting was there. It had not disappeared. The florin sized mould would grow, but why the hell should I have to take notice of it? The rest of my fruit was golden and fine. I shoved gobbets of joy down my throat, wanting to preserve it, to hold it safe for other times. I was a hamster storing food, but not as irascible, not as protective in my cage, I hoped. For a moment I thought of the cool calm face of genuine happiness, the measured reconciliation of the good and bad into the quiet platonic search for enlightenment and then I plucked a pink rose from its stem, snuffed its sweetness and strode back to the kitchen.

"Here," I called magisterially. "Gather ye rosebuds while ye may and stick 'em in a jam jar. It is pinkly blushing like a virgin. I present it to you with all its innocence and all its shining glory."

Peter had his feet on the table, his face behind the local rag. Jane had propped her bum upon the sink. Of Elsie and Elisabeth there was no sign. The ex-sailor and current property developer lowered his paper and looked at me with his left eyebrow marking a question.

"Very kind of you," he said. "You shouldn't've gone to the trouble." He smiled and took the flower from my hand, brought it elaborately to his nostrils and sniffed like an eighteenth century roue with lace cuffs. "Eeeh evvenly," he said in a terrible mock northern accent.

"Don't take the mickey, Pete. He's been that much more himself today." Jane walked across to rescue the flower. She rubbed his black hair and planted a kiss on his crown. Our eyes met above his head and she grinned across as if I were an accomplice. Her kiss might have indicated they were lovers to a less observant eye, but I warmed to her smile. I had touched her. She was alive to me and for me. My normal reaction to meeting the challenge of throwing down a gauntlet was to retract, swallow my words and just stoke the furnace of anger for a later date, but she reassured me and so I managed to speak about the building work.

"Have you told him what I said about the tower?" I asked. Peter laughed and Jane rumpled his hair again. "It's not right," I continued. "It shouldn't come down – listed building I shouldn't wonder."

"Man the battle stations!" Peter laughed. "The friends of the past are gathering their nostalgia weapons for a final defence." But then he spoke quite seriously. "Sorry mate, but you're out of order. That tower is a health risk, a monstrosity and it has to go. I've a demolition order on the way from the council. Write what you like; do what you like, it'll come down as sure as night follows day."

The confidence was ebbing away, but I kept a strong face.

"We'll see about that," I said with as much dignity as I could muster and then Peter shrugged his shoulders and looked at Jane, who shrugged back at him and did not look at me. "It's the beginning, not the end," I squeaked, my bottom lip beginning to quiver. Why did assertion lead to negation? Why did fear clamour at the heels of incredible courage? It took so much from me to articulate the smallest contradiction to those with power over my life, but Jane had surely given me consolation and cause to speak. But there was no arguing now and so I left them and reached the top floor and my bedroom before the deeply insidious doubts began to creep sidelong through my ears into my brain. He'd seemed so sure of himself and Jane had not chimed in to help me. What sort of game was she playing? One moment warm and fruity in my arms, the next stroking Peter's hair as if he were the only toupee in town.

Just feeling tired, I thought – too much sudden excitement – a short nap needed. I shredded off my trousers. They were stuck to me legs with prickly heat. I lay back on the bed so the coverlet smoothed my thighs with initial coolness. The traffic spew hacked outside and I closed my eyes.

I had given myself due warning that extremes were to be avoided, that the dull tenor of even days was safer in the long run, but might as well preach to the wall as expect my dried out brain in my paunched body heed a single note of caution. Just one tiny note of hysteria could sound and it would lodge in my head, bubble and boil on the hod, heat increasing every second. Have you seen milk frizzle and burn on the gas cooker? So I could see the cells of my brain heave and crack into cream pustules. The top of my skull was lifting again and bloody Martin was wrenching up the bone with a crowbar, screaming at me to listen. "For once in your fucking life, listen!" He screamed in my ears, but I could see my face in a mirror and my ears were constructed from thick maroon velvet cloth smeared with gobbets of tar. All sound was muffled. Martin's mouth opened and closed like a goldfish; his eyes spat venom; his cheeks bulged, but my ears were cloth until the man of the cloth squatted by my bedside and wriggled his bibulous Bible words into my head to join the squirming worms of guilt and terror.

"What is your creed?" The theologian in his black cloak asked in reverential tones.

"Niliscience is my vacuum," I answered. The doctor often told me that depression was the worst of diseases. It seemed to strike against an illogical hold on life through faith with a bleak reason that confirmed there was neither God, nor devil, hope nor hell. It was worse than that, for in despair there is no knowing and no understanding, no being and no touch of past or future. When the blackness loomed over the Severn Estuary and Glendower rattled his hilt against tabard, the wild Welsh invaded from the high hills and there would be no escape on the fat flat plains of idleness, but the desperate man, poisoned into acquiescence like a spider victim watching its juices being sucked out in full and impotent knowledge of the loss of life, no longer cares.

"To action stations!" shouted the philosopher, feeding mental flames with ancient tomes. "There is more life in one twitch of a palsied mixi-muscled rabbit than all the thoughts of sages. Sauve qui peutetre is not paralysed." But I was paralysed. All the frantic glee of the day had fled from me. Long, stiff and stark the Oudeis Odysseus Nothing doing man lay on the Eastern bed of nails in a rictus.

Down the stairs, along the corridor, through the shiny white door of the master bedroom in the house, Jane lay with her husband. They were coiled together and there was no distinction between where one part of their bodies met and merged with another. They moved gently like the rocking of infants, self absorbed and open to every sensual touch of living. Theirs was an honourable coupling and I had wanted a small part of their physical pleasure so that I too could be touched with honour and stability. I knew they were happy in their cocoon. I knew Jane, in her generosity, would be able to forgive my crassness, but I would find difficulty in forgiving myself. I, of all people, should have known better than to force my attentions on anyone.

"It is only a touch of flu, Monsieur Pompidou." I mouthed at the frost starch-clad nurse as she leaned over the bed, her hand across her mouth, her eyes wide with fear. It was best to dissemble with doctors and nurses. The stench from black pustules under the arms was temporarily masked by the fragrant pine room-freshener, ozone friendly. I saw incurious thumbs pull down at my eye bags, but I could not move. I felt precise fingers probe behind my ears, but there was no pain. The tingling in my toes disappeared and I left my fakir body far above me, floating on a levitated bed, while the leaden spirit of me sank through the dust mited mattress, through each separate floor of the house from attic to hall, down into the cellars until it stretched on the stone flags. Now above me the black tower rose unknowable and bleak. Below me, the earth festered, anxious to receive me. It was limbo country and my waist and back were too old and too fixed for such contortions.

"You have made a bloody fool of yourself, you fat old lecher." My lips moved in the darkness. "You deserve your punishment, you deceitful bastard."

A square of light appeared and a silhouette of the doctor theologian hovered and then filled the light with blackness. I sensed him pull the knotted flagella from the wet wall and I heard him flex it in his muscular hands. Without waiting for instruction, I rolled face down on the trembling ground. The black-cloaked torturer would fling back his cowl to reveal the red head of punishment. I could not face his burning eyes. The knots would bite into my back time and again, cat o nine tails, cat o nine lives, spat cat claws raking me with continuous suffering, each brand final and each brand new without end.

In suffering there is pain but no death. In death there is an end. Martin was luckier than I. In paralysis I tried to ward off pain. I clenched my eyes and clinched my back, willing the sprouting of wings to help me fly towards ineffable goodness. But each attempted flight into the sky of release was stalled and I came crashing down into the maze of sorrow and suffering.

"You foolish deluded man, speak your pain. Let your agony wail through the long corridors of this night. There is no virtue in stiff upper lips, rigor mortis of the soul." I peered round behind me, through the misty blood haze, to see Doctor Rhodes perched by me like an owl on a branch. He balanced his neat round head, twisted it round and round like an automatic corkscrew and then his narrow sharp beak dipped down to peck away at the liver through my back. I could feel each spurting dagger and my shrieks bubbled up through my larynx. He had been my friend and now he was destroying me. I wailed like a lunatic, howling the wolves away. Betrayed! Betrayed!

"That's better," I heard him say. "Better out than in. Your own torture is worse than any I could bring."

And I howled again, crawling to the attic bedroom

window and making my mouth as wide as the black sky above me and around me, my tongue flickering like a snakes in and out of the window until I could taste each speck of dust clogging up the atmosphere and corroding the stonework. There were people rushing in to my room, grasping at my arms and legs, but I ignored their fettering hands. With just one screech I would break their bands and float far out into the Bristol sky as if in a balloon before plunging down, down like a diving hawk to meet the ground, to pierce the tarmac and cut myself to pieces on the broken ground.

And so I awoke in a hospital ward with all its wincing honest fluorescent light burning through me and my brain sluiced clean with raw surgical spirit.

"For a short time," said Jane, patting my hand. "Just to get your bearings again."

"We'll keep your room, John," said Peter.

"And Elsie and Elisabeth send you their love," said Jane. "And this card."

I turned my head to see a picture of two pink tulips on a blue background.

"What does it say"" I asked. "On the inside."

"Get well soon," said Jane. "With love from Elisabeth and Elsie."

"Who wrote it?" I asked.

"Elisabeth and Elsie."

"Both of them?"

"Their own names," Jane said. I cried, the tears oozing over my lids as easily as oil.

Chapter 15

Such a magnificent pipe this morning – cool and rich, the tobacco furling scented smoke to my nostrils. It was the first step to recovery, surely. I peered through the skylight in my brain and could imagine I could see the top of the tower like a tousled head in dawn fresh light. Crows nested there and their ragged wings blended with the broken brickwork to make the dark tower of Roland's quest. I no longer cared about its preservation, but was this the angle from which to paint it or should I break through its hidden door and create an interior vision?

Perhaps the next day I would be strong enough to travel from the ward to Doctor Rhodes' consulting room or even across the car park to a daubing session with Gladys. The doctor had visited me in the night, given me emergency medication, or had it been the nurse with the scrambled egg hair acting under his orders? Either way, I owed him a visit to show the peace after the storm. And Gladys would say,

"Let it all go. Do not be afraid. You are justified in your own vision, in your own esteem."

"There is a difference between therapy and art, old

fruit," I would say in Eric's voice, testing her waters, testing her acceptance of my story about the Redhead. "I want to paint an ashtray," I would say, "and place disfigured burning babies on the rim like stubbed fags." I could see the picture vividly, but there would be no applause for its brilliant execution. Art critics would peer and tut over crazy juxtapositions. "Where are the characterisation, the solidity of story, the psychological development and the thread of compassion?" They would say in choral unison. "Conceptual art challenges values and all we can see is murder in your work: there is no challenge in destruction."

"There is the lingering smell of stale smoke, " I would say. "Will that do? It is terribly difficult to remove. It seeps into the fabric of the wall and ceiling and no amount of clean white paint can obliterate it. It brings unity to chaos theory."

"Open the window," the chief critic, Jane, would say. "Find freshness." But through the open window would creep the stench of plastic burning, of oil oozing, of lead fumes belching, of diesel particulating into the lungs.

"Open the sky," the chief critic, Jane, might say. "Find escape." And beauty quivered in its secret far retreat beyond the ozone and shot the artist through the head with a needle from a rose.

Doctor Rhodes had said, when I had first met Charlie and argued to accompany him to the gardens, that I might reach a time when I would wish to recapitulate, to recollect my experiences and, in speaking them, come to terms with the damage in my soul.

"But Doctor," I had replied, "such recollection must be done in peace, without the intrusion of now. Otherwise the words would assault me and I am already surrounded by plausible suggestions from the radio, pretending there is importance in armed invasion, that the armoury of conflicting powers may be enumerated and therefore understood. There is a simple truth that rape grows from the powerless, from the nothing people, from the downtrodden, but that truth is ignored. Hordes of complacent crotchety words cut swathes through my mind until they gather in purple clouds of burning to release drops of acid to the earth and on my balding pate."

But I had tried to take his path towards release and to some extent had been successful, but the new sorrows of Monica's visit and Martin's death had thrown me back. I was walking in a smoke filled smog again and clutched at small pleasures like my pipe, the smell of oil paint, solace in a cup of tea and having my own small bedroom waiting for me.

"Niliscience is my creed when chaos looms," I mumbled into my sheets. It was mere selfishness to pluck a tiny joy from the midst of disease. And there was the arch critic, not Jane at all, peering down at me again, his face stretched in a grin of incredulity that any patient should stretch patience to such elastic twanging pain and his hair was burning, his eyes were furnaces and his hand was stretched out like a claw towards my throat.

"All artists need a structure within which to compose their communication with others, within which to think in studied ways about their precise messages. Your indisciplined work shows no framing power."

"It's a good frame," I said. "Found it in a skip down near the fish and chippy. It'll pin and look a treat."

"We were considering the abstract conclusions from conceptual art, not the relative merits of pinewood frames." He may have been considering with his jaw like my jaw and his stern evaluative sneer like my sneer, but I was angry. The omniscience of commentators eroded all self belief. Oh the bloody arrogance of them all! The painting of walls and woodwork in the appropriate shades, the fitting of carpets flush to the wall, the cleaning of windows with spray and swipe and the sanitised window dummies peering both ways lest they be caught in an unmentionable act of humanity are all desperately trying to hide the rot within. I have the rots, the flu, the plague and the cat's fleas are leaping on my ankles in glee, sucking tainted blood.

"Get them away from me!" I scream. "There are too many of them and all they want to do is dragoon me into their own convenient fascist mould. They laugh at those who reject their own brand of control. Control freaks everywhere!" For now there are multiple heads peering in on me, scoffing at the smallness of my brain, the ineffectualness of my living art.

"If you do it our way, you may be accepted, but this way will be yesterday's way as soon as you attempt it, for we move beyond you, the builders of scaffolds on which you stand and on which you die. We alone are the foragers into new worlds, the arbiters of standards and the judges of your worth."

I flap my hands at the faces, telling them that my presence is not worth their attention for they are far above me in the scheme of authority.

"Just leave me alone," I plead. "We all have our own right to live as we wish." And then their laughter! They howl inside me like wolves after their prey. I am a fool to think that I am beneath their concern. They breed their power from the scarcely living husks that used to be human.

The preacher doctor has sent the critics packing and now pats my hand in last rites, but even he will not reassure me with a vision of unity and mutual love. How dare he pretend when the reality is Elsie twitting her needles and imagining them knitting shreds of flesh, men's sinews, into dolls? Inside her room she is planting pins into rich bellies and she speaks to her reflection on the wall, saying, "Pig, pig, pig."

"That is only your fear speaking," Doctor Rhodes said. "She is concerned for you. I have often found that patients have more fondness than nurses inside them, but do not know how to speak it. If you can face down the fear, you will be able to face other people, warts and all."

Then I remembered how Elsie had crawled up to my attic room and stuck flowers in my toothbrush mug after I had stopped her walking down the stairs. I had watched her try to tip toe across the room, the stench and size of her filling the whole space while I'd kept my eyelids mostly closed, pretending sleep. When she'd backed out, she'd looked at me with hammocked eyes and she'd shaken her head at me. It had made me cry to observe her bulk showing me compassion when all I had to spare was self-hatred. You came to my room one early morning, she seemed to be saying, and gave me comfort. I return that service with these flowers, but I knew better. I was the thief, not the comforter. And all the while, tiny in my armchair, Elizabeth's thin bones had shivered in the plastic bag of her skin. She had drawn nicotine into her mouth like milk from a mother's breast and she'd sat at my bedside waiting for me to hear her own litany of sorrow.

"I knew you weren't yourself," she'd said. "It put Elsie out I can tell you. But it's just a touch of flu. Right as rain in two shakes of a lamb's tail." It was shortly after that that I had started screaming and ended up back in here, in the ward I'd reached after running away from the Redhead and Keith. It was as if I'd never been away.

"Do you want to make a statement to the police? Do you want to bring a charge?" Eric had sat at the end of the bed, fiddling with his quicks. I told him to piss off out of it.

"Too little comes too late," I said. He was relieved.

"No names, no pack drill," he'd said, grinning out of thin lips, but his eyes were still scared.

"Coming up to pension are we?" I'd said. "Don't want to risk a fuss?"

"It's what's best for you," he'd said, keeping up a semblance of officer style.

"As long as I'm safe here." Over and over again he'd told me how I was in the best place, tucked away to help body and mind mend. There was no need to worry about Steve. He would be well sorted out, but I did not want to know and had sent Eric on his way. As much use as a string of limp spaghetti, that one.

Once he was gone, I could revert. The jelly in my gut could churn. My fear could speak in long low wailings that filled my head.

"Shove a dummy in his gob," said the man in the bed next to me. "Shove a needle in his bum, but let me sleep." I suppose the nurses did what he asked, but I was past caring. When I tried to roll my own, the paper fluttered from my fingers and the valuable Clan sprinkled to the floor. "He wakes up every bleedin' night screaming – needs a mallet I reckon."

I lay with blankets so firmly tucked in around me that nobody could get in and my eyes scanned every movement in the ward. There had been talk of a stranger assaulting a woman downstairs. I had heard it on the news and even the nurses could have been the Redhead in disguise. The radio headphones talked of women needing gentleness, the shared spirits of compassion, but I needed those things as well, perhaps more than women for I found myself in tears at the smallest intervention and was jeered at for weakness. The man who talked of mallets rolled me up a fag from his sown store and told me to smoke it.

"It might choke you off," he said. "And then we'd have some peace." That made me cry.

He was all right was Jim, even though hair stuck out of his ears through wax and he farted. Bodily things were not important. It is chance that gives the frame in which we move. I knew that then, lying in the dormitory like a beached whale. I had not met Martin and Elsie; I had not faced their spirits and recoiled. My frame was fair enough to look at in a middle aged man, but it was not good to see inside my brain, not deep down.

"Are you coming for a gentle walk?" Nurse Bentham had asked and it was the word "gentle" that touched me. I had not shown it, but managed to dress myself and totter from the ward with the nurse's arm on my elbow. My side, where the rib had been broken, was sore and my legs were old man's shanks. Thinking back, I was embarrassed by this short walk in the hospital garden. I'd babbled like a child over the sun on green leaves, the shooting heads of daffodils like stars and the rich, sweet earth between banks of beaded juniper. I'd told the nurse about Monica's garden, its whitened fence and sweet pea trellis, the clover-edged pond and climbing roses. I'd seen the order in the string-lined plots, the labels for the seeds, the trays glistening with silver budding in the long greenhouse.

"Can I return here soon?" I'd asked the nurse. "Please let me walk here now and then?" I'd thought of the children's book, The Secret Garden, and cringed at my faith in such simplicity. The damage to my side was festering from a Roman lance and, even in its scabbing, poison would accrue. Surely I had run out of new starts.

I'd thought so then and now the same thought reverberated, even though it was Jane and Peter's garden in my head with its lupined fence, the rabbit, Blod, and the shivering sound of Elsie's voice sweetly blossoming into the dusk. How old was Elsie? Where had she been and where was she going? Simple questions to ask of anyone, but I had not asked them. I would ask them. I resolved to put myself beyond myself into another's existence, without intruding. No, it would not do to intrude, but Jane had said she'd been a singer and even now her voice flowed into my brain and soothed me. "You see," I crowed triumphantly at the empty chair by my bed. "There is a new start every day and every moment. You thought I was trapped in here for ever now, but just one note of purity and the fires recede."

There was nobody to answer and I knew I was alone to travel through the history again before I started out on another new route, hoping there would be no hold ups, no pitfalls, no diversions or dead ends.

Chapter 16

"I'm sorry, but it's the end. You know it is." Monica Muriel said on her first and only visit to me in the holding prison. I had chopped at the seams in her body and they gaped wide. The sap of her split wood oozed out in fruitless juices. "I can not explain to the children. I can not explain to myself." She explained and I rocked in dry sorrow at her understandable coldness. "To throw it all away," she went on flatly, "Our house, our children's happiness – I do not understand. I do not want to understand to be truthful. I've tried once too often. You are not the man I married."

"You swore an oath," I mumbled, "for better or for worse and all I've brought is worse each time. I recognize that. You have suffered the seven times seven and more. Leave me if you like." But I had not meant it, nor expected the solicitor's letter quite so soon.

The black haired lad, accused of grievous bodily harm, sharing my cell with his toenail parings and the slop bucket, had looked knowing and nodded when I returned from this unhappy interview.

"If it's kids or you, mate, she takes the kids. When chips are down, a man is just a semen stick. Forget her if you can."

"What do you know about it?" I sneered, him being half my age, the sort of kid I'd tried to counsel in my art teacher days.

"Please yourself shit-face," he answered, flicking his grey sickle moons to the concrete floor.

Doctor Rhodes eased himself from one side to the other on the edge of the bed as if he suffered from piles. I found it difficult to think of him as a doctor because he wore a grey cardigan with bold wooden buttons and corduroy trousers without any shape.

"There are a couple of routes you could take," he said. From the lean of his body and the set of his thin cheeks, the way his eyes crinkled at the edges, I knew these words were part of a set speech and formula.

"Catching a bus am I?"

He'd heard that too, but managed to smile as if it were new. Was there nothing new? Perhaps repetition brings unthinking ease and false security like asking after the weather. The weather words used for rain, sun and wind are without meaning and impact, not even flotsam and jetsam. The floating and thrown up words could hole a boat. Weather words stay smoothly on the surface, like oil. Chuck me the bottle of disinfectant, doctor. I want to sink the oily words. Were routes real?

"You could," he said carefully, putting one finger on his right cheek and then stroking it down to the neat point of his shaven chin, "list each event that has hurt you and try to describe your actions and reactions at the time, fighting through the terrors they invoke and translating them into a more objective journal or …" His right hand dropped to his lap and his left hand rubbed reflectively up and down on the left side of his chin as if he wore a beard there and wished to push his finger through the hair, " … you could put all the crap in one big rubbish bin and start to pick out little threads of silk in the dross to weave yourself a protective skin of self respect and worth."

I looked at him like a stoated rabbit. He had asked too much.

"It's just two approaches to the same problem," he tried to explain. "The first based on therapy through expression and resolution, the second a learning of behaviours by which we cope."

"And never the twain shall meet?" I asked. Either path demanded that I take responsibility. There could be no running into others' dreams, no shifting the blame, no naming of the guilty.

"A factual list of dreams or a dream coat made from facts?" I said eventually when the silence had reached me. "Nothing in between – no names, no pack drill." Why did I use Eric words unless I too had become a ducking and a weaving man like him?

"Even an invented route can bring some enlightenment, as long as there is honesty within it."

"Just a silly game – a stupid bloke I knew – I used his words to hide – forget it," I said.

"A perfectly reasonable behaviour," he commented calmly. "I strongly believe, you see, that there is no guilt, just the products of chance collisions. Somewhere along the road, your brakes weren't checked, no new linings put in. It is a transactional guidance model I use."

231

"When one observes the setting sun," Joshua Reynolds had addressed the academy, "do you not see a shape rather like that of a golden guinea?"

"No!" William Blake had shrieked. "Rather I see the multitude of the host of heavenly angels crying, 'Glory to God in the Highest and on Earth Peace Good Will toward Men.'"

"No," I said to the doctor. "Rather I see the fire of man's agony unfleshing beauty with its acid flame and the hole of oblivion gathering to swallow its heat."

"In your own time," Doctor Rhodes said quietly. "The decorative style for expressing feeling asphyxiated through fear is the patient's own choice, of course. I agree that cars are singularly ugly and inapposite images. We were not born in a car; we merely learn a technical skill for survival on the roads within one. The human frame is an infinitely more intricate form of locomotion. Zen recognition applies."

"No starting handles now," I said.

"You have all the time you need. You will not have to leave this hospital until or unless you wish to do so. This is as safe a haven as we can make for you, but you will be expected to take on responsibility to keep it so."

"May I work in the garden?" I had asked and he had smiled on my request. Nurse Bentham told me that the previous occupant in my bed had been put to washing soiled bedclothes. I had been lucky, but it wouldn't have done to get carried away. There are sticks and carrots behind every doctor. Slowly I had learned to press the brakes and the linings held for very slight gradients.

So this is the rubbish bin theory at work. I've had the

'think of an object', the 'list all your troubles', the 'images of hurt and pleasure', the 'hard physical labour', 'the displacement theory', the 'pleasures of now in the garden', the 'identification with another's problem', the 'call to duty', 'the hypnosis to childhood' and even the threat of electric shock treatment, not from the doctor himself, but from Jim, who ripped the blankets off me one night and told me he'd shove my willy in the wall socket if I didn't stop moaning in my sleep.

"Just grovelling through the rubbish bin," I explained. "Couldn't find anything."
"You had kids, didn't you?" Jim shouted. "Darn sight more than most."

"Most means you, does it?" I said, feeling bitter about the cold air invading my bed.

"Most means men," Jim answered. "Most men don't have kids. They have expenses."

Thank God he laughed then at the wit in his words. He huddled back in his bed, leaving me to tease out the silken thread of my children but I could not be enriched by their undoubted love and giving. Even as they smiled I turned away from them, having no right to impose my pain upon their innocence. In their presence my darkness became obscene, a denial of their right to follow untainted lives. There were good reasons for white sheets; they showed up the skipping frenzy of fleas among the dark flecks of skin droppings.

"For God's sake," Jim shouted. "You don't have to examine your bloody navel at the least word. Can't you take anything on trust? Love, kids, security – those little things you had and chucked down the pan in case they turned out fake? You don't belong in this bloody hospital; you need putting down."

"Thanks a bundle, fart features," I said. "What brings you in here?"

"Hurrah!" Jim bellowed, waking the whole ward, bouncing on his mattress like a walrus mounting pebbles. "Wowee! Who'd have thought it? Prick-scared John here has asked about me. Wouldn't he like to know? Wouldn't he fucking like to know?" Jim suddenly leaned over, grabbed my arm, wrenched it towards him and I had to follow. Then his wet moustache was flapping in my ear and his voice battered my brainbox. "Ask no questions, be told no lies. I've fucking killed for less. How dare you stick your nose in?"

The night nurse was there like a shot. He shoved a needle in Jim's bum and had him quiet and covered in moments.

"What did I do? What did I say?"

"Just settle down," the nurse said, the syringe still in his hand. "Jim won't stand questioning."

"Asks enough himself," I said.

"Smokescreen."

Charlie in the garden told me much later that Jim had killed his only son when his wife had boasted she was being shafted by a mutual acquaintance. Jim had never been able to accept his son as his own after that, thought he saw his mate in everything he did.

"It's like lions," Charlie explained. "New king of the pride rids himself of the old litter so only his own kids go on. Step-parents can't win. They can be sweet as pie and loving as chocolate, but the ancient fear runs deep. Is new Daddy or Mummy going to kill me? The baby is always asking the question. Trust me. I know."

I'd learned from Jim that one did not to ask questions about an inmate's past experience, but his sharp comment set me thinking among the cabbages. Was Monica Muriel already finding another man? Were my children fearful of his genetically selfish rage?

"We're not just animals," I said, squeezing a small ribbed black slug between the fingers of my gardening gloves until the orange squirted out. "Humans work by another book." I knew that humanity was a wide Church. There might be some who aspire to spiritual and moral justification and lifestyle, but the Redhead was always there to deny the argument that man is intrinsically capable of virtue. I had learned to expect the worst and believed I would not go far wrong if I stuck to that belief. How was I to understand that the seven times seven next chance for this chancer was obligatory? The preacher might claim that the gateway to everlasting happiness was open for all, but I could not stomach forgiving the Redhead and stamping his bus pass for clearance.

I knew that Jim's rage was not personal. It was not serious and the nurse was there to rescue me, but the memory of the Redhead was a different kettle of fish altogether. He lurked in the rubbish bin and there were no silver threads to catch him by and reel him in. Just looking at the bin cover brought the dreads upon me. The hairs on my legs were individual conductors of electrical impulses and when I reached down to scratch, the seat of irritation leaped elsewhere. I remembered how I used to sit in the front room, roll my trouser legs to the knee and scratch my calves. Monica used to sigh with displeasure.

"Scratch my back love?" I used to plead and she'd reach at it with stubby competent spades, rub cursorily and say,

"Is that OK?"

It was far better than the nothing now, the rubbing of my spine against the wall as if I were a bear. I bought myself a back-scratcher, but it was hopeless, no sensitivity, no sense of give and take.

"We're still mostly animals," I said to Charlie. "But animals are much nicer than us. Don't wear their hearts on their sleeves."

If I pulled gently at the long curling hairs at the base of my throat, they could be teased into brown, black and grey separate threads as if they sprouted from different sorts of flesh and different colour vats. When I released them they sprang back into one matt of grizzle, so part of me was grizzly bear up on my hind legs, omnivore. This observation kept me occupied for ten minutes at a hand mirror. I noticed the mole on my neck had grown again. The hospital barber had nicked it with his buzzing razor and it had a stiff head on it that wobbled when I touched it. I could push it into the fold of my neck, but it perked and peeked back as soon as I looked the other way. This absorption in the body was most unanimal like. Animals sit at home in their bodies and move unselfconsciously through the days and nights. Their world of now does not admit nostalgia for what it used to be nor plans for the new look next year.

When a child I'd suffered warts on my fingers and

regularly held them in hot water and turps. My father claimed this would cure them. I had watched them minutely to see whether they reduced or changed. They had not, merely moved places if I forgot to look.

"A placebo," Monica Muriel had said when I suggested James should follow in my footsteps.

"What do you know?" I had asked, furious that my father's wisdom had been challenged.

"I am a nurse," she'd said, pulling starch around her like a shield. "Children's warts come and go like veruccae – nothing to be done about them."

"So that's the modern creed," I had snarled. "Let children suffer into adulthood and all their ailments will die of their own accord. There was a time when intervention was deemed appropriate for young illness. Even the jabs are suspect now."

"There is a risk, but in statistical terms, they're safe," Monica Muriel had said.

"Our children are statistics then?"

"Part of the success rate."

"So far," I had said, doom-laden. Risk assessment was just a lottery.

"Oh God, you're so boring. Can't you pull yourself together and look on the bright side?" Then her eyes had widened and she'd clapped her hand to her mouth. "I'm sorry," she'd said. "I know you can not help it. Depression is a disease. It gets you down. I swore I'd never say to pull yourself together. I am a nurse after all."

I had shrugged and pretended to accept her words, but I hadn't. Her real concern had not been for me, but that her perfectionism as a nurse had suddenly failed her. Her feelings had shown. Besides she'd been absolutely right. Pulling together was the exact requirement. I had needed to integrate the strands of hairs in me lest they sprang out of their sockets and fired like rockets to the moon and I had failed. Nothing remained but sudden action to forge an escape.

"I must go to work," I had said and could remember picking up my lunch box; I had even pecked her cheek under the bruise.

"You need to understand how I have felt," she'd said the night before. "You used to sympathise and help with the children. Now you seem all locked away inside yourself, living in a dream. If you were a child, I'd shake you out of it, I would." No, the shell of her nursehood was cracked irredeemably. I had considered the sanctuary of autism and fostered another escape route, but in the morning my pipe and the lunch box had been waiting and no more words had been required.

Rather than return home, I had waited in the staff marking room until darkness and then I had skirted round to my car, the last in the yard, and ferried the petrol can to the science prep. room. Here I'd poured unleaded into my lunch box, placed it under cloths and papers taken from the shelves and had flicked the match from the open door, giving me time to escape through the fire exit to the field. I'd driven my car round the block and parked it on the road. I could have driven straight home, but there was no home to go to and so I'd returned through the public footpath to watch the building from the fence near the old people's flats.

To start with there'd been nothing to see, just the grey

murky building, the cleaners' lights dipping off one by one in the top block and the science rooms in shadow. It had been like watching a firework and wondering whether the fuse had been caught by the flame. I had even thought of tracking back across the playing field to check when I saw the first light creeping into the biology laboratory. It touched the black windows with redness like seeping blood.

It had been a cunningly exercised piece of arson set in the bottom of the school out of sight, but able to infiltrate without notice along interconnected classroom doors and corridors, funnelling flames like insidious spies into the heart of the complex before it had broken out through the skylights in the dining room like monster gas jets on a giant's cooker. Then the sound had crackled over the field as the school splintered. Plumes of smoke and flying debris had lifted into the evening. Windows had exploded and the released heat had scorched towards me with its monster breath.

Then I had not wanted to leave. I had needed to see the fire flecks dance, had craved the bleating of fire engines, the rushing of ants with hoses, the shrieks from the houses opposite as their outside paint began to blister. It had been my experiment in de-schooling – bound to hurt at first, but the dependency trap had to be broken. Learning was not to be trapped inside bureaucratic cages of social engineering, but should blaze out into the free sweep of knowledge and understanding. Fire, the great cauteriser, the cleanser, the friend and intimate foe, blazed its redhead to the sky.

I had thought, when the hand was laid on my elbow, that I had been selected for congratulation, that I had a companion in the glorious venture.

"Just a few questions, sir."

"That's the one. He was stood by that fence watching for a good twenty minutes."

The woman pointing at me had come out of the old people's flats. Now I can recognize that she must have been one of Elizabeth's kin, part of neighbourhood nose, but there is no blame attached, just a chance collision.

"They often stay to watch the fireworks, missus." The policeman had said, but he had dragged me away, not letting me witness the finale when the roof fell through.

Chapter 17

Three days later and I felt relatively steady again.

"I need to come home now," I murmured. This last explosion was nothing compared with previous big dippers. "Nobody was hurt?" I said, needing reassurance.

"Only you," said Jane. "That was bad enough."

How I wanted to go home to my small attic room! If consigned to the hospital bin again, I would never return to the Tower House.

"You've had a bit of a turn," said Peter. "Better off here for a while more."

"Just two days then, only a short time. I'm not on much medication. It was last knockings and the Redhead did not come. He's out of my life for good. I know." I could see my attic room vividly and another tenant was being introduced through the door with Peter smiling his empty hail fellow well met, don't worry old son, flip flop, here we are safe and sound in the eyrie, but it was my home, my place of refuge still.

"My room," I blurted out. "My home!" I cried. "You will keep my place. I will never betray your trust again. There was no fire, was there?" I clutched at Jane's hand. "I didn't bundle old newspapers under the door, did I?

There was no trail of flame. I wouldn't, never would for you. You've been good to me; please let me stay."

From the womb of my birth I had returned to the cold sheets of a hospital bed, its blankets firm about my legs. I had to convince myself, let alone another, that the kernel of self esteem was worth watering, worth nurturing. "Please Jane. Please Peter," I gasped. "This is important to me."

"So you've stopped playing games, have you John?" Jane said seriously, her wide cool grey eyes scanning me and I knew I looked a mess, my hair straggled, my eyes wild, but yes I was whole inside or would be whole inside, knowing her generosity, seeing the card by my bed. "Just a few days more," Peter said.

"Promise me," I pleaded. "I know I can believe you and every word you say, but just give me the promise."

"Oh you poor old man," Jane patted my arm. "We promise, but no tears now, just sleep and rest."

She stood suddenly, brushed her broad hands down her skirt efficiently.

"Don't brush me away," I said. "There's something worth preserving here."

"I know, John. I know," she said and she leaned over, her lips touching my forehead. "It is night-time now – time for some sleep. We'll be back for you when the doctor says you're ready. Don't you worry. But remember the promise goes both ways." And they were gone without a backward glance. I turned on my side, stretched my legs long under the sheet and felt a great sleep flood towards me. I was engulfed in darkness and there were no flames roaring inside me. This breakdown was just a temporary blip and I was resolved on mending every part of me.

An artist creates in the cool complacency of his mind and through his arrogant brush strokes a version of reality that may heal or wound. The Redhead has been my destructive urge. Conjured from the pain of fire and death, he has haunted my footsteps and imposed his art upon me. In so doing, he has made fear where there was confidence and distortion where smooth straight limbs had proclaimed honesty. The artist's own creature can overwhelm him and translate him to monster, not man. It is easy to observe how image becomes evil, but harder to assert that finished art should reflect the best and truest state of being. When Gerard Manley Hopkins held a horse chestnut tree leaf in his hand and wondered whether there was a perfect leaf in a perfect existence on which nature modelled her forms, was he suggesting that the poet should aspire to the model or the all too human imperfectly formed version? I could understand the Jesuit poet affirming his faith in heaven through worldly observation of the most ethereal and heavenly experiences, but when the world reflected the darkest reaches of the human mind and not the finest aspirations, the artist presenting the ideal becomes divorced from the darker side of nature and is rejected. It has to be in small things, perfectly observed and shaped, that the artist can reach the heart of the matter in man. The leaf is tiny in its intricate design. The sense of Redhead's evil is huge, threatening to swallow whole cities in its reach for power. The sense of goodness is not such a cataclysmic element. It is painstakingly built from small to larger awareness.It requires intense hard work and belief in others' desire to fill each vein of living with precise care.

The impossible task was to heal the whole, remove the rotting flesh and seal the join so that a foundation may be laid towards perfection, but I would attempt it, realising I would fail in the ultimate quest for perfection, but I would try to bring the search one step nearer to escape.

The hours I have spent in minute brushwork, looking more and more closely at each fissure in the tower's crumbling edifice until the moss and lichen have seemed the most important and most sweet of the building's components, have brought me to realise that goodness lies in relating the particular to the larger whole. The Redhead has all the power he needs to force his way through the fissured brickwork to reach my secret tomb within and rob me of my last virtue, unless I unite the whole building with strong bonds of cement. The intention and potential are all important when the technician's skills are used. I had turned my skills towards a false intention, creating diseased art through a diseased mind. Art is not revenge, although the actions of the Redhead demanded revenge.

You may believe that I am telling you now that the Redhead is a fiction, an artist's poor creation to rationalise pain. If this were so, Martin Beverall would be standing, waddling and talking today. His death confirms my truth. I have experienced the death's head, the evil blood between the Redhead and me. Unlike Victor Frankenstein, however, I have the means to evade his clutches and regain my balanced humanity. I will create another vision, a closer to perfection and a new warmth from the immediate clay within my grasp. Monsters demand companionship and introduce their lonely poison into their fearful parasites.

Jane had asked my why I was taking notice of Elsie when I promised to act as hospital companion. I replied that she seemed trapped inside her own body and that I sympathised with her. I am convinced my impulse is healthy and I shall use my art to drain away the poison that besets her to find out whether she can be beautiful in the sight of others. My plan is her redemption and in her redemption flows my freedom from the monster that haunts me and would turn me back to murder and fire. Jane tells me Elsie used to sing in a choir, but gradually could not face standing in front of the crowds, thinking that all eyes were turned on her obesity. Elizabeth too could not face the world outside her doors, reduced to frozen huddling inside a false security. I lay in bed wondering what keys existed to bring confidence inside the brain when there was so many reasons for hiding.

The next morning I remembered that I had not asked Jane and Peter how the wedding had gone. I had been too full of my own worry to think about others' lives, but it could be held against me. It was evidence that I was not as balanced as I should be for living in the "real" world. I began to chew over the oversight, worrying it into panic until I remembered the existence of telephones and rang home. Elizabeth promised to pass on my good wishes, but with the phone back in the hook, I began to feel anxious lest she forget or speak in such a way as to reduce my sincerity. I sent a postcard first class and felt that I'd covered myself.

A few mornings later and my heart was still whole. I scrubbed every part of me until the nerve ends of my skin tingled with newness and anticipation. I shaved meticulously. I dressed as smartly as my wardrobe would allow and sat in the armchair by the wardroom door, waiting for release. At four o'clock in the afternoon the previous day I had telephoned home to say that I was feeling much better and would be ready for rescue at eleven o'clock in the morning. Peter had answered the phone. I apologised to him unreservedly for being so trapped in my head that I had forgotten all principles of care and gratitude.

"Plenty worse," he'd said. "Don't worry about it, mate."

"Easier said than done," I'd said, my lower lip trembling, but I had kept control.

"Just take it steady," Peter said. "Keep taking the tablets and be calm as a little Buddha. If you keep your body breathing gently, you'll drag your old mind along with it. Think calm, Jane says, and she's not far wrong."

"See you tomorrow then," I'd said.

"No problem." The phone went dead.

I had slept well again that night, but had awoken suddenly at four in the morning with my forehead beaded with sweat. The part of my brain that exaggerated all plights of betrayal and fear was enflamed, but I recognised it for a false flame, a chimaera. I pretended sleep, not wishing to demand a cup of hot sweet tea to soothe me, refusing to ring the bell lest the powers of nursing and unnecessary medication found my early morning vigil a reason for keeping me in chains. I would not risk a relapse. Then I had slept again, woke refreshed at eight o'clock, renewed my pledge to the new world and was ready, packed and prepared, by ten thirty for Peter's arrival.

By eleven thirty, my eyes were stalks for every new entry to the ward. Workmen were busy pulling up the carpet in the corridor outside. There was a strange smell of dust and rubber-based adhesive. Trolleys scraped along concrete. Nurses complained.

"You could sit by your bed, you know. You don't want to be sneezing all day."

I stayed where I was, holding my faith deep inside me, breathing slowly and steadily. I would not be betrayed, not this time, not after the promises given.

"Time to go home mate," said Peter, appearing from behind green-overalled carpet fitters with a hop and a jump. He picked up my suitcase and offered his arm in one movement.

"Good to see you," I said nonchalantly and took his guidance carefully. I thanked the staff. I waved goodbye. It would be the last time, I knew, and walked out of Daffodil Ward like a new man with a new friend on my arm.

"Do what you like with the tower," I said to Pete. "It's your property – no call for me to be a bother to you."

"You get wound up too much and don't do enough to make a difference. Take it easy and things will happen."

"Not worth the hassle," I agreed.

We reached the car park.

"It's the gentle buggers that cause the biggest trouble," he said. He looked round briefly, identified where he'd left the Peugeot and tracked across to it. "The ones who think everything has to be just perfect, particularly themselves. I tell you this, mate, if something's worth doing, it's worth doing badly." He put my suitcase in the boot and we slid into the seats. "Just do what you can do," he continued. "How can you be expected to govern a country with so many worries inside your head? You thought I was wrong. You said so. I disagreed. You wrote a letter to the planning office. I answered it. All above board, no skin off anybody's nose and no hard feelings. You thought it was worth doing and you did it. Good for you."

He was right. It was time to forget the words and hold to doing what was worthwhile even if I didn't do it very well. Preserving people was worthwhile.

"How is Elsie?" I asked.

"She asked after you yesterday," he said, pulling away from traffic lights towards the Cliffe.

"Did she call me pig?"

"Of course," he said, turning right back on the one way system and then left to Gloucester Road. I laughed.

"Can I buy her something to show I'm not all bad."

"Don't need to do that, but it's a thought. What are you thinking about giving her?"

My idea was still in its early stages and so I didn't tell Peter then, but I did explain that I would need some help from Jane.

"Is the party still on?" I asked.

"We just put it off for another fortnight. Wouldn't miss it for the wiorld." said Peter. "There's a few things to celebrate."

248

Chapter 18

Jane was in organiser mode, cross-legged on my bed as I carefully unpacked, arranged the new toothbrush and paste in the new mug on the shelf by the basin and then tucked the fresh blue towel on the rack.

"Now who do you want to come for this party?" She asked, pencil at the ready.

"No gatecrashers, only a few friends," I said. I was happy with the concept of party, but wary of the social implications. My privacy was dear to me and a party could bring crowds into the house. "A little at a time, I need," I said. "It's not a chance for the whole street to drop in."

"Pete'll see to that," Jane reassured me. "He'll have a couple of mates and we'll be wanting our Sharon and her baby to come along. So who have we got then?"

I gave her four names from the art therapy, Nurse Bentham because she took me to the gardens, Doctor Rhodes, even though he would not come lest it affect his professional distance from a patient, and Gladys Mitchell. I had neither phone numbers nor addresses, but Jane just jotted the names.

"And then there's Elsie and Elizabeth," she said.

"Guests of honour," I agreed and we talked about how we could manage. "Perhaps Elizabeth would take on the baby-sitting role for Jane's sister's new baby." I suggested.

"It would give her a job inside the house, but she might have to come outside to let Sharon know her baby was all right." Jane said and then I asked her for the back-story.

"It was her baby sister. Her Mum died in child-birth when she was just a little girl, but she took on looking after baby when Dad wasn't about being fire warden. She has blamed herself ever since."

Elsie though was a different kettle of fish. How would she feel to have people invading the house?

"She's much better than she was," Jane said. "New medication is having an effect and there's a little time yet. Clothes could be the problem." I smiled because I'd had an idea, but I wasn't telling yet.

Suddenly Jane stood up. It was as much as we could do for now.

"And I want that picture for the party," she said, looking back over her shoulder on the way out. "So get moving."

I painted all morning, putting slug trails over the brickwork like a silver net and turning the unpointed joints into flower beds. I filled the air with dancing seedheads and at the centre of their spoke-stranded hopes I placed a speck of gold. They flew on the drift of wind and warmth, testing and turning until finding preliminary landing posts in the fissures of the broken tower like fragile wisps of hair clinging to a bald skull. From some I painted thin green tentacles sending their roots into rock, the spores of future growth. As I worked I heard Charlie's voice.

"Bloody dandies – stick their nose in where they're not wanted. If I'd a quid for every one of those bleeders I've fed to rabbits, I'd be a wealthy man."

"You already are rich, Charlie," I said, shifting the barrow next to the manure.

"In another life at another place maybe. A fat lot of good it did me, I can tell you. She sweated the lot out of me, she did." He leaned on his shovel, giving me the cue to dump the fork for the time being. "Did I tell you how she worked the books?" He had, but would do so again regardless. "There was yours truly floggin' my guts out on the cars, knowing London like the knowledge and more, keeping the boys happy enough and the cars on the road while she looked after the money side. I never was good with figures, me. I trusted her, you see, and when she upped and left, taking our two girls off with her, I didn't dream she'd salted away the money too – all of fifty thousand nicker it must have been. Enough to send any bloke gently round the twist. But did I tell you what she did then?" He had and would again. "Sued me for maintenance for the kids and I had no comeback, none at all, for where was my proof? She's sitting in a luxury house in Wimble Wombledon, being kept in fodder and fine clothes. I tell you this, she'll not have one penny more out of me. She's bled me dry. I don't want money. I'd give it away rather than feed her face. It makes me sick to think about her. How she can sleep nights I do not know."

"Go easy Charlie," I said. "There's more fish in the sea. Remember what you told me about the girls on Brighton beach when you did the seaside runs in the summer –

good time had by all!"

"When you reach my age. I'm sixty eight you know. They all look the same – all grab and grasses!"

I'd believed every word. He gave circumstantial details of the car hire firm he ran, the names of the drivers, the sorts of fiddles he'd managed and then he'd turn black in the face when he talked of Sylvia, his wife, who fleeced him of his home, his children and his cash and was still bleeding him for more. And so we progressed to the digging ground and cleared a row or two for the late spuds, sifting manure into the deep trenches, cleaning off all but the neatest eyes and dibbing in the tubers. I'd lead him on to talk about footballers of the past and funny items found inside his cars, the way he'd sorted out his drivers' complicated affairs,

"No I can't take that call, gov. She's the one with the wooden leg and the plastic eyeball." It was quite a punch line and Charlie delivered punchlines all sweetness and light as if every silly accident was the most natural thing in the world: dead pan Charlie; master storyteller. But when Nurse Bentham came to bring him back to the ward, he'd close inside himself, not even giving her the time of day.

"I can find my own way," he used to mutter, but she'd smile and say,

"Orders is orders – I've to bring you – gives me a breath of fresh air." Then she'd put her hands on her solid hips and nod happily at our work. "My, you've been busy bees."

She was no beauty that girl-poor complexion and heavy in the rear-but how she cared!

She dropped Charlie off first and then would shake

her head, her top teeth just clenching on her bottom lip slightly.

"Doesn't get much happier, does he?"

"Just shy," I said.

"He hates women."

"With good cause from all accounts."

"Six of one, half dozen of other is the normal thing." Nurse Bentham loved normality. It was her way of coping with abnormality to lay on thick paste to cover the extremes. "You can't go through life with a chip on the shoulder, blaming everyone else for what can't be helped. You have to let go because you just end up destroying yourself," she said. "His wife visits him regular as clockwork and leaves him lovely things. His daughters drop in every month with the grandchildren. They try to love him to bits, but he's got another story in his head."

And suddenly I am back with my picture and find that there is beauty there. The tracery of light against the dark has kept its lustre. I leave the room to find Elsie and Elizabeth down below watching television. I decide to give it a go. It's Fred Astaire season and he flickers across the stage in top hat and tails, dapper from his shining hair to his twinkling shoe. His trouser legs flap and his torso swivels as he whirls Ginger through the old routine. Elizabeth is rooted to the screen, her thin legs twitching to the music and her fag accruing ash on the tray. Elsie is propped in her chair trying to sit tall as she had been counselled I try to see what they see, but the creatures are alien to me, not the same shape as the people in the street, their clothes so different and their voices so strange. When the credits roll, Elizabeth sighs, shakes her head and returns reluctantly to the sitting room.

"He could dance," she said. I agreed. "People don't dance like that nowadays," she continued. "They don't know the rules."

"Make 'em up as they go along," I said.

"No discipline," she said.

I did not want to hear her views on National Service and war years. I went into the kitchen to brew tea for the three of us. I decide, while I'm pouring the boiling water, that we will have some Glenn Miller big band music at my party and that there would be dancing on the patio. I could see my parents at the institute dance sailing in and out of the fox-trot floor, feet moving to an intricate time, balance and poise and togetherness. Nobody would have thought there was a moment's schism between them: all harmony and relaxation.

"That's nice dear," said Elizabeth when I handed her the tea and Elsie pushed her chocolates to one side to make room for her mug.

"Not too many chocolates now, Elsie," I said. Her blue eyes looked startled. "The more there is of you, the more you need to feed, I suppose," I smiled at her as warmly as I could. "Comfort eating is what it's called." She nodded slowly at me and pushed the box to the edge of the table until it began to topple to the floor. I caught it before it dropped.

"Doctor said so too," she articulated clearly. "But not give up everything at once – not good for a pig."

Her words were coming now, as if the door into baby worlds at the back of the brain had been closed and adult worlds were beckoning.

I made a start on the garden then, seating the slabs into sand and beating them down. It was satisfying to feel the muscles in my back working, but I took it carefully, not wishing to tear my rib again. Occasionally I looked up at the tower and noticed how it shielded light from the flowerbeds, how the shadow of it threatened. It seemed to be leaning over the wall and had been an instrument of war. Perhaps it was time for a truce.

It was having the confidence to let go, I decided. It was realising that the only patterns worth making were my own, that trying to please and trying to be perfect were false objectives, that my own morality was worth more than any stuff shoved down my throat by other lost souls eager for power. Then through the back door, as evening drew in still further and the lights from the kitchen touched the fuschias with sulphur light, a huge shape loomed. Boom! The foghorn of a liner belched. I moved silently into the deeper shade by the shed and leaned against the creosoted wood as Elsie moved towards the wall. I saw her silhouetted arm stretched out towards the roses. She seemed to shrink down and I realised she was sniffing the buds. I could hear her breathing and then she swelled up and strongly, purely, above the hum of traffic, she sang that love was a many splendoured thing, that it was the April rose. Her voice was young, light, tuneful and sweet. Each word was clear and the music flowed from her. It was full of delicacy, the tracery of silver that threaded the dusk. I closed my eyes and let her song wash over me as she changed to singing of giving true love, true love. There was such hope, such aspiration in her tone that I felt tears prick my eyes. I had only ever heard her wail except for the scales on the stairs and now the evening had brought her into flower. I knew that if I moved, made one step to intrude on her dreams, she would be destroyed again. The simple communion she was achieving was reaching deep into the heart of her, stripping away her obesity, her self-revulsion, the walls that imprisoned her. And then she was silent and I peered into the holding arms of the dark to sense her return to the house. The back door closed behind her. I decided then to bring a portable tape-recorder next time, to play it to Jane, perhaps use it at my party as a surprise.

Chapter 19

To think about Elsie as a multi-faceted, complex person conjured from clay to assume a specific personality was to deny the fundamental stereotype that she had built around herself as her only protection and defence, but I was convinced the challenge should be made. In Woolworth a small recorder cost only twenty one pounds ninety five pence. The quality of recording was bound to be relatively poor compared with a performance in a fully fledged recording studio, but wheedling through her outer covering to the heart of her had to start somewhere even though there was no guarantee that she would even recognize her own unvarnished voice, unclouded by the barrage balloon of her being. It was a problem, however, because a tinny recording would not do justice to the vibrancy, strength and vulnerability of her voice.

What right had I to steal this woman's voice? It was a theft from one who held her body to be revolting, who had lived within a strange rhythmical baby language of baby clothes. It was a small attempt to help her into the open, but only if she wished to come through the door. But there were times now when a flicker of kindred recognition had infused her face and moments when she spoke lucidly.

When Elsie called me "pig", was she going to market with other little piggies all friendly and fun, or had she realised the hateful term of abuse most commonly levelled at her and turned it back upon the insulters? I had to attempt more healing if the singing were to succeed.

"Who used to call you pig, Elsie?" I asked, expecting the volcano to burst, but ready to duck and weave out of range.

"Nobody," she answered. "Nobody dare call me pig. You're the pig," she said.

"I know," I fully agreed with a smile. "Sweet, frisky-tailed, pink, smooth bellied and very very clever. I almost said 'cleaver', but it is an unkind word for a pig."

"Kind is better than clever," said Jane firmly. "No game playing in my house. It'll end in tears. You know that only too well, don't you John?"

"I play no games now," I said, holding my hands out wide, opening my eyes to hide nothing and nodding my good intentions in all directions: fridge, Elizabeth, Jane and finally Elsie. "It's just that Elsie can't see the good inside herself," I explained. "She knits for your sister's baby. She helps Elizabeth out with fag money. She always lends a hand in the house and we all say what a good person she is, but she can't take the compliments."

"Perhaps she can't trust a sneak like you," said Elizabeth, flicking ash furiously. "Give her a break, Mister Know-it-all."

"I can see where you're coming from, sister," I drawled in laconic Southern State accent. "So many times bitten, your arse is bandaged in steel-plate and your tongue spits rivets, but Elsie? Where's she been to stay so sweet and so hurt?"

"Men! Bloody men!" Elizabeth squawked. "Can't you hear the bastard in them, twisting and turning the knife so it always points away from them? Who does the biting eh? Who does the sticking and pigging?" She hastily lit another cigarette.

"We do," I said. "We take all the blame all the time – no heart and no help, just take and run and the older they are, the easier they come."

Jane stopped loading the cupboard with plates and cups. She moved to the table, arms folded and shaking her head so her bosom trembled.

"Leave him be, Elizabeth," she said. "He's had a rough time."

The old woman stabbed out her fag and then hastily picked it up, tried to straighten it before slipping it back into her packet for later.

"I'm sorry, Elizabeth," I said. "I've been trying to be just me, but you lump me with all the other men in your life and you'll never believe I'm to be trusted. I know I can't be, not by you. Could there be a short truce?"

She looked confused and retreated, her lips working. Elsie began to heave at the arms of her chair as if to follow, but Elizabeth was gone and the door was closed. Jane stood as a protection from the pig and Elsie froze behind her, peering with sharp blue eyes out at the hostile world.

"Cat food," I said, getting to my feet and picking out tins of Katkins from the carrier I'd brought from the

259

coop. "Buy three. Get one free. Can you put them away?" I pushed the tins one by one across the table and Elsie's left arm reached across and stopped them one by one. She put them in a neat row of seven for each day of the week and the eighth she stood on top of the first for the beginning of the next week.

"Cupboard's behind you Elsie," Jane said and she hoisted herself clear of the chair and carefully packed the tins into place.

"Got him a treat today," I said and pulled out a packet of cat nibbles. "George'll like these – letters of the alphabet." I tore off the top and spilled some of the brown scratchy pieces on the table. Quickly I assembled GEORGE for the cat.

"Cats know everything," laughed Jane. "Reading his own name – a bit simple for George." I rummaged on and created each name in turn from Peter through to Elizabeth. Finally I turned to Elsie.

"No more 'E's," I said. She tipped up the bag and sorted through the letters and put three out: PIG. I took the 'E's from Elizabeth and created ELSE. With great care I took the 'I' from the middle of PIG and put it in her name.

"Only a tiny bit of pig in there, Elsie," I said.

Suddenly George scrabbled to the table top and began to munch, but I managed to rescue Elsie's name and handed the letters to her.

"Your name," she said. "John!" Her eyes were bright, but my eyes were swimming and I could not tell whether she was crying or laughing.

"Off to the hospital Tuesday, Elsie," I said. "It's Saturday today and time to prepare. A taxi job – coming at nine thirty – after breakfast and we'll be right as rain."

Slowly Elsie lurched from the room, but she held on to the cat letters and looked back at Jane with a small smile before she left.

"Now what are you up to?" Jane asked suspiciously.

"Taking an interest," I explained.

"Why? Part of your own therapy – pick her up to make yourself feel better and drop her later?"

No can be said in a myriad ways and normally with me it came out with a thread of defensiveness staining it with guilt. On this occasion I denied the charge with a straight clarity.

"No games? I can't be doing with games," Jane continued.

"No games," I reassured her and went on to explain about the singing and how I felt sorry for Elsie, but this was not caused by a selfish wish to appear good in my or others' eyes. "There's something there," I said. "She's trapped and I want to help her out."

Jane stared at me coolly and then nodded.

"Hurt yourself and we'll pick up the pieces as best we can," she said. "Hurt somebody else and you'll be out on your ear – not back here, not back anywhere!" It was stark, clear and totally fair. A fortnight before I would have started pondering whether the borderline between self and others was so clear cut, but I knew exactly what Jane meant and vowed to stay in the giving vein.

On the corner of Froggatt Street beside the erstwhile municipal library, now a coffee and wine bar for the well-heeled and apparently upwardly mobile from the city planning department, there is a two-sided, v-shaped commercial opportunity temporarily called the Oxfam

Shop. Most of my clothing has the benefit of pre-trial to iron out the creases and soften the cloth and I can recommend charity shops in the better end of town. They attract almost new clothes at subterranean prices. A few enterprising managers have even taken to mounting designer label rails for the cognoscenti. A largely white middle class clientele recycles the clothes in the cause of poverty, while the poor wouldn't be seen dead in an Oxfam shop, preferring new Asda to the shame of somebody else's cast-offs.

I dressed up to visit this shop on the Monday, forked out the dark blue corduroys, the brushed cotton blue shirt and the well-worn sandals. I had early recognized the shop manager's distaste for the dirty and down and out. She might be helping the poor, but did not want them near her goods. Big black letters on the door bespoke her good taste: "Leave no bags when closed." It would not do for the shop to look like a jumble sale or a refuse dump. Besides donors should not be ashamed of their offerings, should bring them in during daylight opening hours.

There was a specific purpose in my mind. Evening dresses, although often presented and displayed in charity shops, were rarely sold. I had this treasured information from a volunteer helper on a visit to Dr. Barnados when I had noted the row of old man suits and the line of shimmering long dresses.

"People like these new really," she'd said confidentially. "They're special you see. I don't mean the suits, not the suits. They don't go because the trousers are normally for short-legged fat old men. We do move some of the jackets

262

on students, but that was last year – bit of a fashion fad, I think. But the evening dresses – ever so lovely – but they stick, you know. It's because a woman likes to feel special on a special night out and it needs to be a dress just for her. We've quite a few. They come after funerals, but Oxfams have hundreds. They're in the rich end, you see. Attract a better sort of customer."

"Or a better sort of corpse," I'd said because I had not been very well. She hadn't found it funny.

It was my first time in Oxfams, but the smell of the place was the same as any other charity shop, slightly musty despite valiant efforts to spruce it up like a real shop. I approached the counter where a woman in a blue rinse stood.

"I need the largest evening dress you have in blue and the smallest you have in pink," I said with a huge smile. "And I can't pay more than twenty pounds for each."

"Some of these dresses were over one hundred and fifty pounds new." She pursed her carefully painted lips and whispered, "We have most of the big names here."

"It doesn't matter to me if you don't make a sale," I shrugged. "It's best to keep stock moving, I would have thought."

"The biggest, you say." She was intrigued. "In a blue?" I nodded. "Length?"

I hadn't considered that, but Jane had wanted lots of cloth to work with.

"Long enough for me," I said, winking at her. Her pancaked face cleared, leaving behind little fissures in the make-up.

"Oh it's for fancy dress," she smiled and whisked through the rail turning her eye on my six foot and measuring against the rail until she'd found two. "Either of these do for your first?"

"I'll need to try them on," I said. There was nobody else in the shop and so I took them into the booth and the helper went a little pink and thought it such fun because she remembered when her youngest had acted drag queen in a drama festival at university and how he'd looked the image of herself when she was young. All her family said so. "My husband said it was where he got his good looks, but you could tell Bernard was embarrassed, but I didn't mind at all."

Meanwhile I struggled into the first dress while she talked through the curtain at me. It was long enough in a very dark blue, but was slinky tight for me with a split up the leg and shoulderless so that I could not fetch it over my belly, let alone my chest and yet the feel of the fabric was cool and fresh: a beautiful dress. The second was more manageable, probably bought for a dowager duchess in late Edwardian mode without the bustle. It fitted me with much room to spare on the hips and flopped down on the chest like a sail without wind. Too small for Elsie without significant gussets, but it might be attempted, I thought. The colour – powder blue with silver trimmings at the neck. I would not find a closer fit, but I loved the sheerness of the dark blue gown and wondered about the tall woman who might have worn it once and passed it on to this drab funeral parlour.

"How are you managing in there?" The helper called. "I've found a small pink one, but there's other customers in," she hissed through the curtain.

"I wasn't going to give a catwalk," I laughed. Hastily I dressed myself as a conventional male and wandered out.

264

I'd heard the ping of the doorbell as I'd changed and was ready to meet the gaze of other shoppers with the gowns spread on my arm, but there is none so insular as the casual shopper. I was ignored.

"No point trying on the pink," I said. "It's for a friend – bit of a shrimp." I thought of Martin as I spoke, but his stockiness would have split the dress the woman held up to her neck. She smiled archly above it. She too was small, but more like a peardrop than Elizabeth's flat thinness. She pulled the side of the gown to show its shining cloth. It did not quite reach her hip width.

"It'll do," I said.

"He must be small," she smiled. "It's a Gucci," she said. "You can always tell."

I rather doubted her ability but there was the label – a dead giveaway.

"Can you try it on for me?" I asked because I could tell she wanted to be helpful and, after protestations that she couldn't and who would look after the shop while she did, she called a friend from her tea break and slipped away. And yes, it did her good to wear it and I could say in all honesty that it suited her and would not suit my friend half so well, but perhaps I could return it after the party and she might have it then. She knocked twenty pounds off the asking price then and smiled so much that her eye make-up crinkled.

I bought all three for fifty quid. Jane, Peter and I had put into the kitty, but I found the tenner for the dark blue dress. The helper carefully coddled the dresses into tissue and slipped them into Oxfam bags.

There was a tall slim redheaded girl moving in front

of me as I walked back to Gloucester Street and the Tower House. She was wearing a dark blue gown, her back was smooth as cream and her legs shifted the silk against her thighs like ripples in water. I did not once think of the other Redhead, the one with the hammer and the slug belly. I turned the key in the front door and sensed another companion by my side. It was Martin, his big face smiling at me, and then he disappeared.

Chapter 20

I prayed today. I knelt by my bedside, put the palms of my hands together and made a prayer as if I were a Catholic boy utterly convinced of the magical place for children above the bright blue sky of Elsie's dress. My wish flew into the ether like a released dove. It swooped and fluttered winsomely, pleadingly, urgently. I could not remember seeing such a prayer before. It was the colour of just fallen snow tinged with sunrise pink. It moved like the sweet passage of cool water over rounded rocks. Each time a cloud appeared to chase away its light, it shimmered away into sunshine, crying "You can't catch me!"

And what did my prayer say? A simple thing. Keep the weather fine and the people happy at our party here tonight.

"It won't make any difference," said Pete over breakfast. "You can get the Lord Mayor on your side, but that tower is coming down." I smiled even more broadly. He was on the wrong track totally.

"Is it all right if my sister comes?" asked Jane. "She'll have to bring the baby. She can go in a cot in our room and we'll keep an ear out for her." I knew all this before, of course, but Jane was speaking for Elizabeth.

"You do not have to ask," I said. "It is your house and it is our party. The more the merrier, but I hope we'll be able to hear her if she wakes. We'll be in the garden, won't we? It'll be best to have somebody on hand to make sure she's all right – just run the occasional rain check." Jane and I were conspirators and we grinned.

Elizabeth cracked open the top of her egg and removed slivers of shell with slow and trembling fingers. Her eyes did not move from the crown of the egg and there was an intentness in the gaze most unlike her normal twitchiness.

"I'll listen out for baby," she said. "If you need me, that is."

"That'd be great. Couldn't do without you, Elizabeth!" Jane reassured her. "If we put her carrycot in the front room, you could pop in and out quietly from time to time, couldn't you? Keep us posted how she is."

The old woman peered towards Jane and then across at the windows leading out to the garden.

"I could stay in the room with her all the time. No harm would come to her."

"We'd need an update," Pete said with a grin. "Just out to the patio and back again."

It was weeks since Elizabeth had ventured to look through the glass at the world beyond. Now she would need to move out under the high night sky where the stars shot needles to the earth.

"And how old is your sister's baby, if I may ask?" Elizabeth continued with careful control.

"How old would she be now, Pete?" Pete shrugged. Jane went on. "She must be all of eighteen months because it was only last summer that Lucy came over for the day and she'd had her then."

"A little girl," said Elizabeth as if in confirmation of a long held understanding.

"A little girl," agreed Jane and there was a silence. I waited for Elizabeth to remind us of her little girl and how old she would have been if it hadn't been for the unexploded jerry bomb in next door's back garden and the way it had gone off when the pram had been left in the yard, but she didn't.

"Her name's Tilda," Jane said.

"Like the rice," Peter laughed.

"And she's got lots of dark hair."

"And a big mouth."

"I won't leave her side," said Elizabeth.

"Oh but you must," said Jane. "We'll keep an eye between us. Then we can all enjoy the party."

"Don't you worry about her crying," said Elizabeth very definitely, putting her egg spoon on the table so the goo ran off. "I will rock her to sleep."

"That's the way to do it!" I chipped in with my best Punch and Judy voice. "A rock is better than a mallet any day." "Poor little mite," said Elizabeth. "You'll not go near her."

"Too right. I'll be tripping the light fantastic with dancing Delores, the Bristol beauty queen."

"And who's she when she's at home?" asked Pete. "You must introduce me."

"You'll dance with me, won't you, Jane?" I asked.

"Second choice eh? Well I can't do any of those fox-trot things," she said. "But I'll have a dance or two as long

as I can trust you lot to behave while I enjoy myself."
"It's a promise," I said. "We've all promised."

Elsie sat stroking her new blue dress. It lay over the back of the armchair behind her and she kept twisting round to it against the weight of her body, her fingers stretching to feel its smoothness. She did not know from where it had come. Jane had kept our secret and I huddled my knowledge inside my belly like a chocolate eclair. Oh well done Oxfam shop for outsize outsider people! Not that it would fit her now or perhaps for ever, but when Jane had shown her the two dresses, the one I had chosen for Jane had been Elsie's immediate choice. She had held it to her cheek like a velvet flower, leaving the dowager dress to one side. Her taste was good. Why shroud herself in flounce and taffeta when there was silk and simple lines to admire?

"That dress was for you," I had whispered to Jane, but I couldn't be angry with her when she'd shaken her head and pointed at Elsie's smile. We were both holding up a mirror to Elsie, showing what might be possible.

"It's lovely," said Elsie as clear as a bell and she smiled at Jane because she was her friend.

"Will you wear it for the party?" I asked, but she did not rise to the bait.

"Don't be silly, Pig," she laughed. "I'm still too big. But I will wear it one day soon."

The news from the hospital had been promising. She'd accompanied me in the taxi as good as gold and walked to the outpatients without leaning on my arm.

"You'll be fine," I'd said. "Absolutely fine." And she'd

walked to the consultant's room with her head held high. Ten minutes later, back she'd come, smiling round, looking for her taxi driver. And then she'd talked all the way home, explaining how she'd lost a stone, that the medication was working; the blood pressure was lower and glands were down, that she could start doing some exercises and could she walk out with me, just to the shops or round to the park? She'd take it slowly, but soon she'd manage by herself. She did not want to be a nuisance to anybody.

"Your eyes are so alive," I'd said. "And you're speaking like a queen." I shouldn't have said that. She'd closed up, but her cheeks still burned and her eyes darted out to the roadside as if they were looking at a new world.

"It was those bloody pills," Jane had explained when I told her how Elsie had talked. "Them and depression – and who wouldn't be depressed with that weight hanging on them and everybody treating you like blubber?"

"We're just waiting for your picture," said Pete, interrupting my reverie.

"No picture, no party." Jane capped his words. It had become the phrase of the moment. I knew they knew the painting was complete, but they did not know where I'd left it for safety.

"Gladys," I'd asked, "you will remember it. You will bring it on the night." "Better than a bottle," she'd answered. "Bring a picture to a party – much better than booze. I won't forget."

Gladys had liked the painting; she'd praised the use of colour, the strength of design, the technical accuracy, the fluency of brushwork and even the intensity of its vision. She had called me Pickarso after all and had hoped that more would come from my springs of creation. She'd even shown it to her cat, greatest of honours, and wrapped it in cloth for its protection.

"An inner voice," I tried to explain, my eyes filling with water at her generosity, "can only partially be expressed to an outer world to the satisfaction of the inner man." She'd walked away, propping the painting against the wall. I had followed her. "There are individual values at work derived from external influences working on interior perceptions." She'd squatted down to adjust the cloth and then turned back to grin at me. "I've tried to reach given forms of recognisable, but not replicable, worth.

"Just cut the crap and do the thing," she'd said and I had nodded. I had thought art was any preservative action informed by experience, but now I knew it was action endowed with worth, respect and love. I had stayed quiet in Gladys' smile and was warmed by her pleasure.

There were boxes of Californian wine, bottles of mineral water, cartons of fruit juice and cans of beer on the kitchen cupboards; cheeses and sausages, gherkins and silver onions impaled on plastic sticks, bridge rolls with egg and anchovy. Bowls of green salad decorated the dresser. On the patio the barbeque waited and inside the fridge were wings of chicken, little mackerels, chops and burgers.

Pete had rigged up lighting in the cherry tree and on the shed. The sound equipment was safe in the house, but the speaker system looked out from open windows to the garden. The neighbours had been warned and some invited. I cherished the expectation of pleasure inside like a precious foetus. The vulnerable child of my being was growing in confidence; there were friends around me and no place for despair.

And so welcome to you all! I open my arms to embrace you. I open my heart. It may be naive to wish the world a better place; it is probably a selfish instinct for survival. Better for whom? In this little world of a few seconds and a few friends, with the casual black clouds beyond and a fleeting glimpse of the sun above us ..."

"It's the moon, sunbeam," Pete called out from behind the barbeque.

"Anyway," I laughed. "It's time to celebrate and the buggers won't get us down. They might trip us, wing us, poke us in the eye, but will we be down-hearted? They only hurt us when we see them: just shadows, they are ... no real redheads at all anymore."

"Cut the cackle and pour the wine. " I swung round to spot the voice. It could have been Martin speaking, but it was one of Pete's friends, leaning back on a sunbed with a meaty hand round a hot dog. The company cackled with him, loosening the ritual into life.

"What is that music?" Gladys shouted. Sudden smooth rush of clarinets joined with deeper resonance from the trombone section all in perfect dance hall rhythm ... the big band had started. It flowed over the garden.

"It's the music of my childhood," I replied. "I remember my parents locked together in body and spirit, forgetting the war with Hitler and between themselves, sallying out over the floor together."

"Just pander to him," Jane called over the lawn. "There'll be all sorts later."

"It's my party. I can do what I want to," I tried to sing and Gladys quickly covered my mouth.

"All right," she said. "You may be able to paint, but you certainly can't sing!" And I enjoyed her words because I knew one who could sing, who would sing later will she or no.

Elizabeth was in the pink and flitted mothlike from the shelter of the house to the lighted patio ferrying food and news of Tilda.

"She's sleeping like a baby," she told me, her cheeks as pink as her dress and her eyes feverish because it was still a battle to take those few steps beyond the kitchen door to the dark outside.

"That's because she is one," I said.

"One what?"

"A baby: that's what they do – sleep and feed."

"Don't know a thing, these men," said Jane's sister, Lucy. She pushed herself out of her garden chair to take a plate of vol-au-vents from Elizabeth. "That baby has screamed through more nights than she's had hot dinners. If she's settled, for God's sake don't disturb her."

But Elizabeth was off back into the house, successful in her latest short foray.

Elsie had made herself invisible by sitting in her armchair. Pete had lugged it into the garden and placed it by the side of the shed, away from the light. I strolled across to her, offered a plateful of chicken and salad. She took it, but only pecked a little spiced meat.

"I'm on my diet," she said as if I didn't know the ins and outs of her glands, her hospital visit and her resolution to follow doctor's orders.

"Mustn't go overboard," I said. "Got to keep body and soul together and you'll need a little energy for dancing."

Her eyes flickered uneasily. Was I playing games with her again?

"Will you dance with me, Elsie?" She began to shake her head, but I continued rapidly. "Just over here," I said. "Pretty well got the floor to ourselves." I reached down and took her arm. Slowly she pulled herself up, hoisting herself on the arm of the chair for I could not have taken her full weight. Glenn Miller started a new waltz. I put my hand on her side and held her right hand high. Her body, although massive in front of me, was not a blancmange and her hair smelt sweet. We waltzed over the grass and her feet kept time and rhythm with a natural grace. I have often noticed that big people often have delicate feet and smooth movement. It would be so of Elsie when weight had been shed. I could hear her breathing heavily below me, but we stuck at it and traversed the garden four times before she began to suffer from heat and exhaustion.

"Take it easy," I said, leading her back to her seat. "It's a hot night. We'll dance again later, if you would like that." She settled back in her chair, springs complaining, and smiled up at me. "Thank you for the dance," I said formally. The waltz was coming to its conclusion and I needed to stay with her because the next item on the tape was not to be missed.

The band suddenly stopped, no sophisticated editing features here, and static crackled over the speakers.

"What's wrong with it?" Pete shouted, but there was nothing wrong. Elsie's voice flooded sweetly out over the garden as pure and clean as a waterfall. I watched her face. Her mouth dropped open and the hot blood fled from her cheeks. She put her hand to her mouth as if to scream, but I patted her shoulder and whispered that her voice was wonderful and the whole world deserved to hear it.

"Don't lie to me," Elsie muttered.

"Every word I say is the truth – no more games. Just listen to yourself …"

There was a yearning sweetness and a simple purity in the sound that was both woman and child and when the voice died away, there was a silence in the garden like a moment's prayer. Then the babble of voices rose again and many of them commented on the singing, trying to work out which major opera star from the past could have been filling the garden with her voice. Elsie put her hands over her face. She was crying.

"It is just our secret and Jane's," I said. "Nobody will tell unless you want to." She shook her head. It was all too much and I wondered whether I should have stolen her voice from her body after all. I told her she was brilliant and she managed a small smile.

"Too breathy," she said.

I left her to recover. Jane, dressed by special permission of Elsie, in the dark blue gown, was standing by the edge of light on the side of the patio, her eyes full of the question.

"She's a bit overwhelmed, but very happy, I think."

I claimed my dance from Jane. She held the small

of my back and moved her solid precious legs to my rhythm. When the music stopped, she put her hands on my shoulders and kissed me.

"That is for my picture," she said.

"Not for me?" I asked grinning at her like a schoolboy.

"You and the picture," she smiled. "Can't have one without the other." I put out my hand and touched her cheek. She caught it, patted it and returned it to my side.

"You're quite a sweety," she smiled and I felt like an indulgent father whose daughter had long since moved away into her own realms.

"Brain and body, inward and outward show," I said.

"What do you mean?" We walked along the fuschia bed towards the shed, going the long way back to the patio.

"I don't know," I replied. "Perhaps I have stopped pretending that my existence is more or less important than any other. When brain and body are one with oneself and with others, it is time for another drink ..."
"That's right," she said seriously. "Don't take things to heart."

"I've given up fencing," I said. "If one comes armed with a rapier I shall bare my breast. I shall take the hot steel into my heart without fear. I have spent too many days fearing the consequences of others' fury, stoking my own anger until the flames have burned higher and higher against the dread. The redhead was one such fear that kindled flames."

"You've lost me."

"No," I laughed. "I've lost you, but I don't mind, you know."

"You never had me to lose." Jane stopped and turned

me round to look at her.

"My brain has often said my body wanted to be inside you," I said gently. "But it was because you represented refuge, warmth, safety, the security of womanhood away from the hatred and murder." "That's not your brain talking," she said firmly. "It's mush."

"You're more than right." I was pleased to agree. "You always are. Thank goodness for your feet on the ground!" I bent towards her and kissed her quickly on the cheek. "That one's for luck," I said. "Not that you need it, but I do." She smiled and whisked away in her silken dress, the light catching the red in her hair. I turned back to where Elsie was sitting, her eyes sharp. She had seen and possibly heard it all. It was time for another dance and, once again, we promenaded over the lawn and I told her that her voice was glorious.

"When you are ready," I said, "and not before, will you sing for us in public?"

Elsie seemed to move more freely in my arms and her laughter was real.

And now the close evening brooded over the dark roses. Charcoal glimmered and sausages hissed like feral kittens. Sprawled on the black grass, propped on household chairs, leaning against the sun-warmed wall, the sweet sleepy late night party people crooned. I stood on the patio and looked out towards where the tower gloomed.

"At the risk of interrupting a quiet end to a peaceful night," I announced to a few groans, "may I have your attention for a few moments?" The tape continued to play from inside the house and George stalked across the doorway, furious at the night time invasion of his territory.

"Words, words and more words," said Pete. He was lounging in the door jamb near the barbeque. There were smuts on his forehead. "Cheers!" He said, bringing up a glass of red wine and gulping it down. "Thirsty work."

I felt an arm lace under mine and looked round.

"It's been a lovely party," Nurse Bentham said. "Thank you for inviting me. I knew you'd come out the other end of the tunnel."

"Party's not quite over," I said. "You see that tower. Well Pete here wants it pulled down."

"So Jane tells me," said the nurse. "And you're unhappy about it. I can understand that."

"It's to topple," said Pete. "It's an eyesore."

"But it's a beautiful picture," said Gladys. "Quite an irony." Pete had hung the picture on the side of the house, put two spotlights on it. "Our own private son et lumiere.. well lumiere anyway," Jane explained.

"He wants to build flats there," I continued, nodding round at the women who now clustered near me like pillows. "I said the tower should be preserved, it being historically interesting and important." "And so it is," said Jane. "But there'll be photographs and your picture, John." "Is that enough?" I asked. "Once gone, it's gone for good."

"And good riddance," said Pete, his voice blurred from Bristol wine. "Time can't stand still. Beside Health and Safety says there's vermin in it and the damp cannot be treated without spending thousands."

"Besides," I capped him, "think of the thousands homeless. They need a place to live."

"You trying to be funny?"

"Oh no," I answered. "I know what it is to be without a home, no place to go except where I'm not wanted – shell of a flat and the vermin scratching away at the floorboards. They'd rip your throat out at the drop of a hat or the smallest snore."

"You trying to be funny," Pete asked, coming round from the doorway. He was carrying the knife he used for slicing sausages off the string. "People aren't vermin."

"I never said they were," I answered. "I just thought he was worse than vermin, the man I told you about." I watched the blade move in the spotlights like a white flame.

"Let's not spoil the party," Jane said. "You can put that knife down for a start, Peter Sawyer."

Peter looked at what he was carrying and laughed.

"It's just the sausage knife," he said and put it on the barbeque stand, a little embarrassed.

"You gave me shelter and took the crap I threw at you day after day. How could I not share my gratitude?" I knelt down by the stripy bag I had placed on the ground under my picture. "I want to give you this. I'm not sure it's mine to give, but Martin wouldn't mind. He lived on a building site." I brought out the demolition hammer, hefted the handle until the head nestled cold in my palm. "It's for you," I said and handed it over. "Have a smashing time!"

And then I laughed because his face was such a picture.

There was no cup of the tea in the morning. I woke at nine o'clock and the chimes from St Mary's were ringing in the far distance. The bed was smooth as if my body had stayed fixed upon the mattress in one place all night. There were treasures to be remembered, but no tea. Elizabeth knew how to make it hot and strong and sweet and every day she struggled up the stairs to give her daily treat, but no tea this morning and in the stillness of the Sunday after the party, I realised why.

Slowly I pulled myself out of bed, drew my dressing gown around me and pulled up the sticking flange. The stairs were bright in early sunshine through the landing window. Dust motes shone like stars. I flicked off the night light. Elizabeth's door was slightly open. I pushed against it gently.

"Elizabeth!" I called. "Are you all right?"

The morning shed a dim light through the curtains. I opened them and turned to view the bed. She was flat on her back, the duvet up to her chin and her thin face stared up at the ceiling with unseeing eyes. I remembered her brave passage creeping like a night moth across the lawn towards the lights on the fence to tell Lucy that her baby was crying and would not sleep. By the time she'd reached Lucy, her body was trembling and her eyes rolled in their sockets. She clutched at her body with both arms, holding her desperate agoraphobia inside the tiniest frame of her being.

"I did try," she said. "I've rocked her and hushed her quiet, but still she needs her Mum and that's not me. I thought she might have thought of me as you if I just kept quiet and pretended I was a mouse, but they can tell, can't they? And then I didn't want to leave her. When you leave a baby anything can happen and I should know. It's cot deaths or bombs and I don't know what. You must come back. For God's sake come back!" The hysteria crackled across the garden and heads turned so that she bolted with Lucy running behind, calling that she shouldn't mind so much and then they'd gone back into the house together with Elizabeth dabbing at her pink eyes with a sodden tissue and her shoulders heaving.

Later, after all the guests had gone, Lucy told us that Elizabeth had taken it hard, blaming herself for not helping baby go to sleep. She'd gone to bed unhappy, her spirits low. She'd placed by the bed the flowers Lucy gave her to thank her for caring so much to overcome her fear. The room smelt of mustiness. She put Lucy's card among the trinkets on the dressing table among old photographs of people long since gone and her face too was rapidly becoming one of the sepia ones. She'd been too frightened to open the door to find her way through the world, but now the final door had opened and she had been sent through it will she or no.

Over a cup of coffee, Jane turned to me and said we shouldn't blame ourselves, but I was perfectly in control. The party stayed a happy memory to me, conditioned by the sadness of a death.

I took to bringing tea to Elsie every morning instead.

Chapter 21

An artist creates through arrogant brush strokes a version of reality that may heal or wound. He is the controller, but he is also controlled. I have tried to do my best, but it is circumstance that prevents perfect execution and perfection leads to another sort of execution: the death of hope and the birth of expectation. The Redhead has been my destruction. Created from the pain of fire and violence, he has haunted my footsteps and imposed his art of murder upon me. In so doing he has conjured fear where there might have been confidence and distortion where the smooth straight limbs of my children might have walked. The creature brought to flame by the artist can overwhelm him in his turn and translate him to monster not man.

In order to heal the whole, remove the rotting flesh and cauterise the join so that an impossible perfection might reign, I have spent my hours in minute brushwork, looking ever more closely at each tiny fissure in the tower's crumbling brick until the moss and lichen have seemed the most important components of the structure. I have ignored the whole picture by concentrating upon the particular. The Redhead had all the power he needed to force his way through the unjointed walls to reach the secret tomb within and set the demolition of fire raging anew. I had to act urgently to block the gaps in the mortar.

The Redhead was no mere invention, an artist's creation to represent the furnace of the mind. Although the stress he caused me was raging in my head, he was the man I described in the prison and in the flat. If he had not existed, Martin Beverall would be standing, waddling and talking today. His death confirmed my truth and the fact of the murderer's existence. I too have experienced the death's head, the redhead, and all my art has been transmuted through pain and the evil blood between us. I sometimes wonder why Martin died and I did not. I have felt guilty that I should remain on this earth, while Martin, who had no previous knowledge of the Redhead should have ended his days with brains broken and flesh burning. I have ceased trying to conjecture the reasons and wherefores. If the Redhead imagines there may be a weaker creature, then it is the weaker who dies. I needed to create another vision, a goodness in a reworked woman from the clay immediate to my hands.

Jane had asked me why I suddenly took such notice of Elsie and I had replied that she was trapped inside her own body and I sympathised with her. This too was an arrogance in me to assume I could alter her circumstances, but there was no other impulse and certainly no game to play when once I had quelled the fear and hatred inside myself. The Redhead was singularly effective at infecting my thoughts with his own diseased hatred of the most unfortunate. I do not know whether my impulse was healthy, but there was a beauty within the woman that I had never seen before and I had some magic in my hands to conjure a redemption. Elsie was no monster except when my thinking made her so and, if I could approach her with humility and respect, I might have achieved the only worthwhile alchemy. Was it arrogance to believe so?

It is fashionable to decry romantic notions of Gothic horror and I have never been an aficionado of other world creations. I believe that we create the content and fabric of our lives, but there is a making spirit that is neglected at its and my peril. If repressed, it conjures hatred from the clay and daubs destruction on the walls. If brought into the open and abused, it asserts its power to be greater than others' striving for expression and acceptance. It bullies and is bullied. The Redhead was just such a powerful manifestation. He would have burned the world to gain his recognition and he saw in me his own creature lurking. Had I not taken up the flaming sword of the arsonist? Was I not a conundrum for such as he? To all outward appearances I was weak, a dabbler in paint and a product of middle class values and education. Yet, I was in Dartmoor as a burner, a destroyer. Steve looked at me with contempt, but also confusion, for I was close to madness. The Redhead feared my gentle madness.

Elsie was a frozen creature with a small spark of regenerative artistry left within her. Her voice of angels singing in a broken choir was my small chance to reverse the downward plunge to what Dr. Rhodes might have termed insanity, but I claim is possession by the bully who tried to destroy me and continued to wage war against the weak and tender, the kind and destroyed after I had escaped him. Martin was one such.

I have learned that if you wish to find true virtue hidden from sight search the homes for the saddest and most frightened. If you wish to bring them flowering into light, then work to remove all tincture of revenge from their awakening lives lest in their rebirth they become as angry as those who first destroyed their hopes. I may now appear calm and dispassionate. Our midsummer party has been held. Our party clothes have been worn. My divorce is final, but my children are prepared to meet me. I have given a short statement to the police explaining my last meeting with Martin and the local press carried the arrest of two men for his murder and one of them was called Steve. All seems equable. But I know that if the Redhead were to march through my door crashing his boots into my body, I would want to seize the hammer and batter his skull, shrieking for revenge with every blow. It is best for Jane to wash her hair in henna for loveliness and for Pete to have the hammer. He knows how to use such tools for their proper purposes.

Elsie walked into the kitchen yesterday wearing the blue dress. There is still a way to go before it falls in smooth lines to the floor, but there was pride and confidence in Elsie's stride. She stood by the back door and sang to the flowers in a gentle and private voice. I planted a rose called Elizabeth. It was a tea rose.